T0129208

For a gang of old college buddies, the quaint resort town of South Cove, California, is the perfect spot for a no-holds-barred bachelor party. But for Jill Gardner—owner of Coffee, Books and More—this stag party is going to be murder . . .

After a few months of living with her boyfriend Greg, Jill is still getting used to sharing such close quarters, but she's got no hesitation about joining him for a weekend at South Cove's most luxurious resort. While Greg and his college pals celebrate their buddy's upcoming wedding, Jill intends to pamper herself in style. But when the groom is found floating facedown in the pool, Jill must find the killer fast, or she might not have a boyfriend to come home to any more . . .

Also by Lynn Cahoon

The Tourist Trap Mysteries

Killer Party

Hospitality and Homicide

Tea Cups and Carnage

Murder on Wheels

Killer Run

Dressed to Kill

If the Shoe Kills

Mission to Murder

Guidebook to Murder

The Cat Latimer Mysteries

Fatality by Firelight

A Story to Kill

Published by Kensington Publishing Corporation

Killer Party

Tourist Trap #9

The Boys are Back in Town

Lynn Cahoon

LYRICAL UNDERGROUND
Kensington Publishing Corp.
www.kensingtonbooks.com

First Electronic Edition: July 2017
eISBN-13: 978-1-60183-635-9
eISBN-10: 1-60183-635-X

First Print Edition: July 2017
ISBN-13: 978-1-60183-636-6
ISBN-10: 1-60183-636-8

Printed in the United States of America

To the men in my life who are loving, caring, and a little bit crazy.

Acknowledgments

Men have always been a mystery to me. One day in Chicago, I was having dinner in an outdoor café. At a table nearby was a group of guys, enjoying the early summer evening and telling tales, like men are prone to do. As the meal progressed, I watched their interaction closely. So when I started writing Killer Party, I knew how the book would start. Thanks for the muse and the strangers who pointed me the way into this next Tourist Trap story.

Writers tend to be magpies, picking up shiny bits and pieces to add to our collection. I hope you enjoy the latest design as I had fun bringing Jill and the gang along for the ride. Huge thank you to the Kensington crew who have taken the Tourist Trap series and made it shine. Esi, Michelle, and Alex—thanks for keeping me on track and getting the word out for the books. You guys all rock.

CHAPTER 1

Whoever wrote the line *you can't go home again* must have been staying in a luxury hotel at the time. I stretched out on the king-sized bed and sank into its glorious softness. The Castle was less than ten miles away from my house, but we'd checked in for the weekend. Or at least, our host, Levi Walters, had done the checking in. In fact, the tech millionaire had rented the entire place for his bachelor party.

"I'm just staying in bed for the entire weekend," I told Greg as he unpacked his suitcase, hanging up the slacks and dress shirt he'd brought for the formal dinner tonight. Greg was my boyfriend and as of a few months ago, my roommate, too. I still wasn't totally comfortable with the entire couple cohabitation thing, but I did appreciate having him around. Especially when he mowed the yard. "Throw me a book and the room-service menu, and I'll see you when we check out."

He jumped on the bed next to me, his baby-blue eyes sparkling with humor. He brushed back a wayward curl from my face. "No such luck, buttercup. Where I go, you go. At least this weekend. We have to show the upcoming newlyweds what a proper couple acts like. I'm pretty sure Levi works all the time, so Jessica must be alone a lot."

"Sounds a little like us. Except I work as much as you do." At least sometimes. Now, that we were back to full staff at Coffee, Books, and More, my hours had been limited. Which worked great for me since I was way behind on my recreational reading after starting classes a year ago for my master's degree in business.

"No, Levi works more than both of us together. He's always either on the phone or his laptop, even when he's home. Look, I know this weekend will be touchy. I'm not even sure why Levi was so insistent you and I come. I mean, we were close as kids, but that's a long time ago. The last time I came to one of these, I was still married to Sherry. And, well, that weekend blew up in my face."

"Do you want to talk about it?" I rolled over onto my side and pushed a lock of hair out of his eyes.

"Honestly, no. I just want you to be prepared. I'm going to owe you big for this weekend." He glanced at his watch. "We have an hour before the first event. You want to stay here and fool around a little bit or go check out The Castle? We have full access to all the public rooms."

"Brenda must really like Levi. The last time Aunt Jackie tried to get her writers' group an all access pass for an afternoon, Brenda turned her down flat. Aunt Jackie's going to be so jealous." Brenda Morgan was the manager of The Castle, the site of our weekend gathering. The Castle had only a few rooms they rented out and often didn't even open the hotel section. Most weeks, it was a museum only. Brenda had been having trouble with the old buildings and the lack of air conditioning, not to mention a lack of adequate staffing to run a real hotel full time.

I ran my fingers through Greg's sandy-blond hair as I considered the options. Brenda Morgan had been The Castle administrator since her husband, Craig, had been murdered out behind one of the cottages in the complex. I wouldn't have been able to work in the same place where a loved one had died. On the other hand, Brenda and Craig had been separated at the time. Maybe the term, *loved one*, was out of place here.

Greg watched as I jumped off the bed and slipped on my flip-flops. "So I guess fooling around is off the table?"

"When it comes to making my aunt green with envy, I'll go without for a while." I put my phone in my capris pocket. "Are you ready yet?"

"Can we discuss how long a while is?" Greg sighed and then pushed himself off the bed. "I hope this satisfies your need to one-up Jackie. You two fight like sisters. Maybe you should try being nice."

"Why do I have to be the adult?" Don't get me wrong, I loved Aunt Jackie. Sometimes our relationship got a little tense as she could be overbearing and controlling, but nothing like what had been happening lately. My aunt had been on a holy tear for the last month. She was planning a June wedding to Harrold Snider. Jackie carried around a three-ring binder so she could write down notes as she thought of them. From what I could tell, everyone in the country was being invited. Well, everyone but Josh. He was still a little miffed about the Jackie and Harrold thing. Even though he was now officially dating Mandy Jensen, manager of South Cove's new produce and fruit stand, the man still held a soft spot for my aunt.

Greg leaned down and kissed me. "Because you love your aunt."

Well, he had me there. Even at her worst, she was still my aunt and my only living relative. I opened the door and stepped into the hall. "I'm still going to post these pictures on my Facebook page. I just won't tag her."

"Maybe she'll be too busy looking at seating charts for the reception to notice. I could call and give Harrold a heads up to try to keep her away." He checked his pocket for the room key, then pulled the door closed behind us.

"You're a little OCD with checking if you have the key. You know that right?" Moving toward the elevator, I linked my arm with his.

"Who always locks herself out of our hotel room when she goes for ice?" He pushed the down button and the ancient elevator motor whirled to life.

"No one remembers to take their keys when they get ice." I shot him a dirty look and then hesitantly stepped inside the elevator. "Besides, you're usually in the room when I leave."

"The last two times you locked yourself out, I was taking a shower. Luckily I heard your frantic knocks." He pressed the lobby button and the doors slid shut with a bang.

"I wasn't frantic. There were just people in the hallway and I was in my pajamas." I looked up at the lights that showed us slowing making our way down the three floors. "Maybe we should take the stairs. I'm not sure this elevator is going to last the weekend."

"Izzy works on these things and he says it's safe." Izzy was one of Greg's friends and lived in Bakerstown. From the way Greg quoted him, Izzy knew everything about anything mechanical. As we stepped out into the lobby, a cool breeze flowed gently through the room. Greg picked up a flyer from a side table. "Do you want a tour pamphlet?"

"Sure." I studied the map on the flyer and pointed to a spot to our left. "Let's start in the dining hall. I hear they have tapestries from the Middle Ages."

We found the room and as I walked inside, a sense of peace filled me. The place was stunning. If Levi was planning on hosting a dinner party in the room, he could invite all of the residents of South Cove and still have room for relatives and friends of the bride and groom. I pointed to the tapestry with the castle scene. "I saw that in a history book when I was in high school. I didn't realize it was owned by The Castle."

"There are a lot of antiquities housed here in The Castle." A man spoke up behind us. "The original owner had boatloads of art and architecture shipped over when he visited Europe. He'd find old churches being torn down and take every last choir pew and piece of stained glass. He rescued this stuff and now everyone wants it back."

I turned and looked at the elderly man watching us. He was doing the comb-over hairdo. I don't know why men think we can't tell they're bald if there's a few strands covering the top. I introduced myself and Greg, trying not to look at the top of his head. "I'm very interested in The Castle's history. Are you a trustee for the place?"

He barked out a laugh as he shook our hands. "Not on your life. I'm John Anderson. I'm kind of a museum guide. I work for Brenda. Those trustee farts are all Wall Street types with their eyes only on the money. I swear, they'd take this place apart and sell it off, piece by piece, if they could figure out a way to break the trust."

"It's amazing. I don't know why anyone would change a thing." A female voice cut through the tension.

We turned toward the newcomers and I saw Greg's eyes light up. He stepped toward the man and woman who had just entered the room.

"Levi! Hey man, thanks for inviting us." He walked over and gave the taller man a bro hug. "I can't believe you finally found someone to put up with you."

"I could say the same thing about you, times two. Of course, I told you the first one wouldn't work out when I stood up for you at that Vegas chapel. Didn't we have to wait for Elvis to get done with his drive through couple?" Levi Walker slapped Greg on the back. "You should have listened to me and run that night."

"You're right there." Greg turned toward me. "Levi, this is Jill Gardner. Jill, meet my best friend since seventh grade. Even if the guy doesn't call, email or visit me unless one of us is getting hitched."

"Jill, so nice to meet you. Greg has told me so much about you. And Jim had nice things to say too." He came over and gave me a quick hug. "This is the love of my life, Jessica soon–to-be Walker."

The woman came up and held out a hand. "Jessica Cole. I haven't decided on if I'm taking Levi's last name or not. It feels so archaic, like I'm property."

"Jill Gardner. So nice to meet you." I took a step toward Greg who pulled me into a hug. "Are you originally European? I can't place the accent."

"Jessica's family is from Germany and we just came back from a tour of Europe. I told her that she was picking up the local flavor." Levi beamed with pride at his fiancée.

"That must be it." Greg shot me a questioning look, but I ignored him.

Holding out the map of the building, I asked. "We were just starting our tour of The Castle. Do you want to join us?"

Her smile was wide, with too-white teeth. I hadn't been expecting someone so beautiful. Especially since Greg talked about Levi as the ultimate computer nerd. I guess I'd thought his fiancée would be more geek goddess rather than beauty queen. Her black hair glistened in the room's dim light.

"I'd love to—" Jessica started to say, but Levi shook his head.

"Sorry dear, we have to go to the room. The lawyer's calling in a few minutes with the last changes on the pre-nuptial agreement. It's just a formality, but my company's insisting on it so if anything happens to me, the business has a clear right of succession plan." Levi winked at me. "I wanted to elope and just surprise the shareholders with a mailing announcing: *He put a ring on it*. But Jessica wanted the big production."

She grinned at me. "I've been dreaming of this day since I was five and my Barbie had to marry Ken at least three times a day. No one wants to just elope."

Well, I didn't. Especially now that I knew that Greg and his first wife, Sherry, had tied the knot in Vegas. But I thought it was a great idea for some people. Aunt Jackie should have just eloped. The wedding would already be over and she could have sent out announcements. But no. "I'm sure the wedding will be lovely."

"It better be, for all it's costing me." Levi slapped Greg on the back. "Don't think you're getting out of doing shots tonight. That's why I rented the whole place. No one has to drive anywhere and take a chance of getting pulled over for a DUI."

"I appreciate your concern. My night deputy watches the roads pretty carefully out here. He'd love to nail me on an infraction." Greg looked to me for confirmation.

"Really, we need to go, but tonight. We'll get caught up tonight." He put his hand on Jessica's back and led her out of the room. "Nice to meet you, Jill."

And then they were gone. Sometime during the last few minutes, John had also disappeared. I looked around the too-large empty room. "Wow, he kind of fills up a place, doesn't he?"

"Levi's always been over the top. Think geek with actor attitude. Of course, none of the girls saw his good side, just the class clown and a too-smart-for-his-own-good kid." He stared out the doorway where they'd just disappeared. "I hope this Jessica has Levi's best interests at heart."

I stood on tippy-toes and gave him a kiss on the cheek.

"What is that for?" He turned his attention away from the door.

I shrugged. "You're a good guy. You worry about everyone and everything. It's part of your charm."

He put his arm around me as we walked through the room. "Just wait until you meet the rest of the guys. We were tight in school. We were the nerdy kids who read Tolkien and wanted real light sabers for our birthdays."

"I'm looking forward to it."

I really wasn't. Greg's brother, Jim, barely tolerated me after my dating Greg made it impossible for Jim to hold on to his fantasy of Greg and his ex-wife, Sherry, getting back together. Who knows what camp these guys would join. And from what Levi said, Jim was still in touch with at least him. I looked down at the map. "There's supposed to be a great hall through this door. Ready to go see how the rich folk relaxed back in the day?"

"Sure." He followed me through the next doorway. He scanned the room the way he always did when we entered a new house or room in a store. He was always looking for the worst rather than let it sneak up on us. Toby did the same thing. They called it being hyper-vigilant, according to a book I'd read. Cops were cops even when they weren't in uniform.

We spent most of the rest of the afternoon wandering through the display rooms. For the place being so big, there wasn't a speck of dust anywhere. Brenda must keep a tight rein on her cleaning staff. We stood waiting for the elevator, when the doors opened and Jessica walked out in a too-small white bikini.

"Hey, again. You guys still down here?" She nodded to the French doors leading to the back pool area. "I'm heading out for a swim before dinner. Do you want to join me?"

Greg looked at me. I don't think he trusted his voice. Whatever accent I'd thought I'd heard had been replaced with the voice of a sultry stripper. I leaned closer to Greg, letting her step around us. "Maybe. I'm not sure we brought suits." It was a total lie. I'd bought us both new suits just for the weekend.

She turned her head back to us and laughed. "Darling, we have the entire place to ourselves. Suits are totally optional."

CHAPTER 2

We didn't talk on the elevator ride to our floor. Greg started to say something, but I shook my head, not wanting to be overheard. When we got to the room, I flopped on the bed. "What was that?"

"I'm not sure, but I know I either need to turn in my man card for turning her down or my badge for not arresting her. Levi has himself a firecracker there." He opened the closet and started digging through the suitcase.

"What are you looking for?" I peered at him from my reclining position. He looked over his shoulder back at me. "Our suits."

I threw the pillow and hit him right on his head.

"Hey, what's that for?" He stood straight and threw the pillow back at me. "Does this mean we're not going swimming?"

My phone rang, which saved me from killing him. He grabbed the remote and turned the television on as he took my place on the bed. Glancing at the caller ID, I saw Coffee, Books, and More's number. There must be a crisis. Mentally, I went through the supply orders I'd completed the first of the week and tried to guess what hadn't come in.

"Hello?"

There was silence on the other end of the line.

I looked at the room clock, Aunt Jackie should be on shift. Had she fallen? Heart attack? Was someone robbing the place? I tried to keep the panic out of my voice, "Hello? Aunt Jackie? Is anyone there?"

Greg muted the television. I saw concern on his face as he sat up, ready to spring into action if we needed to leave. My aunt might like to pretend she's young, but in truth, the woman is getting up in years. I'm not sure how old she is exactly as she doesn't celebrate birthdays anymore and she won't let me see her driver's license or her employee file at the shop. But she's been in my life since I could remember. I repeated her name, "Aunt Jackie?"

"Sorry, dear, I dropped an earring." My aunt's voice came on the line and I felt my heart rate slow. She'd dropped an earring?

I bit my lip, not wanting to yell and making eye contact with Greg, I covered the phone and whispered, "Everything's fine."

"Jill, dear, are you there?" Aunt Jackie asked. She didn't like being kept waiting.

I sank down on the chair by the bed. "Yes, I'm here. What's going on?"

"I wanted to talk to you about the wedding reception. I'm thinking of having the florist put small bowls of roses on the tables. You know those little white ones that are so pretty? He says he'll do a mock up for me, but I wanted your opinion before I told him to go ahead."

"Aunt Jackie, the wedding's six months away. You don't think this conversation could have waited until I'm back on Tuesday?" I rolled my eyes and Greg chuckled, folding his arms under his head and getting comfortable. He was watching a show on alligators. Right now, I wanted to be cuddled up next to him, and not talking to my aunt about her upcoming nuptials.

"Pre-planning an event makes it run smooth. I thought I'd taught you that by now." She sniffed, apparently put out by my lack of enthusiasm. "Oh, and Tina Baylor stopped by. She said Marvin wants you to invite our new business owner to the meeting on Tuesday. Personally."

"The Russian doll shop guy? I didn't think the shop had opened yet." Actually, I'd gotten a fax from the mayor a week ago, but like most of his charming missives, I'd trashed it after I'd skimmed the message.

"Oh, yes, the grand opening began this morning. I didn't realize there were so many people who liked those things." I heard the pause in my aunt's voice. "Don't tell Harrold, because the dear man stopped and bought me one on his way here to have lunch, but I think they're kind of creepy."

I'd always wanted one of the stacking dolls as a child. It was like having a whole family of identical playmates. Of course, I'd never gotten one, mostly because we didn't have the money to spend on an imported toy. "I'll try to stop by on Monday when we get back from the party. You realize I'm away for the weekend, right?"

"You're a few minutes from town. I don't think that qualifies as away. Besides, you could come over tomorrow morning and take the owners a dozen cookies and the invite." I heard my aunt greet a customer as they walked into the store.

"I'm not coming into town just to invite them to the Business-to-Business meeting. If Marvin's that worried about it, he can do the honors."

"Tina and Marvin are in the city for the weekend. She only stopped by for a book to read while they relax poolside." I heard the bell over the door chime again and I knew the shop was getting busy. "Look, I've got to go. Just make sure you invite the man and his daughter. I have their names written down on a piece of paper in the cash register for you."

"Aunt Jackie," I started but realized I was talking to dead air. She had hung up on me.

I sat the phone down and lay on the bed next to Greg.

He put his arm around me and pulled me close. "So you going into town tomorrow?"

"No, I'm not." I watched the alligators fight over some sort of deer that had gotten too close to the water. *Probably just trying to get a drink*, I thought. Wrong place, wrong time. Just like my mini vacation. "We should have flown to Hawaii for this weekend."

"Probably true. But Levi didn't want us to worry about being away from South Cove." He rubbed my arm. "Besides, for him, this *is* a vacation spot."

Levi and Jessica lived in Raleigh, North Carolina. Apparently, that was a hot spot for computer geeks.

The room phone rang and Greg answered it. "Hello?" He paused, listening. "Okay, see you in a few."

When he replaced the handset into the cradle, he grinned at me. "We're being summoned to the pool. Everyone is down there but us and from the sounds of it, the drinking has started."

"In suits?" I closed my eyes. I wasn't a prude, but a pool filled with thirty-somethings in their birthday suits didn't make me want to jump up and join them.

"In suits." He kissed me. "I'm sure Jessica was just teasing."

I wasn't so sure, but I changed into my swimsuit and slipped on a cute cover-up I'd bought just to match. I added my flower flip-flops and then we left the room. Greg had been ready in two and a half seconds. This weekend was for him and his friends. I was just along for the ride. I'd never been arm candy before and compared to Jessica, Greg wasn't winning that competition. But I didn't care. I was going to have fun this weekend, even if I had to turn my phone off to keep my aunt from calling.

First stop, pool party. I brought a bag with our room key, sunscreen, and a book I'd been wanting to read forever. In two weeks, classes would start up again, and my free reading time would be filled with text books about business stuff. I wasn't sure that I was learning as much as my aunt thought I would, mostly it seemed like the curriculum was focused on big corporation, not small town stores like ours. I had no interest in franchising, and yet, that was one of the core classes I had to complete. And this semester, included a math class for business decisions. I was hoping I'd at least get a 'C' so I wouldn't have to re-take the course. Math and my brain just didn't mix.

"You don't really think you'll be reading, do you?"

Greg had seen me stash the book. "It could happen. Maybe the other women will be swimming or something else?"

"Then you could talk with me and my friends." He held open the door. "I want them to get to know you, not just see you with your nose in a book."

"Books are my business." I reminded him.

He pulled me close. "But we are on vacation, dear. You can't have it both ways."

He was right, of course. I'd just told my aunt that I wasn't working this weekend, and yet, I wanted to justify my reading by pulling in my store. Sometimes I was complicated, even in my own mind.

The pool area was beautiful with most of the tables and chairs stored away. There were just a few scattered around the patio area. The wisteria drooped over the wooden pergola, the blooms a deep purple and they filled the area with a floral scent. The men were all gathered around one table and the women were mostly on reclining chairs, sunbathing. One woman swam laps in the too blue pool. A small bar was set up near the entrance.

"Can I get you a cocktail? We have frozen strawberry margaritas or a full bar." The bartender was young and must have been from Bakerstown, as I didn't know him. Of course, there weren't a lot of young people in South Cove. Most of them went off to college, then found jobs elsewhere. I was lucky that Nick Michaels, my friend Sadie's college-aged son liked working at Coffee, Books, and More during his college breaks, although Sadie had mentioned an internship he was looking at for next summer. One actually in the kid's field of study.

I realized Greg and the bartender were watching me. "Sorry, I was thinking about something else. I'll have a margarita."

"Good choice. The strawberries are fresh from Jensen's farm, right down the road." The bartender turned toward the machine that swirled the iced mixture. Greg sipped on his beer and pointed to the line of chairs. "Looks like you might get some reading in after all. The women don't seem to be all that interested in chatting."

I shrugged. "We don't know if we have anything in common besides you guys. Give the group some time to feel each other out and I'm sure we'll be inseparable by the end of the weekend."

Or we'll hate each other. But I didn't say that part aloud. Let Greg have fun with his buddies. I'd deal with the other women, even if they were all wannabe beauty queens like Jessica.

I'd dealt with that type before. Kathi Corbin who ran Tea Hee across the street had come into town with a distinct handicap. The real former beauty queen was knock out gorgeous. But as I'd spent time with her, I'd also found out she had a quick wit and kind heart. We weren't best friends, but I trusted her and enjoyed spending time with her.

"I'm not sure that's true, but..." Greg moved me toward the table. "Come over and meet the guys, then you can go mingle and read."

I loved how he knew me too well. The bartender handed me a plastic glass filled to the brim with the red ice mixture that looked more like a slushy with a dollop of whipped cream over the top.

I took a sip of the drink and choked a bit. The alcohol level was strong for the fruity mixture. Good, but strong.

"Greg," the group chimed in almost perfect unison when we walked toward the table.

"Where have you been, man?" A blond man with glasses and a bit of a tummy pooch stood and gave Greg a bro hug. His skin was the color of a codfish. "I haven't seen you since your wedding."

"I've been here in South Cove since the divorce." Greg took my arm and stood me in front of him. "Guys, this is my girlfriend, Jill Gardner. She owns the coffee shop and bookstore in town."

"Hi, Jill!" Again, the group responded in unison.

The standing man flushed. "Sorry about bringing up the whole wedding and Sherry thing. It was just the last time I saw you."

"No worries." Greg kissed my head. "Jill knows all about Sherry. In fact, she opened a store here in town selling clothes. She and Jill are almost friends."

I was taking another sip of courage when I choked again on Greg's "friends" comment. I looked up at Greg who was grinning. He shrugged, "It could happen."

"Well, I'm just glad you saw the light and left that woman." Levi smiled at me. "I'll tell you a secret. She always gave me the creeps."

"Let's put my romantic history aside, okay guys?" Greg nodded at Levi. "You know our host. The guy standing next to him with his foot in his mouth is David Rock. The behemoth over there is Butch, and that's Mikey, with the beer in his hand."

"You're a few behind," Mikey grabbed a can from the bucket of ice and held it out to Greg. "Finish that beer you're nursing like a little girl and let's get this party started."

Greg squeezed my waist. "You want to join us?"

"I think I'll head over to the pool. You get caught up with your friends." I held up my glass in a toast. "Have fun and I'll see you at dinner."

"I'll be five steps away." Greg shook his head. "You just want an excuse to pull out a book and read by the pool."

"You know me too well." I kissed him. Walking away, I surveyed the women tanning by the pool. Jessica lay so still, I figured she was asleep or passed out already. There was a lounger near a woman who had her own book open underneath a large sun hat. Her hair was curly like mine, but blond. And she had a white sunscreen nose.

I grabbed a towel from a table and then spread it out on the chair next to her. "You don't mind if I join you, do you?"

The woman looked over her sunglasses at me. "Another cast-off wife or girlfriend? For this couples' weekend, they sure like their bro time." She held out a hand. "I'm Lois. Butch is my husband. We had to make it official before he went down state so we could at least have a few special visitations."

"Oh? I'm Jill Gardner. I'm here with Greg." I wasn't sure where down state was, so I jumped into the fray. "So where are you guys from?"

"Louisiana. We live in Shreveport, but Butch works on the docks. It's hard work, but he makes good money." She cocked her head toward Levi. "Well, not great money like the computer nerd over there. According to the upcoming bride, Levi's not just a millionaire anymore."

I'd found out more about two of the couples in less than five minutes than Greg had told me since receiving our invitation. "Greg and I live together."

Lois laughed. "I take it you just started shacking up?"

"Well, yeah, why?" I wondered if Lois had known Sherry too.

"Just the way you say it. I remember when Butch moved into my apartment. I didn't know how to describe our relationship. I mean, boyfriend sounds too casual, and yet, you're not married. Relax, you'll get used to it. When we got hitched, Butch went off the deep end. Like he was responsible for me or something. I told him he could get off his high horse and just be himself."

"I don't know if we're even ready to talk marriage yet." How'd we get so deep into the personal stuff so quickly? Of course, I'd starting thinking about the future, but honestly, I liked where we were right now.

"I'll stop bringing it up then." She nodded to the other women on the lounge chairs. "Jessica's the bride to be. MaryAnne is with David."

MaryAnne waved a hand to me, but didn't turn her head. "Nice to meet you, Jill."

"The one swimming is Allison. She's Mikey's new wife." Lois leaned closer and whispered. "Number five. Mikey has problems with commitment."

"Preach it," MaryAnne called from her lounger. "At least this one actually talks to us. The last wife thought she was too good for us."

"So you guys know each other?" I hadn't expected that.

"Every September we get together at someone's house." Lois looked at me. "Greg hasn't shown up for a few years. I'm surprised he didn't just bring you along."

I tried to think back to last fall. Had he invited me to some trip that I'd turned down? "I'm sure we must have been busy on those weekends. Greg works so hard and I've got the shop."

"Oh, don't feel bad about it. He rarely showed up with Sherry either. That woman wouldn't let him out of her sight." Lois stood and wobbled a bit on her flip-flops. "Let's go drag the boys inside and get dinner started."

I watched as Allison stepped out of the pool, water dripping off her blue bikini which was just as skimpy as Jessica's. The women were in great shape. Except for Lois. Yet, she seemed more comfortable in her plus-size body than the other woman did in their model size ones.

"Throw me one of those towels, please." Allison looked at me since I was standing next to the table.

"Sure." I tossed her a towel.

"Thanks." As she wrapped herself into the large towel, she grinned at me. "Looks like Greg found someone who wasn't a flake."

"Just because I can throw a towel?"

Allison stepped closer and held out her hand to shake. "Actually, just because you responded to a request. From what I heard, Sherry would have ignored me completely. I'm Allison and I'm so glad I'm not the new girl anymore."

"I guess that role falls on me now." I liked Allison and Lois. MaryAnne seemed nice or at least funny. And Jessica? Well, she was the bride, so I'd let her have some bridezilla moments for the weekend.

Lois stood at the edge of the table, her hand on Greg's shoulder. "Nice to see you stranger."

Greg looked up and gave Lois a quick kiss on the cheek. "Did you meet my girl?"

Lois patted him on the shoulder, then smiled back at me. "I did. She's lovely. You did good this time."

"I hope so." Greg leaned his head back and made eye contact. "Oh, honey, I didn't see you standing there."

"Whatever. Apparently, it's time to eat. You guys done talking about glory days?"

Mikey jumped up and into a sumo warrior stance. "Never. But I am hungry."

As we made our way into the grand hall where Brenda and her crew had set up dinner, I heard Jessica whisper to Levi. "I can't believe I let you talk me into this snooze fest. Tell me we won't be doing this every year."

A glance up at Greg and I knew he'd heard the comment too. He pulled me close and nuzzled my neck. "I guess we're more of an acquired taste."

"Or the rest of us are too polite." Bridezilla Jessica had two strikes against her. One more and she'd be officially on my list. And not the one where I keep all my best friends.

CHAPTER 3

Brenda's staff served the dinner party in four courses. When the dessert course, strawberry shortcake and coffee, was served, Levi stood. "Let's take this party back out poolside. The bar is open and Greg's behind on tequila shots."

The group stood and followed Levi, leaving Greg, Allison, and me staring longingly on the uneaten plates. He sat his fork down on the table and turned to me. "Do you mind?"

I shrugged. "I get it, you want to go play with the boys. But seriously? You're turning down one of Sadie's desserts? I'm going to have to rat you out the next time she visits."

"Don't. She'll stop bringing her leftovers to the station for the guys." He looked at the group as they disappeared out of the dining room. "I'll stay and wait if you want to finish yours."

I shook my head. "Go. I'll be there in a few minutes."

Greg kissed me on the cheek and almost ran out of the room.

"These guys act like little boys when they get together. You'll get used to it." Allison took a bite of the shortcake. "You seriously know the pastry chef who made this? She must be crazy in demand. We don't have anyone this good in Boise."

"Sadie's a friend and owns her own bakery here in South Cove. She supplies wholesale accounts like my coffee shop and catering jobs, like this." I took a bite of my own dessert and smiled as the flavor exploded in my mouth. "They don't know what they're missing. I might just eat their servings as well."

Allison giggled. "I'd help, but I'm already going to have to swim for an hour just to help negate the calories in my own. So you own a coffee shop? That's cool. Mikey wants me to be a stay-at-home mom."

"Oh, you guys have kids?" I sipped my coffee. "How old?"

Allison dropped her eyes. "That's the thing, we don't have kids yet. Mikey says it happens sometimes and we should just relax, but seriously, we've been trying for six months. In high school, girls got knocked up after one back-seat mistake. I'm having sex every freaking day and still I get my monthly visitor."

I wasn't sure how I felt about Allison's personal sharing, but at least she was nice. "I didn't realize you and Mikey had been married that long."

"Six months. He made it clear when we got hitched that he wanted kids. And not just one or two. The crazy nut wants at least six. He's talking about even more." Allison looked at her empty dessert bowl. "Of course, I have no idea how to take care of even one."

"I think that comes with time. You probably weren't a perfect swimmer the first time you got in a pool, right?" I eyed Greg's untouched dessert.

"Actually, I was kind of a child protégé. I trained for the Olympics, but I never could get my times down to where I was a serious contender. My dad said I had too much body fat to really compete." She shrugged and pushed away the empty cup. "I won a few national titles, but nothing important."

"Wow, I've never met a competitive swimmer before. Did you grow up in Boise? Were there a lot of swim programs there?" I took a sip of the coffee and tried to push Greg's uneaten strawberry delight sitting within arm's reach out of my mind. It wasn't working.

"I started competing in junior high. We traveled a lot for events. It got me a college scholarship, so I went to Cali State. I loved living in California, but Mikey didn't like it here. So we're back in Boise." She stood. "It's a great place to raise kids. I'm heading back to the pool for some lap time. I'll see you out there."

As she left, Brenda Morgan walked into the room. She eyed the uneaten plates and sank down into Greg's seat next to me. "People are funny about desserts. Some don't eat because they're on a diet, some people would rather just drink their calories."

"I think you've got both in this group. Don't tell Sadie her creation went to waste." I sipped my coffee. "What's been going on in your life? I haven't seen you forever."

"I've been busy here at The Castle. I really enjoy my job, even if it is becoming clearer by the day that Craig didn't know what he was doing."

"I'm glad you're finding your spot. But don't forget your friends. I'd love to have dinner with you sometime."

"As soon as I get a break, I'll give you a call." Brenda took an unused coffee cup from the table and filled it from a nearby carafe. She nodded toward my cup and I shook my head in affirmation. With filled cups, we leaned against the chair backs. "So I heard about Jackie's upcoming nuptials. What about you and Greg? Has he mentioned making your living arrangement permanent?"

"I'm still getting used to having him around all the time." I sipped my coffee. "Not sure I'm ready for the big white dress. At least not for a few years."

"Well, I can relate to that. After the way Craig treated me, I don't think I'm going to give anyone else that power again." She held up a hand. "I know what you're going to say. All men aren't crazy like my ex-husband. The problem is that they don't wear warning labels and I'm bad at reading a man's mind."

"You have plenty of time to find love." An echo of laughter came in through the open patio doors. "I guess I should get out and be sociable."

"No worries. We'll take care of this." Brenda stood and picked up the carafes off the table. "By the way, I'll have a van here at nine for your use."

"A van?" Had there been a discussion of the couples going somewhere that she'd missed out on?

"Sure, for your tour of South Cove? All the women have been talking about hitting the shops tomorrow. Don't tell me Greg didn't mention that you're leading a tour group." She studied my face. "Okay, then, maybe he didn't know either. According to the itinerary they sent me last week, the guys are going out on a charter about five tomorrow morning. And you and the women are going into town. Seems a little sexist, but I'm just the host here."

"I'm not sure we didn't get the better end of that deal." I'd gone out fishing with Greg and his brother once. I loved watching the ocean and even the sun come up, but mostly I got a lot of reading done. At least I'll be able to do an errand for Mayor Baylor while we're there. Now I wanted Greg's dessert and maybe a few more. What did I know about leading a tour? At least it should be interesting. I'd start at my shop. That way I could check on Deek, my newest employee who was taking my shifts this weekend.

I wandered out to the pool area where the boys were back at the table and the women were scattered around the patio. Allison was swimming. Jessica appeared to be sleeping. And Lois and MaryAnne had taken over another table, frozen margaritas in front of them. I ran a hand over Greg's shoulder as I passed by the table. I thought about stopping and asking who had volunteered me to babysit the female side of the party the next day, but the pecking order was becoming clear.

Boys rule, girls wait for boys to get done.

Not exactly the type of life I lived or even wanted to play at for a weekend. Greg and I would have to talk about future visits if we were still together for next year's reunion. I can only hold my tongue so long and then I know I'd say something. But I'd give him this weekend.

At least I'd try.

Lois pointed to the bar. "You look like you need a drink. Go get one and join us. We're talking about MaryAnne's trip to Boston next month."

I nodded. "I'll be right there." At least these two were friendly. Three if you counted Allison, but it appeared that she spent most of her free time in the pool staying in shape. The girl just needed to relax.

Taking the frosted glass filled with the frozen drink, I made my way to the table. "Boston, huh? I've never been. What are you going for?"

"My business. I run a beauty supply company and I'm speaking at the convention. You know, the typical motivational stuff." MaryAnne sipped her drink, her long nails painted pink with flamingos drawn on the polish.

Lois leaned closer to the table. "David doesn't know, but Levi is a silent partner in the business."

"Seriously?" I didn't know how anyone kept a secret with this group.

MaryAnne laughed at my reaction. "I should tell him, it's been years now, but Levi keeps telling me to keep it between us. He doesn't want David to feel uncomfortable in their friendship."

I took a sip of my drink. "That sounds reasonable. So your business is doing well?"

"We've really taken off this year. I should be able to buy Levi out by the end of next year; that is, if he'll sell. The beauty business is hot right now and he's getting a great return on his money. I can't really blame him, I wouldn't have been able to start up without his help, but I'd like to be sole owner someday." MaryAnne stole a glance over to the guy table. "At least he doesn't mess in the day to day operations. Some people I know with silent partners are ready to kill them by the time they get control of their business again."

"Anyway, she's going on a dinner cruise in Boston Harbor," Lois changed the direction of the discussion, apparently bored with the financial talk. "You should take some tea bags to throw in the water."

MaryAnne gave Lois a dismissive glance. "I don't think they allow that." She turned back to me. "So will we get to visit your little shop? I'm considering opening some retail stores next year, but I'm not sure I want to get into the customer service situation."

"You have great customer service now, it's just a different level of customer." I pointed out. A confused look passed over MaryAnne's face so I went into how as a wholesaler, she had customers, they were just the retail stores that actually sold the product to the end line consumer. I realized I must have been paying attention in some of my classes lately as I participated in the discussion. Thank God for Aunt Jackie and her insistence I learn more about the business side.

The evening was winding down and Lois stifled a yawn. "I'm heading to bed. I'm looking forward to seeing your little town tomorrow. I'm so glad the boys are going out on the boat. Butch loves fishing. He goes out on a local charter during the weeks he's working too."

I was glad we were going into town, even if no one had asked my opinion before the plans were set. Or after, for that matter.

Raised voices cut off our discussion of tomorrow's activities. The noise was coming from the table where the guys sat.

"You think you're so smart. Just because you make more money than the rest of us." A raised voice came from the other side of the patio. I looked over and Butch was standing, or actually, swaying, pointing a finger at Levi. "You think you can get away with anything. But it's not going to happen on my watch."

"Butch, calm down. I didn't mean to imply…" Levi started, but stopped when Butch slammed his fist on the table, knocking over beer bottles.

"You never mean to imply or sleep with someone's wife, or even give a shit." Butch moved closer to Levi and I saw Greg step in between the two. Lois ran by me and grabbed her husband's arm.

"Honey, can you take me upstairs? I'm not feeling well." She raised her voice to be heard over Butch's heavy breathing. "Honey?"

He broke eye contact with Levi and looked down at his wife. Then he glared at Levi again. "You are so not getting away with this. I'll kill you if I have to."

"Hold on, Butch. Levi didn't do anything wrong." Greg said in the voice tone I'd heard him use with drunks at the bar when a fight had broken out at the winery during one of our date nights.

Butch turned his anger to Greg. "You don't know. You think he's that skinny kid we went to school with? No, he's a schemer and we're all just players in his personal game. But he's not getting away with this. Not after all we've been through. Someone has to put their foot down."

"Butch, I need you to help me upstairs. I'm not feeling well." Lois stepped in front of him and tipped his head down so she could see in his eyes. "Please?"

I could see the tears in his eyes as he studied her. His voice dropped a few octaves and he asked, "Are you sick?"

"Probably one too many margaritas. Can you walk me to the room?" She pulled on his arm, leading him away from the table. Greg didn't say anything, just stood, blocking Butch's view of the target of his anger.

As they walked past, I saw Lois pat Greg's arm and nod her thanks. I waited for the couple to reach the hotel entrance before moving to Greg's side. I looked up at him. "That was intense."

"Butch can be a little over-the-top at times." Levi slapped Greg on the back. "I appreciate the support, dude, but there was no way Butch was going to hit me. He and I have an understanding."

Greg put his arm around me. "I've got to get some sleep. Especially if we're heading out on the boat tomorrow. Talk to you all in the morning."

We heard the good-night calls and he waved a hand behind us, acknowledging the words but not slowing down. I hurried to keep up with him. When we got into the elevator, he slumped against the wall. "Now, I remember how crazy those guys are. It's like being back in high school."

"What was the fight about?" I brushed a lock of hair out of Greg's eyes. He looked beat.

He didn't look up, instead he sighed. "Something that happened over twenty years ago."

CHAPTER 4

Greg promised to tell me the story before he left the next day, but after enduring his tossing and turning during the night, I'd slept through his four o'clock alarm. When I'd finally woken, he and the fishing boat had left hours before. I stretched in the too-soft bed, enjoying the softness of the high thread-count sheets. Brenda knew how to run a high-end hotel. I thought about Emma and hoped my dog was enjoying her sleepover with Toby. Toby Killian lived in the shed turned apartment behind the house along with being a part time barista at my shop, the guy also served as one of South Cove's finest. Basically, the guy never slept. But Emma loved him and he was good with her, so I didn't feel uncomfortable with leaving her for the weekend.

However, I missed her. We typically ran first thing in the morning down on the beach. She loved pretending she could catch the sea gulls. And the gulls loved teasing my golden retriever. They had a history and a system.

A lot like the group I'd met yesterday. They definitely had history. I wondered: *What had gotten Butch worked up that fast?* I'd blame it on the alcohol, I saw way too many buckets of beer and shots flowing to the boys' table yesterday. Except Greg had mentioned their high school history. Or at least that's what I'd assumed he'd meant.

I opened up my laptop and typed in the town where Greg had grown up: Sioux City, Iowa. I got a lot of hits, but when I added all the men's names, I got articles from the local paper about them and their lives since the accident.

"Accident?" I racked my brain to try to remember if Greg had ever mentioned being in an accident, but I came up empty. I had just clicked on the first article, which seemed to be a summary of the others, when a knock came on my door. I bookmarked the link and leaving my laptop open on the bed, went to answer the door.

"Hey, sorry to bother you, but the van's waiting and everyone's inside, but you." Brenda studied me with a concerned glance. "Are you okay? Should I send one of my volunteers with the group to do the tour? I have them all on call this weekend to help me with the group."

I glanced at my watch, the morning had gotten away from me. "Let me run under the shower quickly, then I'll be ready. Sorry about the delay." I stepped back, intent on closing the door, but Brenda blocked it with one hand.

"One more thing. One of the women looks like she's been crying all night. I heard there were some loud voices at the pool last night. Is everything okay with that Lisa?" She looked at me with understanding gaze.

"You mean Lois." I shrugged, not wanting to get involved in the whole thing. Besides, how would I know, really? I just met the group. "I think so, I'll try to pull her aside today to talk to her."

"I'd appreciate that. I hope everything is okay. I have some referrals to the women's safety council, if she needs help." Brenda shoved a card into my hand. "Maybe you could give her this."

I held it up and nodded. "Sure, if she says anything to make me think she's not okay, I'll pass these on."

"Sometimes they don't say. You should pass them on no matter what." Brenda said through the narrowing slot where I was trying to close the door. Brenda had used a women's network to leave her husband. I didn't know all the facts, but even I could see Craig Morgan had been a bad man. Now, Brenda volunteered with the organization that had saved her life.

"Gotcha. I'll see what I can do." I pointed to the pajamas. "I really need to get ready now, the ladies are waiting."

"Oops, sorry." Brenda flushed and turned away toward the elevator. I closed the door and looked at the card. How did I explain handing off a card offering battered women's services to not only a total stranger, but to one that was married to a guy Greg went to school with and still considered a friend?

Yep, my life just got more complicated and mostly because I didn't know how to say no. Ever.

The driver was the older man we'd met yesterday at the beginning of our tour. Joe, James, no, John. I smiled but he narrowed his eyes and took off as soon as I had closed the door. As the van accelerated, I bumped my shoulder into Allison who helped me find my seatbelt after I got settled in the seat next to her.

I had him drop us off at Coffee, Books, and More, with a promise to pick us up at the winery no later than 4:00 p.m. At least I thought it was a promise. It was actually more like a grunt. At least I had my cell and I could call Brenda if John didn't return for us.

The plan was for us to hit the shops on the way to lunch at Diamond Lille's, our one and only greasy spoon in South Cove. Then continue shopping on the way back to the winery where we could get a few drinks before heading back to see how the guys had fared on the water. But first, I, I mean, we could get a coffee from the shop.

I had a touch of a hangover from the margaritas last night. Sugar and alcohol were a bad mix, especially since I loved the darn things so much. As I walked in the door, Toby looked up and horror filled his face.

My hands when instinctively up to smooth down my hair. "What? Do I have a bug in my curls? I know I didn't put any makeup on, but I can't look that bad."

"I told the vet not to call you; that I'd take care of it." Toby walked over to meet me. "It's really not as bad as they made it out to be. She's just a little sick right now. I caught her before she ate the whole thing."

I stared at him, confused. Deek should have been working, right? I glanced at the clock, it was after ten. Deek must have just left. Then I realized who Toby was talking about: Emma. Something was wrong with Emma. That could get me out of this crazy couples' weekend without a backlash. Greg knew my dog was important to me. Heck, it might be the excuse to get him out too. "What happened to Emma?"

"She got into my bag of chocolate chips. Man, she had a mouthful before I could stop her. Sissy down at the vet's in Bakerstown says Emma's going to be fine in a day or so. They're keeping her overnight for observation, just in case. And I told them I was covering the costs." Toby threw the barista towel over his shoulder and then smiled at the women crowded around me. As soon as they'd seen him, they'd all come running to my side to meet the cutest member of my staff. At least in the male category. "Hello, ladies. Can I tempt you into a coffee and a treat?"

"We're not done talking about Emma. Why weren't you watching her?" I wanted to kick him in the shins, but his next words made me pause.

"Sasha called and we got to talking. Okay, maybe we were fighting. I'm really sorry Jill. I don't know what I was thinking." He nodded to the other women. "Let me get these orders done and then you can yell at me all you want."

"Jill, you can't be mad at this hunk of perfect male flesh." MaryAnne grinned at me. "Seriously, if guys like this worked for me, I would have divorced David years ago."

"I have to make a call." I ignored the women who flooded around Toby and marched to the office. I used the land line to call the vet. After being assured Emma was fine after being given doggy ipecac to get the chocolate out of her system, I felt my shoulders relaxing. Toby stood in the doorway, watching me.

"Jill, I really am sorry."

I wiped away the tears of relief now that I knew my dog was okay. I can be strong and detached during emergencies, but when they're over, I'm a pile of mush. "I know. Sissy said you did the right thing, bringing her in so quickly. She said you were a mess."

"Emma threw up on me twice before I got her to Bakerstown." Toby laughed. "I guess it was my fault since I'd been feeding her chicken strips from the diner before Sasha called. I really liked having the company. I thought maybe I'd get a dog, but now, I don't know. Maybe I'm not responsible enough."

"Or maybe you are. Thank you for taking her into the vet so quickly. I don't know what I would do without her."

He blushed and then looked out the doorway. "Looks like your group is getting antsy to leave. Are you staying here or going with them?"

I sighed and stood up. Now that the emergency with Emma was taken care of, it was time to get back to the fun. *Not.* I was never part of a group of girls. I had my few friends in high school, but we did things in pairs of two, not five. "I'm going back to the fun."

"Don't make it sound like it's a death march. You could use some vacation time." He glanced back toward the dining area. "They look like they could be interesting."

"I'd say I'd trade you places and I'd work your shift, but I'd never hear the end of it from Greg."

"She's coming," he called out to the group. Then he turned back to me. "Better go now, the kids are getting restless."

I gathered the group together and outlined my game plan. We'd hit one side of Main Street down to the diner, then work the other side when we came back to the winery. Our first stop was Antiques by Thomas, the store next door to my shop. Josh Thomas, the owner and former boyfriend of my aunt, was nowhere to be seen. Instead, Kyle the intern turned full time associate, was manning the store.

As the women walked from room to room, oohing and ahhing over the collection, I stayed in the front and talked to Kyle. "Where's your boss this morning?"

"Mandy took him to a wine tasting up in Napa. I'm in charge of the store all weekend." Kyle puffed his chest out. "And I even get to make the deposit tonight."

The last time Josh had left town, he'd asked me to make his store's deposits so Kyle wouldn't have to. Now it looked like he was trusting his employee more and more. "It just takes time to win Josh's trust. You've been doing a great job."

He blushed, then looked over my shoulder. "Something I can show you?" Jessica stood at the counter next to me.

"No, something you can sell me. I'd love that old wooden bedroom set you have in showroom number five."

"Good choice. It's eastern European and our records show it was brought over to the states a few years ago when an immigrant family settled nearby. I have several items from that estate sale if you'd like to look at more." He opened a large notebook, scanning the pages until he found his notes. "Can I show you the rest?"

"Don't bother. I'll buy all of it." She handed him a black credit card and then took out what looked like a business card and scribbled on the back. "This is my home address. Have it all shipped to me there."

"Don't you want to know what pieces you are buying?" Kyle asked, but instead of answering, Jessica grabbed her cell phone and dialed a number as she walked out the door. He looked at me. "She has money."

He didn't ask it as a question, but instead, stated a fact. I nodded. "Her husband to be is a tech millionaire. I'd say don't look a gift buyer in the mouth."

Kyle took a photocopy of the card and then started ringing up the items on the list he'd found in the book. "I'm going to charge this and then maybe you can get her to come back to sign the receipt?"

"Hurry, up. The group is getting ready to move on to the next shop."

I watched as Jessica finished up her call. I didn't think the guys would have cell service out on the ocean but I guess Levi's phone was more advanced. She came back into the store and waited by the counter.

"Nice furniture?"

Jessica looked at me. "What?"

"The furniture you bought. It must be nice to purchase so many items." I didn't say sight unseen, but the implication was there. It had taken me months to buy the just right antique bed for my guest room, and even longer to find the right quilt to cover the bed. I guess I was picky, or basically couldn't make up my mind.

"The set reminds me of one I had when I was a child. Besides, it's a piece of history. You can't put a value on that." She took the photocopied list of items and her copy of the receipt from Kyle, signing her name with a swoosh. She tapped the pen on the counter. "I'm serious. If anything else comes in from that source, I want it. You kept a copy of my card, right?"

"Yes, ma'am. I'll call if something else comes in."

She waved away his words. "Don't bother about calling. Just send me the stuff."

As we walked out of the store, Lois pointed to Dustin Austin's bike rental shop. "If we had another day, we should talk the boys into taking a trail ride with us. I hear there's a trail that runs most of the coast."

"You're right, it's called the Mission Trail and there's a trail head here near the beach. It's a great riding and walking path." I fell in step with Lois as we window shopped Main Street. By the time we'd eaten lunch and then started back up Main, I'd forgotten about Jessica's over-the-top purchase at the antique store.

The new Russian Collectibles was next and the group gathered around the window display, pointing out the stacking dolls they loved. I fell in love with a blue and silver doll who looked like she was a princess. As we talked, a little girl, about four, ran out of the store and wrapped her arms around Jessica's legs.

"*Cectpa*," the little blond-haired girl said over and over.

Jessica kneeled down at the girl's level and as she accepted a hug, I saw her whisper in the girl's ear. As she stood, a man came out of the door.

"Alana, come here and stop bothering the women." The little girl ran to her father and clung to his leg.

She looked up at him. "*Cectpa*, Papa, *cectpa*."

He smiled and stroked her hair, mimicking the motion I'd seen Jessica just perform. "My daughter says you look like her sister."

Jessica smiled, meeting the man's gaze. "I'm afraid I'm an only child."

"Alana's sister is back in the home country with her mother. I brought Alana with me to help set up the store. She loves dolls."

I stepped closer. I'd be able to knock out this favor for Tina and Marvin while I was doing the tour. Multitasking at its finest. I should write a book about my techniques. "I'm Jill Gardner, and I own the coffee shop down the street. Tuesday is our monthly business meeting and we'd love to have you visit."

He looked at her gravely. "The mayor said you would be coming by. I will be at this meeting."

"It's kind of casual, we have treats and coffee and typically start at nine before the stores open. Besides, Tuesday is kind of slow, unless we have a tour bus scheduled to arrive. But mostly, it's slow midweek here." I felt like I was rambling. The man's deep blue eyes searched my face for the truth in my words. I ended with another invite, even though he'd already said he'd come. "We'd love to have you."

"Then I will be there." He pointed to the window display. "Have you all seen the stacking dolls? Alana can demonstrate one for you."

The group left after purchasing five stacking dolls. I bought a smaller one than the one I'd wanted. The price tag on the one I'd loved at first glance had given me sticker shock. But no one could turn down the child's soft-sell tactics. I needed to rent the little girl for the children's side of the book store. Alana was going to be an excellent business owner or salesman someday.

As we reached the winery, the men piled out of the van and joined us for a drink before dinner. Stories of the ones that got away circled the table and had us all laughing. Riding in the back seat of the van back to The Castle, I told Greg about Emma.

"Are you sure she's okay? Do you need to cut this short?" He held my hand as we talked.

I shook my head. "Sissy says she's fine, they are just keeping her overnight to make sure she doesn't react to the chocolate. They gave her an IV and they want to make sure it doesn't cause any problems. Toby's a mess." I smiled at the way his face had looked that morning. "I think he about had a heart attack when I walked inside the store."

"He should have called us." Greg settled into the seat next to me for the short ride.

I kind of liked the way he said us. Maybe this cohabitation wasn't so bad after all.

Dinner was wonderful, a fresh-caught salmon as the main course that Brenda had purchased from a local fisherman since the guy's trip had been unproductive. The group seemed to be enjoying the company along with the meal. I saw Brenda study Lois and remembered I'd never asked if she was all right, but from the night's activities, it looked like the storm had passed, if there had been one between her and Butch.

As we retired to our room, forgoing the invitations to drinks poolside, I sank into Greg's arms. "Today was crazy. How was fishing?"

"We always have fun together, at least at first. Of course, the fishing was incidental. We didn't even get a bite all day. It's when the alcohol flows a little too freely that people start talking about things they should leave private." He yawned as he opened the door. "Sorry, I'm beat. You can go down and talk to the women if you want."

"I'd rather stay here with you." I picked up my bag and pulled out a mystery I hadn't even cracked the spine yet. "You don't mind if I keep the light on and read a little before bed, right?"

"Do I ever?" He got ready for bed, then threw an arm over my leg. "Love you."

He was so tired; his words were almost unintelligible. But I'd heard them. "I love you too, Greg."

A series of frantic knocks on our door woke us the next morning. Greg groaned and looked at his watch. "Four a.m. If that's Levi, I'm going to shoot him. He wanted me to run with him this morning, but I'd told him no."

He threw a T-shirt over his boxers and opened the door a crack. Brenda pushed the door inward and almost fell as it swung open. Greg grabbed her arm and pulled her upright. "Are you okay?"

Her eyes wild, she shook her head. "You've got to come down. I've called 911 but you have to come down now."

Fear crept over the back of my neck. I'd never seen Brenda this upset. Had it been vandals? Or something worse?

"What happened, Brenda?" Greg had on his police voice now. Calm, but demanding. "Take a breath, and tell me."

She sank onto the edge of the bed. "In the pool. There's a body in the pool."

Greg grabbed his jeans and headed to the bathroom to change. When he came out, he had turned from my boyfriend on vacation to the chief detective for South Cove. He looked harder somehow, the jut of his jawline completing the look. "Show me what you found."

I stood to follow them but he glanced back at me. "Go change. If you have to come downstairs, stay away from the pool area. We don't want to contaminate the scene."

I could see the unspoken mantra in his eyes. Don't be someone he knew. Finding a dead body was hard. It was impossible to deal with if that body used to be one of your best friends. So far, I'd only stumbled onto dead people who I'd hadn't cared for. Except for Miss Emily of course. And that had been a few years ago. Before Greg and I were even dating.

When I arrived downstairs and saw Greg slumped in a chair, trying to process what he'd seen, I knew it was bad. Looking around, I'd found everyone from the dining table last night, including a sobbing Jessica. Brenda must have gotten everyone out of bed. Except for one person. Levi Wallace. And from what I could see in Greg's eyes when he looked up at me, I knew who had been floating in the pool.

Levi.

CHAPTER 5

"This is total crap." Greg paced the small hotel room, running a hand through his hair. "I should be out there, trying to figure out what happened to Levi." The Bakerstown police department had been asked by Mayor Baylor to step in to investigate the death, effectively taking it out of Greg's hands. For once, I agreed with the mayor's decision. Greg needed to be a friend of the victim, not the cop investigating his friend's death. Terrance Duskant had arrived on scene a few hours ago with Doc Ames and sent us all up to our rooms while the crime techs investigated the scene and they removed Levi's body.

"You know that's a bad idea. You are—I mean, were, too close. You need to let Terrance deal with the investigation. Anything you'd do would be suspect." I sat on the edge of the bed, watching him pace back and forth. "Besides, you need to grieve."

"You don't know what you're talking about. Just because you like to meddle in things that don't concern you doesn't mean I couldn't be objective. I am trained in law enforcement, remember? Besides, sometimes doing something is better than just sitting." I just stared up at him until he sank next to me on the bed. "I'm sorry. Levi was my first real friend in middle school. We rode our bikes everywhere. And when we stopped, Levi always had a story to tell about the rocks, or the area, or even the haunted house down the street."

"You had a real haunted house?" Now I was intrigued. I'd never heard this story before. Maybe keeping him talking about their good days would keep his mind off Levi's death.

Greg ran a piece of fabric from his shirt back and forth through his fingers. "Probably not. It was an old abandoned farmhouse. No one had lived in it for years. We told our folks we were staying at Butch's house even though we knew they were out of town on a summer trip to the beach. Then we took our sleeping bags and sat in the living room and told ghost stories until we fell asleep."

"Any ghosts show up to liven up the party?"

Greg grinned. "Not a one. And we even stole his sister's Ouija board to call on the spirits. When Angelia found out we'd taken it, she was so pissed. She said we'd probably scared away all the spirits because we were just dumb boys."

"Do his parents still live in Iowa?" I could see Greg growing up wild in a small town. No rules except everyone was watching and would report bad behavior back to parents, so kids stayed in line. "His sister?"

"His folks died a few years after Sherry and I broke up. One right after the other. Some sort of cancer, but I figured the one didn't want to live in the world without the other. They were a super tight family. Their deaths hit Levi and Angelia hard." He grabbed for his phone. "I should be the one to tell Angelia, not some stranger."

I put a hand over the screen. "You know you can't. Let Terrance do the hard part then you can call with support. I assume they'll bury him in Iowa?"

Greg shrugged. "Not sure what plans he'd made, if any. Who plans for their death at thirty-seven? And Jessica. I don't know if they will even consider her part of the family. What's going to happen to her? They've been living together for years. Will she lose the house?"

The same questions had run through my head. Especially when they came to Greg and me. If something happened to him, at least I wouldn't be left without a place to live. We hadn't comingled any funds. But if there were medical decisions to be made, I wasn't his next of kin. His brother was and that guy would do anything to keep me out of Greg's life.

This is not about you, I reminded myself. We could have that conversation another day.

"I'm sure he protected her in case of his death. I mean, they just signed a prenup. Maybe that covered situations"—I paused, not wanting to say the words. I settled on a generic—"like this."

"Could you do me a favor and reach out to Levi's attorneys? I'd like to know if Jessica is taken care of. I mean, we can't do much, but maybe we could run a fundraiser in town if she's not." He closed his eyes and lay back on the bed. "The number is in my notebook. Levi made me an appointment to go in and talk about my will. He said it was foolish not to plan ahead."

"I'll run downstairs and order us some room service for lunch and give him a call in the lobby. Are you going to try to sleep?" I ran a hand over his chest, hoping my touch would comfort him.

"I doubt if I'll sleep or eat for a few days. I just feel numb." Greg grabbed my hand and squeezed without opening his eyes. "Thanks for being here. With everything that's going on, it helps knowing I can lean on you, on us."

My heart warmed and my lips curved into a smile. "I'm glad I'm here too. No matter what, we're a solid force against the storm." Crap, now I was sounding like a greeting card. The one with the floating ship on a stormy sea on the outside. "I'll be back soon. Try to sleep."

The hallway was eerily quiet. I wondered where the other couples were. Terrance, the police chief from Bakerstown, had made it clear we were not to leave The Castle. At least not until he talked to each one of us. I felt like I was playing some part in an Agatha Christie movie. You know the ones where one guest after another dies, until they find the murderer was the butler who hated the world, especially if it came in the form of happy couples. The thought sent a shiver down my spine.

When the elevator opened, the lobby was almost empty. I walked up to the check in desk where Brenda sat with another woman I didn't recognize. Her eyes filled with sorrow as she watched me walk up. "Jill, how is Greg? What a stupid question, I bet he's just stunned about this. I mean, I didn't know the victim well, but he and Greg seemed to be close. They were always huddled up in some nook or cranny talking this weekend."

"They were?" *Where had I been during these talks?* I wondered.

"I'm sorry. You didn't come down here to gossip, what can I help you with?" Brenda turned on a small-business-owner smile. I'd worn it and seen it on the people who practiced customer service, even when they didn't feel very welcoming.

"I'd like to order some food for Greg. Maybe a soup and sandwich? Nothing too much. I'm not sure he's up to actually eating. And throw in a few Cokes. I don't think he's had anything to drink for hours." I held my hand out for the menu Brenda had pulled out.

"We have a full kitchen on staff today and tomorrow for your group. Just tell me what you want and I'll have it sent up."

I ordered a bowl of clam chowder along with a chicken tortellini soup. I figured whatever Greg didn't want, I'd eat. Then I ordered two sandwiches and to round out the tray, a cheesecake brownie and a stack of Sadie's chocolate chip cookies. Then I added in iced tea and a carafe of coffee along with the sodas. There had to be something in the order he'd enjoy.

When that was done, I went and found one of those cubbies that Brenda must have been talking about. The small love seat was comfortable and I dialed the toll-free number on the piece of paper. When Jimmy Marcum answered, I almost squeaked. "You're Levi's attorney?"

A warm chuckle filled my ear. "You didn't see that one coming did you? You probably thought it was some big shot in New York or something. What can I do for you Miss Gardner?"

"How did you know it was me?" The first time I'd met Jimmy was when he handled the paperwork for Miss Emily's estate. Since I was the main heir, I worked closely with him during the probate process.

"Caller ID is a modern miracle, especially for someone in my line of business. You wouldn't believe how many people call and hang up before they actually reach me. Tell me, what's going on?"

I told him about Levi being found in the pool and about Greg wanting to know if Jessica was going to be taken care of in the will. "Anything you can say to ease his mind right now would be great. He's ready to set up a South Cove fundraiser to keep Jessica from having to live on the streets."

Jimmy sighed over the phone. "I'm not sure what I can tell you about Levi except for what you already know. Now that he's passed, his business has a big say in what is actually going to be released to the public."

"What about Jessica? Doesn't she have any say so in Levi's affairs?" To be truthful, I was thinking about Greg and me. What rights would I have if he was seriously hurt—or worse? The shock of Levi's death was making me realize he and I needed to have this conversation, as morbid as it might feel.

"Believe me, Jessica will be involved in all the decisions and he left her more than comfortable. Too many people ignore the fact that death comes to all of us. Your boyfriend could take a lesson from his friend. I know he has an appointment set up for next month, maybe you should come in with him."

"I don't know. I'll talk to Greg." I paused, thinking about what Jimmy Marcum had said. "Did Jessica know that Levi had provided for her in case of his death?"

"Of course she did, she insisted on it."

By the time I got back upstairs, the food had already been delivered and Greg was actually eating the Philly cheesesteak I'd ordered for him. It was one of his favorite lunch choices so I had guessed it might tempt him into eating. He waved a hand over the table set up by the window. "Did you order enough food?"

The window looked out over the ocean and I could see the waves crashing on the beach as I sat down next to him. I took the chicken parmesan sandwich and took a bite. Crunchy breading and a just right tomato sauce made me sigh just a little as I sat it down on my plate. "I wanted you to have choices."

"Well, you accomplished that." He wiped his mouth with a napkin. "I'm sorry I was so down. I promise, I'll deal with my emotional crap without affecting your day."

"Your emotional crap is mine too. You are always the strong one. Let me be in that role for a little bit." I nodded to the soup. "Which one do you want?"

"I'll take the chicken one. I know you like your chowder." He nodded to the view. "This is a great spot. We should come up here for the weekend more often. It's crazy that it's so close, yet it feels so far away."

"You're making small talk to make me feel better. Do you want to know what Jimmy Marcum said?"

He wiped his mouth and leaned back in his chair. "I guess so. How did you find out so fast?"

"He just told me. I guess he's been expecting a call from law enforcement to help clear Jessica's motives." I took a spoonful of the soup, watching his reaction.

"You're not in law enforcement." His bluntness made me choke on a piece of potato.

After I got my breath back, I grinned. "Yeah, but I sleep with someone who is. He didn't break any attorney-client privilege, but he did tell me that you can stop worrying. Jessica is well provided for."

"So why did you mention it could be a motive?" He stirred his soup, absently. "Wait, it's because she set up the will, right?"

"Exactly. How much do you know about this fiancée?" I dug into my sandwich. When I came up for air, I noticed he was staring at me. "What? It's typically the spouse or a family member, right?"

"Have I told you recently that you're kind of good at this investigation thing?" He ate some of his soup.

"Watch it, buddy, or I'll forget you're sensitive and throw this pillow at you." Greg always teased me about my investigation skills, especially when he wasn't trying to solve a murder. While he was in full cop mode, I believe he ignored the nagging concern that I was snooping around too.

"Not a dreaded pillow attack." He held his arm up to defray the strike that never came. "I know he's been living with her for a few years. Levi said she came from back east, some sort of model."

"I wouldn't have put her accent as eastern. But it's not Southern, either." Maybe she had a speech problem when she was younger and the residuals of that was what I was hearing?

"Maybe you could do some looking into her background. I'm sure Terrance won't mind you poking around an open investigation." He opened a soda. "At least until he finds out."

"And it keeps you out of the limelight, right?" Greg was totally sneaky. I hadn't seen this side of him before.

"I'm not sure what you're talking about." He nodded to my plate. "Finish up your food and we'll plan out how you can get the information we need. And while you're doing that, I'll reach out to some of my old contacts in Iowa to see if there's some skeleton left in Levi's closet that I don't know about. Maybe it will explain why Butch blew a gasket at the pool."

"I could talk to Lois some more. Brenda thought she and Butch were in an abusive relationship. But I think it had more to do with the Levi thing." I finished my soup and then opened a soda for me. I went to my tote bag and grabbed a pen and notebook, opened it to a new page and sat down on the bed. "Tell me what I need to find out. Maybe I can figure out more ways to get the information. Google is a great source, even if you don't think so."

"Investigation by Google. It could be a whole new line of business for you at the shop." Greg sat down next to me, one of Sadie's cookies in hand. "Let's get started."

When we got the call that it was our turn to talk to Terrance and the officers he had on the investigation, I had a list of to do's in my notebook along with a list of questions to try and ask both Lois and Jessica. I figured I'd start with whoever was easiest to get alone.

When we arrived in the lobby, Terrance took me to one side of the hall and a uniformed officer whose name I didn't know took Greg into a separate room. The room Terrance led me into was a small sitting room, decorated in the style of the early Middle Ages. We sat on large, uncomfortable pews facing each other. "Thanks for staying around to talk to us. I know you probably want to get back to your shop."

"It's closed. We stop opening on Sundays after Labor Day." I wasn't sure why I was telling him my shop business. Clearly I was nervous. It wasn't like I hadn't been questioned in the deaths of others before, but this felt personal. I realized he was watching me. Watching me think? Wondering what I could even know? Or wondering why I was blabbing. I decided to get right to the point. "Anyway, what can I answer for you?"

He looked down at his notes. "According to what I'm hearing, you hadn't met any of these people before this weekend. Correct?"

"That's right. These were Greg's friends, not mine." I relaxed a little in my chair. This should be over in minutes. I didn't know anyone or anything.

"So why was that exactly? You and Greg have been a couple for what, two years now? And you've never met any of his friends before this weekend? How did that make you feel?" Instead of him leaning back, relaxing, he leaned forward and watched for any reaction. I wanted to slap him.

"We just hadn't. Greg said the group was intense. I don't know why Greg hadn't invited me before this weekend. Maybe you should ask him?" I didn't want to be argumentative, but how was I supposed to answer that question? "I'm sure there are friends of mine that Greg hasn't met."

"Do you always keep so many secrets from your boyfriends? Or is Greg special in that way?" He made wrote something on the small notebook in his hands.

"I wouldn't call them secrets. The information just didn't come up yet. Like Levi and the rest of the crew. We just hadn't talked about that part of Greg's life." I knew I sounded defensive, but I just couldn't stay Zen when it felt like the guy was almost accusing me of actually killing poor Levi. He hadn't asked those specific questions yet, but it was only a matter of time before they came up. I focused my gaze on Terrance as he wrote more in that stupid book of his. "Besides, when did you introduce your childhood friends to Althea? You know we talk at the county police get together trivia nights. I've heard her say you didn't even share where you went to school before the two of you got married and she found your yearbooks."

He squirmed in his chair. "It wasn't one of my friends who was murdered, Miss Gardner. I think we should keep the questions on the matter at hand."

"As long as you stop digging for an easy way out of this. Neither Greg nor I killed Levi. That's probably all you need to know. Can I go now?"

He smiled, but the humor didn't hit his eyes. "Sorry, I have a few more questions. Tell me about your weekend. When did you get here and what happened, right up to the time you found Mr. Wallace's body."

I walked him through what had happened up through this morning when Brenda had knocked on our door. He scribbled notes as I talked. "So you didn't know you were hosting a walking tour of South Cove? That must have made you mad."

"Believe me, I've been roped into doing a lot worse things than shepherding a group of women through town. Besides, I stopped into the shop and talked with Toby for a few minutes." I didn't mention how he'd almost killed my dog. I didn't want to be suspect number one if something happened to my barista in the next few days.

"Toby Killian? Your roommate?" This time Terrance didn't even look up from his notebook.

"He rents the shed out back, he's not my roommate. I thought we'd already established that Greg was living with me?" I rolled my shoulders. "I feel like we're diving into my personal life here, not dealing with the issue of who killed Levi Wallace. I know I didn't. And Greg was sleeping next to me last night. So I think we're done here."

He leaned back and watched me stand up. "If you think so. I just want to have a clear picture of what went on up here in The Castle this weekend."

By the sound of his voice, I was pretty sure he thought the group of friends were either wife swapping or worshiping the devil. One or the other or maybe both. I decided I didn't like Terrance. Not one bit. I walked toward the door.

"One more thing Miss Gardner. You're free to return to your home and work. However, please don't leave the area on an extended vacation until this matter is wrapped up."

"Seriously? I'm a business owner and a member of the South Cove community, where would I be going? Unless you have someone who can cover my shop for a while?" I paused at the door, meeting his gaze. I'd missed his point, originally, but now, realization hit me. "Wait, are you saying I'm a suspect in the death of Levi Wallace?"

He walked toward me and held the door open. "Let's just say person of interest."

CHAPTER 6

Aunt Jackie arrived at the house minutes after we did. She bustled in the front door, then stopped and looked around the living room "Where's Emma?"

"At the vet. She had an issue with some of Toby's chocolate." Typically, Emma would be sitting at a very jumpy attention, her tail wagging softly behind her. My dog loved Aunt Jackie. I couldn't figure out if it was because she typically ignores Emma or if they shared some sort of connection I couldn't see. I flopped onto the couch. I should call Sissy and see if I could bring her home today or not. "What are you doing here? We weren't planning on coming home until tomorrow."

My aunt sat her wedding planner on the coffee table with a thud. I suspected it weighed a good five pounds now. By the time the wedding came around in June of next year, the book should be heavy enough to need a wagon to pull it around. "That poor dog. You should have left her with me. I would have watched her better."

I hadn't even considered leaving my dog with my elderly aunt. Even if Emma worshiped her. It made my heart swell a bit that she'd think about taking on the almost one hundred–pound dog for me. "Don't say that to Toby, he feels bad enough."

"As he should." My aunt settled on the couch. "I saw you drive by the apartment so I thought I'd come over and see how you are. You don't have to explain what happened, everyone has heard about Greg's friend. That poor bride, she must be heartbroken."

"She's hurting, that's for sure." I looked up the stairs toward the bedroom where Greg had disappeared with our bags. I was sure he was avoiding coming down right now to avoid being drilled on the murder

gossip by my aunt. Right now, I hated him just a little. "Greg's a little beat
up too. He hadn't seen Levi in years."

"There's something about childhood friendships that stay with us.
Give Greg my condolences." She stood and turned toward the kitchen.
"Do you have coffee made?"

I leaned back into my couch, trying to enjoy the fact I was home.
Home is where you could relax and chill. I opened one eye, she was still
standing there, staring at me and waiting for my answer. "It's almost four
in the afternoon and we just walked in the door. Why would I have a pot
of coffee going?"

"For guests." She waved me back on the couch. "Don't get up, I'll
make it. And I came by yesterday and put a cherry cheesecake in the fridge
for you. We had leftovers at the shop and Harrold doesn't like cherry."

"I could go for that." Greg's voice boomed down the staircase.

When he reached the bottom, I looked up at him. "Sure, now you come
downstairs. You'd do anything for Sadie's cheesecake."

"I don't know what you're talking about. And I'd do *almost* anything."
He kissed me on the top of the head. "I was talking to Toby. He called
to let us know he's on his way back from Bakerstown with Emma. He
should be here in twenty minutes. Should I get some burgers out for
dinner? Looks like we're going to have a full house."

Aunt Jackie came back into the living room. "No need. Harrold is at
Diamond Lille's picking up fried chicken. You two just relax. You've had
quite a weekend."

I made eye contact with Greg and he responded to my unspoken,
"WTH?" with a shrug that I interpreted as, "Don't look a gift horse in the
mouth." My aunt was being nurturing, which was so not like her. But I
liked this surprising side of her. Home, family—this is where you went
when you were broken. I hoped Greg would feel the love as well.

We could read each other pretty accurately. That was one thing I
noticed when we were at The Castle. The other couples did the same
thing. Except Levi and Jessica. I rarely even saw them talking, let alone
casting glances that soon to be newlyweds should be casting. Like, *I can't
wait to get you to the room and take off that skimpy bathing suit* glances.
What was up with that?

I turned toward Greg, wanting to share my observation. "Levi and
Jessica didn't look at each other."

"What are you talking about?" He plopped down on the leather recliner
he'd brought from his bachelor pad. I had to admit, it was comfortable
and kind of went with my sofa set. Especially if Emma would stop eating

the throw pillows I tried to decorate the leather monstrosity with. "I'm pretty sure they knew what each other looked like. They'd been living together for a while now."

"No, I meant like the glance we just did when we talked without talking." I leaned forward. "All the other couples were throwing those kind of looks to their partner all weekend." I had to admit, a lot of them were eye rolls when Levi was pontificating on one subject or the other. No wonder Allison swam all the time. She was probably tired of hearing her host's stories. I'd only been to one event and I had gotten tired of the Levi show.

"Sure they did." But now I could see Greg reeling the tape of the weekend back in his head. When he'd looked at me again, he'd remembered I was right. "That's so strange. I didn't notice it while we were there. I guess I was too involved in Levi's world but you're right, they didn't."

The doorbell rang and my aunt appeared out of the kitchen to answer it. On the way to the door, she paused and looked at the two of us. "Who didn't what, Greg?"

She didn't wait for an answer, just continued to the door and opened it for Harrold. He walked in and kissing Aunt Jackie lightly on the cheek, announced, "I come bearing food."

Greg jumped up to take the bag from our new guest. "Let me take this into the kitchen."

Aunt Jackie held up a hand. "No need. You two need to relax after your trying weekend. So who wasn't talking?"

"It's nothing." Greg tried to take the bag from Harrold again. "You sure I can't help?"

The older man shook his head. "Son, if I've learned anything this last few months is never argue with the woman. You can't win."

Greg put his hands up in surrender. "I guess they're cut from the same cloth then."

"Hey, what is that supposed to mean?" I threw one of my pillows at him, hitting his legs.

Greg picked it up and tossed it back on the couch. "You throw like a girl, for one. And you know you and your aunt have the same stubborn streak."

"I don't know what you're talking about, Greg King." Aunt Jackie stomped toward the kitchen. "And there's nothing wrong with throwing like a girl. Women can do anything now; we're not just housewives waiting on our man's arrival home from work."

"No, but you were awaiting my arrival from Diamond Lille's." Harrold grinned as he held up the bags. "Shall we get dinner started?"

"Toby should be here in a few minutes." I looked at the clock. "I bet he'll walk in right when we sit down."

"Then we'll set a place for him." Harrold sat the bags on the counter. "Lille filled my bags a little too full. Have you seen her new photo collection? She's calling it the wall of fame. Right now, she had Mayor Baylor and that actor from the sixties sitcom that came into the place a few years ago. She thinks once she starts the wall, other people will want their pictures to be added."

"I'm not sure she should have the mayor as one of her first additions. Maybe no one will want to be on a wall with him." I grabbed plates out of the cupboard.

"That's not nice. Marvin and Tina have done a lot for this town." My aunt pulled out a pitcher of iced tea from the fridge and sat it on the counter as Greg grabbed glasses. Harrold cut up a lemon and put it on the counter

I smiled as I set the table. Somehow over the last few months, the four of us had become comfortable as family. It showed as we prepared to eat Sunday dinner together. Maybe we should make this a weekly thing?

I reconsidered my thought. Maybe monthly.

"I'm with Jill on with this one. Marvin can be kind of a hard ass." Greg grabbed silverware. "And, I don't think he's much of a celebrity."

"Well, Lille's happy with the start of her wall, so that's all that matters." Harrold started pulling out the food from the bags. "That girl has worked her butt off to make that place successful. She deserves our support."

Greg and I shared a look, again. Harrold and his now deceased wife, Agnes, had been friends with Lille probably since she opened the diner next to The Train Station years ago. Harrold acted more like a father figure than just a neighbor to the woman who was now as hard as stone, at least to everyone else but Harrold. I'd gotten a glimpse of what had started to harden her heart a few summers ago. The fact I knew her secret didn't make us closer, just gave her one more reason not to like me.

"You're right, dear." Aunt Jackie laid a hand on his arm. "We should be more supportive. I bet Nathan Pike would send us a photo for Lille's wall. In fact, we might be able to find one where he was eating dinner there on his last trip?"

"I'm sure he'd love to. Nathan definitely considers himself a celebrity." I put paper napkins on the table by each plate, followed by Greg who was placing the silverware as we rounded the table. As I finished, I turned into him, putting my hands on his chest. "Maybe you should call him, honey? He'd love to hear from you."

Both Jackie and Harrold laughed as Greg shook his head, squeezing me into a bear hug. He chuckled as he squeezed. "I needed that laugh. It's been a long day. But you are totally evil. You know that right?" Greg and Nathan hadn't quite got along during Nathan's last visit. Well, Nathan thought everything was peachy, but Greg had been happy to see the guy go. He'd been like a puppy dog, hanging on everything Greg did and said for over a month while he did research for his next book.

When I caught my breath, I went to the counter and poured myself a glass of tea. Greg joined me and I watched him reach for a glass. He looked better. The grief was still there, hanging on him, but he looked more settled. Maybe the impromptu meal was doing its magic. "It's a good thought anyway. I'll e-mail him tomorrow and see if he'll send Lille a photo."

"Two celebrities down, a whole wall to go." Greg filled his own glass. "Harrold, Jackie, can I get you some tea?"

"That would be lovely, dear." My aunt and her beau sat down at the table and started filling their plates.

The front door opened and Emma bounded into the room, finding me at the counter. I leaned down and gave her a hug. "I'm so glad you're okay."

She licked my face and gave me a puppy smile. My dog had the best expressions. Sometimes I thought she was more like a human toddler than a dog, especially when she was happy.

"Jill, I'm so sorry about this. I've paid the vet bill already and Sissy says she should be fine." He held out a piece of paper. "Here's her visit record so you can see exactly what they did."

I took the paper from him and sat it on the counter. "I'll look at this later. Now, it's time for dinner. I looked at my dog. "Emma, do you want to go outside?"

She wagged her tail, code for "Yes, please," and I opened the screen door. Greg pointed to the extra place setting. "Have a seat. Iced tea?"

Toby looked a little anxiously at the screen door, then nodded. "Sure."

As we ate, we talked about everything but Emma or the murder that had happened less than a day ago. Mostly we talked about a wedding that wasn't happening until next summer. I couldn't help thinking about another upcoming wedding that, now, would never happen.

When everyone left, Greg and I cleaned the kitchen as Emma snoozed on her bed in the corner. "Poor Jessica. I mean, I know she's taken care of financially, but I would be devastated if anything happened to you."

He came up behind me as I stood rinsing dishes in the sink and gave me a quick squeeze. "The same here. I watch Jackie and Harrold plan for their wedding and wonder why they don't just elope. We could tag along and be witnesses, maybe even spend a week in Las Vegas and get Elvis to marry them off."

"Believe me, I've offered to pay for the trip." I sprayed hot water, cleaning off a plate to get it ready for the dishwasher.

Greg took it from my hand and put it in the rack. "You got nowhere?"

"Aunt Jackie wants a proper wedding and reception." I turned off the water and put the last glass into the top rack. "She said she was only doing this one more time, she might as well get the kind of wedding she always wanted. She did her first one at the courthouse, just before Uncle Ted left for his basic training."

"I can see how a woman wants the big production. Sherry was just like your aunt, we had a huge wedding. But Ted and Jackie's marriage did better with a trip to the courthouse than my first one did with the expensive show. Greg held out his tea glass I'd missed. "I didn't know Ted was in the service. What branch?"

"Army, but that's about all I know."

"You ready for a beer and some deck time?"

"I'd love a beer before I crash. It's been a long, exhausting weekend. For both good and bad reasons." I thought about the fun we'd had on Friday, before everything fell apart. The entire weekend had been packed with emotion and activity. No wonder I was beat. I took his glass and put it into the dishwasher, starting the machine. Emma and I followed him outside and I sat on the swing. Emma circled the porch, then finally sank into a spot, her head between her paws, watching us. "I think Emma's worn out too."

"I just can't believe he's gone. I know I haven't seen him for years before this week, but I knew he was there. And that we'd get together someday. I feel like I'm abandoning him by letting Terrance run the investigation. And then there's the problem of you." He considered me as he took a sip from his bottle.

I narrowed my eyes. I could see the wheels turning in his head. "What? What about me?"

"Just wondering if I'm making a mistake getting you involved in this investigation. I'm usually trying to keep you out of trouble. Now, I'm sending you into the lion's den." He pulled me closer, laying my head on his chest. "You stay safe, okay? I may not be there to protect you."

"I'm perfectly able to protect myself." I snuggled closer. "I've got the day off tomorrow and thought I'd take a trip into Bakerstown. I haven't seen Doc Ames in weeks."

Doc Ames was our local mortuary owner and, the county coroner. Greg chuckled. "I'm not sure what you'll get him to tell you, but anything at this point would be more than what we have. I feel so out of the loop. I know I shouldn't be investigating Levi's death, but on the other hand, I can't just stay out of it. It feels like I'm turning my back on him."

"I think as long as we don't go crazy, we might be able to help Terrance out with a few things. I know he's probably not half the detective you are and when you add me into the mix, you know we can solve the mystery of who killed Levi in half the time it would take the Bakerstown group to even get all the players right."

"I know you're right, but still, I'm breaking protocol here." He pushed my hair back from my face. "I just feel like I have to figure this out. I owe it to Levi."

We sat out on the deck, watching the sun fade from the sky. Emma snored from her bed. And except that there was a murderer running around South Cove, at that moment, all was right with the world.

The next morning, Greg had already left for work by the time I sat downstairs at the kitchen table with my coffee and a notebook in front of me. I'd told Greg I'd visit Doc Ames today. And I needed to go to Bakerstown for groceries anyway. If I timed things right, I could be back in town in time to have lunch with my best friend, Amy. Usually, we had brunch on Sunday, but this weekend we'd put it off due to the bachelor party. I texted her my morning schedule and told her I'd try to be back by eleven thirty. She responded quickly asking if I'd stop by the local event planning shop and pick up the list of local venues. Apparently the list was too long to fax. Her boyfriend, Justin, had proposed last weekend and Amy wanted to celebrate with five hundred of her closest friends. Between her, Aunt Jackie, and the ill-fated Levi and Jessica, I was surrounded with happy couples planning their future lives together. I was just as happy sitting out on the porch with Greg last night.

Moving in together had been a big emotional step for me. Mostly because I felt like a failure in the happiness area, at least where my love life was involved. I'd been married once, but it was more like we were friends who lived together. He didn't seem at all interested in my life, and I was too busy building a road to nowhere at the law office to notice.

Greg and I were different. I got that. At least my head did. My heart was still scared of committing. I'd made myself a promise that if I did remarry, this would be the last one. So I had to be sure. Besides, I wasn't comfortable with setting up events—not like Aunt Jackie and Amy. I'd rather do the spur-of-the-moment thing. In high school, we had to put together a notebook with all of our wedding planning. I got an A. Then a friend loved my setup so much, she had borrowed the book and copied all my ideas for her upcoming wedding. I was great at the planning part; I just didn't like implementing the plan.

I added Amy's stop to my list and then went through the refrigerator to plan for this week's meals. The good thing is Greg insisted on helping me cook the nights he was here. If we'd been cooking a lot, he'd suggest a night out. And several times, he'd brought home pizza, especially if he was in Bakerstown on business that day.

He did the laundry on Saturday when I worked. If we were out of town that weekend, I did it on Monday. As far as our life together, I thought we'd divided up the chores pretty evenly. I suspected Jessica and Levi had never even talked about things like this. Mainly because Levi's wealth put them into a lifestyle that included servants and cooks.

I felt sorry for them for a moment. Building a life together took trial and error. They didn't have time together for any of the little fights to learn about each other and what was important. Their fights, if they had fought, would probably be about big things. I tried to imagine what rich couples fought about? Maybe how many kids, what nanny to hire, and what the prenup would say. Of course, all those topics were over and done with before they'd even come up. Except for the prenup. And Jimmy had said that Jessica would be kept in the manner she was accustomed to. Which meant to me, the girl was rich. Which gave her reason to be on the list of suspects for Levi's murder. I thought the ultimate list we put together would be pretty long. The guy didn't seem to have social skills or the willingness to go along with the crowd. That could have made him unpopular with a lot of people.

I guess you can never put your own expectations on another couple's relationship. What happens between a man and a woman made sense to them and shouldn't be questioned. Except by the time the investigation was over, Levi and Jessica's relationship would be examined, torn apart, and left open for all to see. I just hoped they didn't have any skeletons hanging out in their closets.

CHAPTER 7

As soon as I walked into the Party Palace, I knew I was in trouble. The woman at the counter took one look at me and came around to greet me like we were old friends. "Jill Gardner, I'm so excited to see you. I've heard that you and that man of yours are starting to take the next steps." She must have seen the confusion I felt in my face. "Or maybe you are here about your lovely shop? I do all my book shopping there. I'm not much of an internet kind of girl. I do love your little author meet-and-greets. I have some great ideas on how I can help you expand your business."

I held up a hand to stop the verbal on slot. "Actually, I'm here as a favor for a friend. Amy Newman said you were holding some kind of list for her?"

"Oh, Amy, she's such a sweetheart. I'm so glad Justin has finally seen to take her off the market. Women like her don't stay single long." She turned to a file cabinet, then spun around. "Oh, my gosh. You must think I'm a terrible person."

Actually I thought she was stuck in the fifties, but I hadn't gotten to terrible yet. She looked a little younger than my aunt, but apparently had the same philosophies about the roles of men and women in this world. Girls were made to be married. "No," I said, hesitantly, not sure what to follow up with.

"Now don't be polite and pretend you didn't notice my error. I didn't even introduce myself. I'm Martha Folks. I've run this party planning store for over twenty years. Of course, back then, we had some crazy parties, not expensive, mind you, but imaginative." She held out her hand. "I make a point of knowing most of the people around the area including South Cove. But it seems like every time I go into your coffee place to introduce myself, you've just left."

"I'm sorry about that." Actually, I wasn't sure why I was apologizing to this woman I'd never met before. I'd read a book that said one of the ways women give up their power is by saying I'm sorry for things that weren't their fault. I decided right then and there that I was going to make a rule not to apologize unless it really was my fault. I'd start a sorry jar and every time, I said those words inappropriately, like just now, I'd throw a dollar in.

"Oh, no need to apologize." Martha squeezed my hand. "Meeting people happens when it's supposed to happen. I believe Fate keeps a close eye on our comings and goings."

Okay, now I just wanted to throw up. The sugar water was getting a little deep. I gently took my hand out of her grip. "I hate to cut this short, but I've got an appointment soon."

"Oh, dear, I didn't mean to keep you. Me and my jabberwocky mouth. I guess I'm just alone here too many hours a day. I really should just work from home, but what fun is that?" She turned and opened the file drawer and started digging. "I think I might have put that book aside in the back. I'll be right back."

Great, now I had made her feel bad and lied to boot. Thank goodness I hadn't set up a lie jar. Maybe this paying my way to good manners wasn't going to be as easy as I'd thought. "Maybe I could come back some time, you know, when I wasn't so rushed. Or you could come to the coffee shop."

"I might just stop by soon." She disappeared into the back.

I sat my purse on the counter and knocked off a stack of papers. I knelt to get them and found a proposal addressed to Levi Wallace. Maybe Martha had put together the bachelor's weekend or she was going to produce the wedding that now wouldn't happen. I peeked around the counter, but she was still in the back room. So I read the first page, and the second. Greg needed to see this. I took my phone out of my purse and snapped copies of each page of the five-page document. I'd just stood and returned the papers to the counter when Martha returned and handed me a three-inch binder, so heavy, I almost dropped it.

"I'm still a little shaken up about what happened at The Castle. You don't know what happened, to that poor man, do you?" Martha peered at me over the piles of loose papers.

"The Bakerstown police department is handling the investigation. I guess with Greg being friends with the victim, it just seemed more appropriate." Apparently, my reputation for sticking my nose into things like local murders had traveled. Okay, now I'd have to figure out how

I was going to stay and chat when I'd just said I had to leave. I painted myself into a wall this time.

Martha took out a rag and dusted off the top of her counter. "I was just wondering."

She was playing cagy. "Had you met Levi and Jessica?"

Martha stopped wiping and considered me. "No, sorry. All I know is what I saw on the news. Why do you ask?"

"I thought maybe they'd talked to you about their wedding plans."

As I walked out of the shop, Amy's notebook heavy in my arms, I decided to show Greg what I'd found out over dinner. My mood lightened as I got into the Jeep. I liked being able to investigate out in the open. In the past, having to sneak around Greg's back when he had asked me not to get involved had been hard. Now that he was benched, he wanted me to find out the things he couldn't. Maybe he could give all the murder cases to the Bakerstown Police Department. Then we could be like those couples who investigate on television. Aunt Jackie had loved a show like that when I was in high school, but I think it was in reruns even then. I'd have to ask her what it was called.

I made a U-turn and headed toward the other side of town where Doc Ames had built his mortuary years ago. When he'd been approved by the county for the crematorium, the ten acres had been in the middle of farmland. Now, a subdivision and an industrial complex sat on either side of the funeral home. The parking lot was empty except for Doc's black hearse. Before I'd left town, I'd stopped at the shop and picked up a bag of ground coffee and an assortment of the desserts from the display case. It was blatant bribery for information, but I didn't think Doc would mind. Much.

The front door was open and I could see light coming from the hallway leading to his office rather than the other business part of the building. I'd never been down to where Doc did his autopsies or prepared the body for burial, and I hoped I never would have to look for him there. Have I mentioned that I threw up in third grade when my science teacher was talking about how the blood pumps through your body?

I swallowed hard and made my way toward the office. "Doc? Are you in there?"

"Who's out there?" Doc Ames came to the doorway of his office, his serious look turning into a smile when he saw me. "Well, if it isn't Nancy Drew. Why are you here, he asks, as he eyed the coffee shop bag?"

"Sue me, I'm transparent." I held out the bag. "I'll take one of those if you have some coffee made to go with it."

"There's not anyone else I'd want to share with." He motioned me inside the office. "Come sit down. How's Greg? Does he know you're here?" I plopped down on the couch. "I'm shocked you're asking. I wouldn't hide things from him."

"And I wasn't born yesterday." He went to the coffeepot and poured me a cup. "You take it black, right?"

"I do." I leaned forward and took the coffee. "Let's get the formalities out of the way. Yes, Greg knows I'm here. He's been taken off Levi's murder case and so…" I paused and Doc Ames finished my thought.

"He thought you could find out unofficially what had happened to our poor groom." He opened the box. "Éclairs. I love éclairs."

They weren't my favorite, but Sadie was going through an éclair stage. She had made at least ten different kinds in the last few weeks. This recent experiment had a pumpkin cream filling and a maple frosting. Basically it was seasonal autumn heaven.

I waited a few minutes, letting the conversation focus on Sadie's Pies on the Fly business, and how much Doc Ames wished she would open a full time shop in Bakerstown. I didn't think that would be happening any time soon. Sadie liked her freedom to work in the morning and then have the afternoon off to do her church work. But I wasn't going to be the one to burst Doc's bubble.

He finished off the éclair he was eating and looked down at the box. "One left, do you want it?"

"Not unless I want to run by myself this afternoon. Emma's on injured reserve for a few days." I went on to tell him about the incident when Toby was babysitting since I was at the bachelor-party weekend. Then I decided to jump into the real purpose of my visit before he finished the last éclair. "Speaking of the weekend, do you know how Levi died? Maybe he just slipped and hit his head when he fell into the pool?"

"An accident like that could be possible." Doc Ames wiped the side of his mouth with a finger, removing a dot of the maple frosting. "However, that wasn't how Mr. Wallace died. From the evidence, I believe he was dead before entering the pool. I'll be getting tox screens in a few days and I'll have an official cause of death to the Bakerstown police then."

"You still haven't mentioned how he was killed." I knew I was pushing our friendship and the power of the éclair, but Greg had given me this assignment and I wasn't going to let him down. Especially since this was the first time my investigation habit had been green lighted by my boyfriend. Everything was situational, I guess.

He closed the empty box and stood, taking it back to his desk and putting it into a nearby trash can. He sat at his desk, opened a file, and read aloud. "The victim appeared to be strangled with some sort of rope or fabric, yet to be determined."

"Strangled?" Someone had been angry enough to squeeze the life out of him. Someone strong like Butch? This was no accident.

Doc Ames closed the file and looked at me, his eyes twinkling with humor. "Oh, I didn't see you still sitting there. I thought you'd left. You know I can't release an official cause of death to anyone except the officers investigating the case."

"I better be going anyway. I still have shopping to finish and I'm having lunch with Amy later." I stood and crossed the office to the doorway where I paused. "Thanks for having breakfast with me."

"Anytime. But I'd like it if I saw you more often than just when someone has died." He turned back to his computer and booted it up.

"I'll stop by soon, I promise." As I walked out of the office and back into the public area of the mortuary, I wondered if Doc Ames was lonely. His wife had died years ago. And since then, the only time I saw him was when he was investigating a murder. Maybe he needed a girlfriend.

Driving back to South Cove, my mind worked on possible hookups for Doc. I hadn't come to an answer before reaching the house. But I had made a plan. I'd do an engagement dinner party for Aunt Jackie and Harrold, and Amy and Justin. That way, I could invite Doc Ames and a suitable date choice without looking like a setup.

I let Emma outside while I put away the groceries, setting aside the ingredients I needed to make dinner tonight. Since Greg wasn't involved in the investigation, he'd be home for supper. I tried to do something new and different on Mondays since I had the day off. Most nights we grilled meat and added a salad. Tonight, I was making a clam fettuccini with garlic bread and the rest of the cheesecake for dessert.

My stomach growled and I realized I had ten minutes before I was supposed to meet Amy for lunch. Food, it ruled my life. However, it wasn't always a bad thing. Like this morning when a few éclairs got me information about Levi's cause of death. I made a quick note about the morning conversations, including the information I'd found at the event planner's shop about the future of The Castle. Then I let Emma back inside, and walked into town.

The fall weather was soft and beautiful. Of course, that's why I loved living in central coastal California. Most days the weather was soft and beautiful. If I wanted winter, I could go to Tahoe and experience enough snow in a weekend to last me the season. I'd rather be in short sleeves and capris than bundled in snow suits and boots.

Amy was already at our favorite booth when I walked in. I glanced at the "Wall of Fame" Lille had set up near the cash register. Our mayor had a framed 11 by 17 signed picture of him in the middle of the wall. Then a few other Polaroids surrounded it. I needed to contact Nathan Pike like I'd promised, and maybe a few other authors who had visited recently, such as Cat Latimer. The woman had been extremely nice, especially to Sasha who had been nervous as a cat on a hot tin roof when she introduced the author.

"I'm here," Amy called out, impatient for me to pay attention to her instead of the almost empty wall. I so hoped she wouldn't turn into a bridezilla like Aunt Jackie had. I couldn't take two people with that kind of attitude in my life at the same time. A girl only has so much patience.

"Hey, I brought you the list." I handed off the heavy notebook. "It's going to take you days to get through all that. Isn't there an online listing somewhere? One you can sort and filter?"

Amy squealed, patting the cover like it was a rare copy of *Harry Potter* or maybe a signed Hemingway. "You would think so there would be, but no. Martha has more knowledge in her head about venues around the area than anyone else in the business. She needs someone to help her update her business but for now, this is the bible of event sites."

"What are you planning, anyway?" I paused as the waitress came by and sat two iced teas in front of us. "Carrie, how are you?"

"Old and my feet are killing me." She took out a note pad. "Let's see, it's Monday so Amy will have a double cheeseburger with a vanilla milkshake and you'll have the usual fish and chips?"

"Actually, I'll have the Cobb Salad. Italian dressing on the side." Amy pushed the menu away as both Carrie and I stared at her. "What? I'm trying to lose ten pounds before the engagement party. I have my eye on a designer dress over at Vintage Duds, and it's a four."

"You're dieting to get into a smaller size?" Amy was slender and didn't have an ounce of fat on her body, especially since she and Justin spent most of their weekends at the beach, surfing.

"Ten pounds won't kill me and it's an amazing dress. Just wait, you'll agree it was so worth it when you see me. Pat has put it aside for me so the sooner I can get the weight off, the sooner I get the dress." Amy sipped her iced tea. "I was dying for a milkshake today, though."

"I guess I'll have the Cobb too." I shrugged as Carrie stared at me. "I'm making pasta with white sauce for dinner and won't be running for a few days."

After Carrie left the table, Amy leaned toward me. "Thanks for the support. I don't know if I could have resisted stealing some of Lille's fries. And I heard about Emma. Are you ready to kill Toby?"

"He's so upset. It's been hard to give him a lot of grief. But for a minute there, when I found out, I wanted to wring his neck." Our conversation continued, but my casual words gave me chills as I thought about what I'd learned from Doc Ames. Someone had been angry enough with Levi to choke him and leave him dead in a pool. The questions I needed to answer was what had Levi done to inspire that kind of anger?

CHAPTER 8

I had been planning on telling Greg about my day and the information I'd found, but after dinner, he got called down to the station. Toby was having trouble with a driver he'd pulled over on a DUI. Apparently the guy was a big shot in the financial world and his lawyer had hit the station soon after Toby had let the guy call out. So Greg had to go and calm everyone down. I knew he'd back his deputy, but Toby needed someone on his side. Especially before the mayor got wind of the arrest. Our mayor liked it when people with power owed him a favor. And apparently, the guy who'd been drinking all afternoon at South Cove Winery was in a position to help the mayor in the future.

Greg kissed me on the lips as he grabbed his keys. "Sorry, I know it's my turn for dishes."

"Go, save the world. I'll be here cleaning up like a good little wife." The words came out of my mouth before I could stop them. I felt my face heat as I tried to backpedal. "I mean, cohabitant, shack-up partner, roommate…"

"Relax. The only person you freaked out with that word was you. I'll just pretend I didn't hear the 'W' word until I need something to tease you about." The keys jangled in his hand. "Are you opening tomorrow or do you have time for breakfast with me at Lille's?"

"I'm opening. Besides, you probably don't want to have this conversation in a crowded diner. Come by the shop on your way to the station and we'll talk then." The coffee shop was pretty dead during my shift, except for the commuters who liked to grab a large coffee before heading into the city for work. The nice thing is most of them also picked up a book or two at least once a week. I didn't know when they found the time to read, but I wasn't complaining.

After Greg left, I cleaned off the table, leaving the dishes for later and spent some quality time with Emma, the couch, and my DVR, all before heading to bed. The bad thing about the morning shift is it came too early. The good thing, my workday was done long before most everyone else's. Tomorrow would be longer than normal since I also had the Business-to-Business meeting to coordinate.

Thinking about that, I e-mailed Amy at her work address and asked her to send me the business license file for our new member. That way I could review it prior to the meeting and maybe have a few tidbits to feed Bill as he introduced Vladimir Petrov to the group.

I knew he had two daughters, one still back in Russia. Was it still called Russia? I pulled up a Google map and familiarized myself with the area. After an hour of getting lost in the internet research on Russia and the little stacking dolls he sold, I tried to take a sip of my soda, but it was empty. Emma nudged my foot. "You want out girl?"

A happy bark confirmed I'd understood her doggie language so I closed my laptop and took the empty soda can to the kitchen. After letting Emma out into the fenced back yard, I cleaned up the kitchen. The bird clock in my kitchen chirped its way to ten so after I was done with the dishes, Emma and I headed upstairs to bed.

* * *

After my commuter customers stopped coming in to the shop the next morning, I curled up on the couch with the latest Stephen King. I only read his books at work in the daylight because most of the time his writing scared the crap out of me. Promising myself I'd only read a couple of chapters, I was jerked out of the story when I heard the bell over the door chime.

"Busy day, I see." Greg sauntered over to the couch and plopped next to me. "So tell me what you found out?"

"No 'Good Morning' or 'Hello, I love you' pleasantries?" I cricked my head toward the counter. "I could pour you some coffee and plate up one of Sadie's éclairs."

"I'll take some to go, and by the way, good morning, but I've got a meeting with our mayor in ten minutes. I probably should have just talked to you tonight when I got home, but our time together has been limited lately." He ran a hand through his hair. "For me not being involved in the murder investigation, I sure have a lot of paperwork to fill out. What did Doc Ames say?"

I filled him in on the preliminary cause of death. Greg sank into the couch. "I knew it wasn't true, but I was really hoping this was just a tragic accident. Poor Levi."

He stood to go, but I pulled him back down. "One more thing. I sent you a few pictures you may want to look at."

"Pictures of what?

I squirmed a little. I knew it wasn't evidence that could be used in a court but we weren't really supposed to be investigating either. "Copies of what looked like a proposal for this event planner of Amy's to promote a nightclub at The Castle?"

"Wait, Brenda's opening a nightclub? I don't remember seeing a permit to serve alcohol coming through the council."

"The proposal wasn't for Brenda. It was for Levi and Jessica. They were planning on turning The Castle into a bar." This time I stood. I needed a drink of water, and Greg needed time to process what I'd said.

"Why would the proposal be to Levi who's just a board member? Are you sure?" He followed me to the counter. "Stop. That was rhetorical, let me read the proposal. Besides, there's no way the board would let that happen. That place is historic. Isn't it on some list?"

"Brenda's been trying to get the place listed. She told me that Craig put the first packet together over five years ago, and still all they get is a letter every six months saying they're on the list. Just like me." I'd been waiting for close to two years for an official decision from the historical society as to whether the stone wall in a corner of my back yard was actually the remains of the original South Cove Mission .

"Interesting." He nodded to the pots behind me. "I'll take you up on that coffee."

I filled a large travel mug with coffee, then put several different éclairs in a box. "Interesting, that's all you got?"

"I'll have Amy check to see if any applications have been filed with the city. I'm surprised you didn't ask her yesterday. I'll see you tonight." He leaned over the counter and kissed me.

Deek came into the shop and held the door open for Greg. "Nice to see you, police dude."

He ambled over to the counter where he stood at the sink, washing his hand.

"You can call him Greg. You know who he is." I crossed over to the couch where I'd left my book. It was time to set up for the meeting.

"Police dude is a term of endearment and respect." Deek glanced around at the dining room. "You want me to set up the tables first?"

I pointed to the office. "Yes, and handle any customers too. I've got to check my e-mail."

"Multitasking at its finest." Deek waved a quick salute then went around the counter again to move tables and chairs. I'd wondered how the laid back perpetual student would do in our staff family, but I shouldn't have worried. Toby and Nick thought he was cool and Aunt Jackie had made it her personal mission to fatten the new employee up a little. The two book clubs he ran for teens and the middle-grade kids loved him as much or maybe even more than they'd loved Sasha. Although I'd never tell her that.

I flipped open my laptop and checked my e-mail. I had one from Amy. *Score!* But when I opened it, I realized she hadn't sent me what I'd requested. Instead, it was a quick response saying the file on the doll seller was missing and she was looking for it. Bill wouldn't be happy about it, but he was going to have to wing it when he introduced Vladimir Petrov as our newest town resident.

Vladimir had purchased the building where Killing Time, the clock shop that had opened and closed just as fast this summer, had been located. Amy had said he got it for a steal since the former owner needed the money to pay his defense counsel. I just hoped all the bad juju had left the building with Ian and his clocks.

Since I had nothing to give Bill, I googled Vladimir Petrov but came up with so many hits it was impossible to determine which ones, if any, were related to our new shop owner. So I googled stacking dolls instead and typed up a few notes for Bill to use to describe the new store, Russian Collectibles.

I thought about his daughter and wondered if he'd bring her along. She and Deek could hang out in the children's section of the bookstore unless a customer wandered in during the meeting. Typically, I saw people peek in and after seeing the group gathered around the table, they'd slowly step away from the door. Between the lost customers and the cost of coffee and treats, the meeting cost me a fortune. At least the town always paid the invoice for the catering when I sent it over. Bill always overrode any objections the mayor brought up to paying the costs at the council meeting.

"Shouldn't you be out there with the group?" Aunt Jackie stood at the bottom of the stairs, watching me.

"I was putting the final touches on Bill's agenda. How long have you been standing there?" Aunt Jackie's arthritis seemed to be doing better the last month or so. According to Harrold, her new doctor had her on a better medicine for the pain and she looked brighter and more settled.

"Just a few minutes. I'm always struck by how deeply you get involved with things. Even as a kid, if you were reading a book, you wouldn't move until it was done." She crossed the floor and ran her hand down my unruly hair.

"I'd meant to pull it up before people came," I started but it was too late now. I could hear the group milling around the dining room.

"You look fine. Beautiful even." My aunt kissed my cheek. "I just want to tell you how much you mean to me."

I side eyed her suspiciously. "Thank you. Now what do you want?"

She jerked back. "Why did you ask that?"

"Come on, you never throw out compliments, even when I've almost been killed." According to the clock, we were starting in less than ten minutes. I needed to get this agenda to Bill. I stood, waiting for her answer.

"I guess I just want you to be happy."

Okay, now she was worrying me. "Look, I've got to get in there. Can I come up to the apartment after the meeting and we can talk?"

"Of course, dear." My aunt smiled and for once, I didn't hear a trace of sarcasm in her tone. Had meeting Harrold and getting engaged finally thrown her over the deep end? Did I have the right to place her in the happy farm if need be? Or did engagement trump niece and that was now Harrold's responsibility?

I watched her turn around and head up the stairs. When the door to her apartment closed, I whispered, who are you and what have you done with my aunt? A knock sounded at the door and Deek poked his head inside.

"Dude, you really have to get out here." He disappeared and then came back inside the office. "Am I supposed to make more coffee if the carafes aren't all filled?"

I hit print on the wiki I'd found about stacking dolls and grabbed the pages as they printed. I couldn't really be mad at him since he hadn't worked a Business-to-Business meeting yet. I should have been out there directing him. "I'll be right out, and yes, make more coffee."

I took a big breath and walked into the fray.

People were clustered into small groups, talking. I saw the plates of éclairs Deek had set out were almost empty. Sadie had a winner with these. I leaned closer to Deek. "Fill these and then watch for ones on the table to empty during the meeting. Normally, they'll signal you, but sometimes you'll just see them try to pour from an empty carafe."

I took the carafe Deek had just filled and walked out to the table where Darla was talking to Bill. "I hate to interrupt, but here is some information about Vladimir's new shop. I didn't get the business license file from Amy yet."

"It's so cosmopolitan for us to have a real life Russian in our town." Darla beamed as she gushed. "I've been trying to get him to agree to an interview, but no luck so far. You can bet his arrival will be the highlight of my report on the meeting though."

Darla wrote for the *South Cove Gazette*. She was their only reporter, and if her editor, Rusty, had anything to do with it, Darla would be the *only* employee as soon as he decided to retire. Of course, living on the beach and publishing a small weekly newspaper had been the original retirement plans for the *New York Times* editor when he moved here ten years ago. Now, I heard he was planning on spending the next ten years traveling the world. Just as soon as he found someone to take over.

Which he'd been talking about for at least two years. I got it. Some people don't like change. I count myself in that group. I looked around the room for our new member. "I thought he'd be here by now."

"Actually, I got a call from him this morning. His daughter is ill and he's going to have to skip this meeting." Bill pocketed the paper I'd printed. "Make sure you put his introduction on next month's agenda. I'm sure you'll be able to get me additional information by then."

As he walked away, Darla huffed. "What's got his goat this morning? He was all grouchy when we were talking."

"I don't know." I watched as Bill made his way to the front of the table which was his nonverbal cue that the meeting was about to start. "Looks like we're getting started on time for once."

"Shoot. I was going to ask you if you knew anything about the guy who was killed at The Castle. Rumor is that he was gunned down in a mob hit." She pulled out a small notebook and waited for my reaction.

"Seriously? You need a better gossip source. Levi wasn't gunned down and I don't think he was on the mob's hit list. He was a software designer." I studied her as she quickly scribbled notes on a clean page. Feeling suspicious, I asked, "Did you really hear that or was it a ploy to get information from me?"

"A girl's gotta have her tricks." Darla shrugged. "And as usual, you don't have any better information than I do. I guess since Greg isn't investigating, your pillow talk hasn't been about the murder."

"Our pillow talk is never about murders." That was the problem with living with someone in law enforcement. Everyone thought you knew everything. But I didn't want to look like an informational gold digger.

"Jill, can you and Darla take your seats?" Bill called from the front of the room. "We're waiting on you."

Everyone turned and watched as Darla and I made our way to the table. Whispers filled the room, but I made my face as calm as possible. No way was I going to let rumors fly about any catfight between the two of us.

"Sorry, Bill. Just catching up." I slipped into a seat next to Amy who raised her eyes in an unspoken question. I shook my head and she turned back to her laptop. Amy had started coming to the meeting as our official scribe. This way, the notes went directly to the council and the mayor and I didn't have to make a monthly appearance at the council meeting to report.

Although I had been voluntarily attending those meetings lately, it was interesting hearing the different opinions about city projects and festivals. Of course, I wanted to speak up at times, mostly to disagree with the mayor, but I kept my mouth shut. I was finally beginning to enjoy my role as the business liaison to the South Cove Council. I didn't want to jeopardize it by speaking my piece when the mayor was just blowing stupid smoke.

"So we have a short agenda today." Bill started the meeting and we moved into talking about the holiday festival. Darla ran South Cove's festivals with an iron fist. Tina, the mayor's wife, had tried to usurp the position one year, but bailed when it got hard. Darla had graciously taken back over with the promise from the council and the mayor that she would be given total authority over any festivals she wanted to develop.

Mary, Bill's wife and copartner in the bed-and-breakfast they ran, stood first and talked about what had worked and what hadn't based on comments from our visitors, both in the drop box by Santa's Village and online. She'd also done a comprehensive survey of the business owners a few months after the event which included sales estimates and customer numbers. At the end, it was clear that having the festivals increased customer traffic for all of the businesses that were open during the last holiday season.

"I can't say we got a lot of increased traffic." Sherry King, owner of Vintage Duds—and Greg's ex-wife—spoke up. "Our sales were down in December."

Mary flipped through the notes she had. "That's odd, I could have sworn that everyone had increased sales."

"Maybe your sales were down because you and Pat took that two-week cruise right before Christmas and closed your shop during one of the busiest retail times of the year." I pointed out Sherry's error. The girl didn't want to work, but man, she liked to whine.

Mary pointed at a sheet. "Here it is, Jill's right, Vintage Duds was closed from December 15 to January 5. But the sales you made between Thanksgiving and when you closed were higher than the year before." Sherry glared at me. Apparently she'd forgotten it was hard to be profitable if the doors weren't open and the owners were cruising the Caribbean.

Darla took over and laid out her plan. We were going to have a traditional fifties Christmas theme. Josh beamed as Darla pointed out that he and Kyle had submitted the winning proposal from last month's contest. "There were some great suggestions, but this one just felt right."

I leaned closer to Amy. "And I bet Josh has a huge supply of vintage Christmas items he'll have on sale during the period."

Amy snorted and Bill frowned at us. That was twice I'd gotten dinged for bad behavior during the meeting. I needed to settle down.

I leaned back and focused on Darla's presentation, thinking about ways the coffee shop could participate. Maybe a special coffee drink for the season? We typically did a peppermint hot chocolate or coffee, but I could figure out something else. Like the old hot toddies my mom had made as soon as the weather turned cold. Sans the alcohol that is. Or maybe some kind of eggnog-based treat? I'd have to talk to Aunt Jackie. Since she'd been working in a café in the fifties, maybe she'd have some ideas. I'd invite Sadie to the meeting also and we'd brainstorm treats to sell alone with the drinks.

Amy elbowed me and I looked up from my doodling. "What?"

She nodded toward Bill. I'd missed a cue or a question.

"Are you with us now?" Bill asked and this time, even Mary looked at him questioningly. I wasn't the only one hearing the snark in his voice.

"Sorry Bill, I was brainstorming about Darla's idea." I forced my lips into a curve. "What did you ask again?"

"I asked if you wanted to be part of Darla's design committee. It sounds like you are very intrigued by the idea. We'll just put you down on the list."

I smiled, even though I wanted to throw my cup at him.

Darla clapped her hands, a big smile on her face as she spoke. "Then the committee is all set. Thank you all for graciously volunteering your time. The committee will meet here tomorrow to get this thing rolling. If that's okay with you Jill, around ten?"

"Of course." I was going to have to figure out a way to bow out or better yet, get Aunt Jackie to take over. This would keep her busy and out of my hair or over planning the wedding.

"The Castle representatives were going to present a proposal to the group, but with all the fuss there this weekend, that project is on hold." He held up a gavel. "If there is no other business…"

Josh held up a hand. "I'd like to discuss the trash receptacles we have on the streets. I think they make the area look dirty."

"Then we'll close." Bill banged the gavel as if Josh hadn't spoken.

As people got up to leave, Josh lumbered toward me. "I hate it when he does that."

CHAPTER 9

I wasn't sure what project Bill had been talking about, but by the time I'd promised Josh that trash cans would be a hot topic on next month's agenda, Bill and Mary had already left. I helped Deek put the dining room back in order and asked him if he'd had any questions on the process.

"No, dudette. It seems simple. I set up the room, pour coffee, set out food, and then keep them in coffee until the angry guy bangs his gavel." Deep pushed the last chair back under a table.

So he'd picked up on Bill's attitude too. I wondered what might have put our chairman in a bad mood and the only thing I could think of was The Castle project. Amy had closed her laptop and hurried out almost as soon as Bill's gavel descended. Maybe Greg would be able to push her to find the information. But the first file I'd asked her about this week had disappeared. I wasn't holding my breath for the second one, even if Greg was the one pushing for it.

The bell over the door chimed and Lois and Allison walked in. I walked over to greet them. "Hey, what are you doing here?"

"The police won't let us leave town, so we thought we'd come visit and get some reading material. Everything at The Castle is years old." Lois squeezed me tight. "How are you doing with all of this? I mean, what a welcome to the group."

"At least she'll never have to deal with drunk Levi's wandering hands." Allison picked up a book off the rack. "Ooh, I've been meaning to read this. Do you have the full series?"

"I think so." I waved Deek closer. "Hey, take Allison over to the YA section and see if we have the rest of the series."

After they moved away, Lois sank into a chair. "Sorry about that. Allison's new to the group too so she doesn't know we don't air our dirty laundry in public."

"Was Levi that bad?" I sat down at the table too, wondering if this had been the subject that sent Butch off that night.

"Why do you think Mikey has been married so many times?" Lois pushed her hair back. "I hate to speak ill of the dead, but we were so happy Levi was finally settling down. Jessica didn't put up with crap from him. And he needed a strong hand."

"Is that why Butch was upset the other night?"

Lois shook her head. "No. Levi never saw me as a conquest. Probably because I shut him down hard the first time he even tried to be funny with me. He brushed it off as a joke, but I think if I'd let him, he would have pushed. Typically, what Levi wanted, Levi got."

"Then why was Butch upset?" Allison was coming back to the table with a pile of books. I didn't think Lois would be this open in front of another wife.

"He thought Levi cheated him out of a new project he was working on. Look, I don't have the details, Butch is pretty tight-lipped when it comes to Levi." She looked past me and grinned at the returning Allison. "You won't be swimming for a week."

"The outdoor pool is closed anyway since that's where, well, where they found him." Allison pointed to Lois. "Do you want a coffee? Deek says he makes a mean mocha."

Lois stood. "A mocha would be lovely. Excuse me, Jill. I need to pick up some books for me and MaryAnne. Jessica, of course, is way too upset to focus on reading."

I'd been dismissed for breaking the group's cardinal rule. Don't talk about the group. I watched as the women chatted at the bookcases. Then I waved to Deek. "I've got to take off. You okay here alone for a few?"

"A man is never alone as long as he has a book to read." Deek waved his hands indicating the bookshelves. "I'll be fine."

I was still thinking about Butch and his fight with Levi. If his wife didn't know what it was about, maybe Greg did. Just because the men didn't talk to their wives about group business, maybe they did talk to each other. I remembered watching the five men surrounding the patio table, shaded from the afternoon sun by a large striped umbrella. Most of the time, they'd been laughing, but once, when I'd looked over, they were more quiet—heads bowed together like they were sharing a secret. Don't let them fool you, men gossip even more than women do. I always heard the best rumors from Toby, my midday barista. Of course, the fact he also worked nights as a deputy for Greg made his gossip more accurate, and a whole lot juicier.

Esmeralda was at the front desk on the phone when I came in. "Mrs. Davis, you know we can't arrest a five-year-old for peeing on your bushes." I grinned and pointed to Greg's office. Esmeralda nodded, then returned to her phone conversation. "Look, I know it was a lot quieter on your street before the Jacksons moved in, but having kids isn't a crime." "Well, it should be."

I could hear the elderly woman's answer from across the room.

Greg was sitting at his desk, working at his computer. "Hey, didn't I just see you? What's the occasion?"

"Did Watson ask Sherlock Holmes what he wanted when he showed up at his work?" I plopped down on the couch and sat my tote bag next to me.

"As I recall, both Sherlock and Watson were men of means and didn't have a dreaded day job." He came over and sat next to me on the couch. "So no. He didn't."

"You're wrong, Watson was a doctor. Maybe I should have used the couple from *Bones*, they both have real jobs." I tried to remember the woman's name, but then gave it up. "Look, I'm here to ask you a question."

"Shoot. But I'm knee deep in approving time sheets and duty logs so I can't spend long with you." His cell started to ring and he looked at the number. "I'll let that go to voice mail."

"Your girlfriend?"

He chuckled. "Kind of. Mrs. Davis. Esmeralda has been screening her calls. Now, when she doesn't like the answer she gives her, she calls my cell. I'll go out and talk to her on my way home. She's been in a tizzy ever since her neighbor went into the retirement center and sold her house to the Jacksons."

"Because they have kids?"

He shook his head. "I hate to say it, but I think it's the color of their skin. They moved here from Spain as the husband's family lives in Palo Alto, but she thinks they're Mexican. Of course, she won't go over and talk to them. The Jacksons are pretty cool. You'd like the wife. She's an attorney at some big firm in the city."

"Maybe we should have a dinner party soon and introduce them to the gang." Although if I had a big party or one with my aunt, I'd have to invite Bill and Mary since they were best friends. With the way he was acting today, I'd rather not spend much time with the guy.

"Anyway, you have ten minutes before my next meeting. What's up?" He moved my tote to the table and moved closer to me, brushing my hair back away from my face.

I could feel the heat of his breath on my neck and a shiver ran down my back. "Definitely not that."

He laughed and moved away, holding his hands up. "Sorry, I know that was totally unfair. Really, what's up?"

"I need to ask you a question without you getting angry or asking me why I'm asking. I just want you to be honest, then I'll tell you what I know." I turned my body toward him so we were facing each other on the couch.

"Does this have anything to do with Levi?" His face turned a little pink.

I didn't know if he could do this, but I guess it was a good test of our relationship. "Seriously, you have to just follow my lead. Just answer the question."

He didn't say anything for a long minute. Then he nodded. "What do you want to ask me?"

I knew he was taking me seriously then. I took a deep breath and dove in. "Did you know anything about a deal that Levi had kept Butch out of? Did either of them talk about something that was supposed to be a sure thing?"

Greg scratched behind his ear, a sure sign that he was trying to remember something. "They were always talking about money making schemes. Butch did whatever Levi told him to do, from investing in a certain stock to taking on a new client. I don't think the guy did anything with his money if Levi hadn't told him to do it."

"So you think Butch might have hurt Levi?"

"I didn't accuse him of anything." He held up a hand. "And before you go off on me for a technicality, neither is Terrance over at Bakerstown. He's as stumped in the list of suspects as I am. Especially now that we knew he was strangled rather than just falling into the pool and hitting his head on the concrete."

"Lois says she didn't know anything about the other deal or Levi's chance at some quick money. Would Butch really hold something that important a secret from his wife?"

Greg thought about his answer. "Honestly, the boys have some sort of pact. What happens in the group, stays in the group. Butch and Levi go way back. I wouldn't be surprised if there was something he held back from Lois."

"Did you keep the group's secrets from Sherry?" What I really wanted to ask if he held something back in our relationship, but I didn't know if I was ready for that level of honesty.

Greg shook his head. "I always seemed to be on the outside with the group. I mean, they liked me, and included me in the parties and the weekends, but I always felt like there was some subtext I didn't understand. Especially once I started working in law enforcement. I guess I always was the rule follower."

"You don't think they were into anything illegal, do you?"

He laughed. "That group? No. If anything, Levi was getting Butch into some risky investments and they didn't want Lois to gripe. Most of the time, Levi's business strategies were spot on, but it didn't mean he didn't lose money now and then."

A knock on the door caused us to look up. Esmeralda poked her head inside. "They're ready for you in the conference room."

He stood and kissed me quickly on the lips. "Time to make the monthly report to the executive committee. Did you know South Cove has had no break-ins for the last two months? It's a freaking record."

I grabbed my purse and followed him out of the office. "I'll see you at home."

As I walked home, I realized the last break in or attempted break in must have been at my house in late summer. Emma had stopped the guy from getting inside and had even kept a piece of his suit pants as evidence.

I decided to curl up with a book on the porch. I wasn't getting anywhere with this fully Greg sanctioned investigation so it was time to let my mind chill. Maybe things would be clearer after I read a book or two. Or I'd just feel calmer.

As I passed by Russian Collectibles, Alana ran out of the building and grabbed my legs. She grinned up at me and asked, "Do you want to see my dolls again?"

I reached down and stroked her long curly hair that hung loose around her shoulders. "I would but I'm on my way home to check on my dog. Are you feeling better?"

She stepped back and clapped her hands in glee. "You have a dog? Is he named Rover? I want a dog, but Papa says they are too much work for a little girl."

"He's right about that. You have to feed them, and walk them, and give them baths." I knelt down to her level. The kid didn't look sick, but what did I know about kids. "My dog is a girl. Her name is Emma and she loves to run."

"Alana, come back inside." Vladimir's voice boomed through the doorway. "You know you're not allowed outside alone."

"I'm not alone Papa, my new friend is here and her dog's name is Emma. Isn't that a pretty name?"

Vladimir stepped outside and paled as he realized who his daughter was talking to. "Miss Gardner, so nice to see you." He took Alana's hand and scooted her toward the doorway. "Go inside now, you don't want your cold to worsen."

"But Papa, I'm …"

"Alana, I said go inside, now." Vladimir didn't raise his voice, but the tone changed and the little girl nodded and disappeared.

I was certain she had been about to say she wasn't feeling sick at all. Of course, the doll-store owner could have had a dozen reasons that he didn't want to attend the Business-to-Business meeting that morning, but one thing was clear. The reason he'd given Bill for his absence was a complete and total fib.

CHAPTER 10

"Can you come down? I need to talk to you." I called my aunt the next morning after an evening spent alone. Greg had some sort of meeting with the Bakerstown police. I'd been asleep when he'd come in and when I got up for work, he looked at the clock and rolled over. He didn't have to go into the station before eight. I on the other hand, had to open the shop at six. I had one commuter who was on the early shift at her job but she didn't want to leave town without a hazelnut coffee. I'd told her that I'd sell her a batch of coffee to make at home, but apparently Julia didn't own a coffeepot. She was one of the reasons I'd fought with Aunt Jackie for keeping the early opening times.

I knew catering to one customer probably wasn't the best business practice but for now, I wanted to be available when we were needed. Today, after Julie left, I had a full hour of steady traffic to keep me busy. I go by the motto, if we're open, they will come.

Aunt Jackie broke into my thoughts. "I'm sure we could just talk about this over the phone."

I looked at the clock. The meeting started in less than an hour. I needed her down here and invested in the committee before Darla showed up with the rest of the team and I was stuck as part of the committee. "Please? I really need a favor."

A pause at the end of the line let me know she was actually considering my request. "Okay, but I hope that this won't take too long. Harrold and I are having a quick lunch at Diamond Lille's before my shift starts."

"What time?" Darla had said the committee meeting would be over in an hour.

"We're meeting at noon." A sliver of hesitation went through the line. "Don't tell me Deek called in sick already. That boy feels a little unreliable."

"He hasn't missed a day yet." I opened a box of books that had delivered yesterday from last week's order. "Just come down. I've got an assignment for you."

I hung up the phone, not letting her ask more questions. If Sasha had still been here, I would have thrown her to the planning wolves. But she was off in the city, learning all about marketing for a big computer search company. Even as an intern, she was making more money working part time than I could have paid her on a full time shift. I felt proud of her accomplishment, but that didn't mean that there wasn't a hole in the Coffee, Books, and More work family.

I'd already finished my morning prep and had settled onto the couch with a recent thriller release when I heard her voice over my shoulder. "I hope you're ready to talk about setting different hours for your morning shift. I don't see why we should pay you for your reading time."

"One, you aren't paying me for my shifts. As the owner, I get a salary, no matter how many hours I work in the shop. And two, no, we aren't changing the open time. The commuters would riot and set fire to the building." I set the book down and patted the couch next to me. "Come sit down. I'd like you to take on a new assignment."

Gingerly, she sat next to me, turning her body to match my own in posture. "What is this new assignment?"

"Are you okay? Your arthritis isn't flaring again, is it?" I'd been really worried about her health all last summer. But with the fall's arrival, Aunt Jackie had seemed to bounce back. I was also sure that her increased mobility was due to the new drug her doctor had prescribed for her to try.

"We're not talking about my health," Jackie snapped at me. "Tell me what you need or I'm going back upstairs. My game shows are on."

"Coffee, Books, and More needs a representative on Darla's holiday planning committee. This is more up your alley than any of the other staff members and I'm starting school next week. Can you be our representative?" I looked up at her, hope filling my eyes. She looked at me, a little suspicious at my request.

"That's it? You want me to be on some city committee?" When I nodded, she went on. "Fine, I can do that, I guess. When's the first meeting?"

"Today at ten." I grinned at her. "I appreciate this so much."

Aunt Jackie consulted her watch. "I guess I can make it. It's really short notice though."

"I know, I'm so sorry. I just found out that we needed a rep." I shrugged. I didn't want to throw Darla under the bus, but a girl's gotta do what a girl's got to do.

"Well, I guess I better go get ready. I'll be back down a few minutes before ten." Aunt Jackie stood and looked down at me. "How is your investigation going?"

"What investigation?" I decided to play dumb but I didn't raise my gaze to meet her eyes.

"The one where you figure out who killed the dead guy. What do you think I'm talking about?" She sighed. "No matter, I get better rumors outside my own family."

"Fine, I am trying to find some stuff out, but I don't know much." I leaned back against the couch. "Except Greg's friends are all psychos."

"Could be true, but that's not a very nice thing for you to say. Especially since you might be joining him in his future, which includes his friends."

I thought about what Jackie had said long after she'd left the dining room to return to her apartment. Apparently the dressy kakis weren't dressy enough for a meeting with other South Cove businesses.

Deek showed up thirty minutes early and I asked him to get a couple of carafes filled. I explained that these sub committees could get free coffee while they were meeting there. However, no free treats, no exceptions.

As I watched Deek set up for the committee, Butch came into the shop. He had a backpack and headed toward me and the counter. "Can I get a large coffee to go?"

"Sure, how are you and Lois doing? She came in a few days ago for some reading material. Did you get released to leave the area? Or are you still stuck here?" I poured the coffee as I peppered him with questions.

He handed me a five. "No such luck there. I thought I'd come in and check in with my boss. You have Wi-Fi, right? Lois gets all bent out of shape if she thinks I'm working off the clock. So let's just say I came in for coffee."

I gave him his change and watched as he set up near the door. He took out a pile of papers, groaned, and wadded them into a ball, making a rim shot into a nearby trash can. I'd planned to leave as soon as Deek got here, but now I was curious. What had Butch thrown away? In a few minutes, he closed up his laptop and shoved it into his back pack. He waved at me and disappeared out the door. When I saw him walk out of view, I causally walked toward the trash can and scooped up the wad of papers. I could see Butch's back as he made his way back toward The Castle.

Turning around, I found Deek's gaze on me. He waited until I returned to the counter to ask: "Something interesting?"

I did a noncommittal, I hoped, shrug. "Nothing really. We should be recycling paper, not just throwing it away."

Deek seemed to accept my response or he knew when to stop asking questions. The bell over the door rang and pointed toward the new arrivals. "These ladies love to visit with Toby. Maybe you can win them over to your side as well."

He shook his head. "Girls like that don't go for guys like me."

I laughed as I made my way to the back office. "Don't sell yourself short. Girls like bad boys just as much as too-hot guys."

"You think I'm a bad boy?" Joy filled Deek's voice. I guess I'd hit the look he was comfortable with.

I decided to bring him down a notch. "A bad boy that still lives with his mother. At least you have one thing going for you."

As I closed the door, I heard the first of Toby's girls order a double shot, soy latte, no whip. Then she said in a voice loud enough to carry to the back room. "You're no Toby, but you'll do in a pinch."

I sat down at the desk and smoothed out the pages.

"What are you doing?"

Aunt Jackie stood in front of me. She'd made her way down the stairs without hitting even one of the squeaky stairs that typically warned me of her approach.

"Just following a hunch." I sat a folder on top of the pages, hoping to keep her from reading them.

Just then Deek poked his head inside the office. "Hey, glad you're down. Your committee chair is here."

"Darla? How did you know she was committee chair?"

Deek shrugged. "You can tell with those types. Their aura's scream power. And anyway, that's what she told me."

"I guess you better get out there." I smiled sweetly and sat my arms down on the table, trying to hide the pages. After the room was empty, I read over them. It was an outline of what the new corporation intended to do to The Castle to make it more commercial. "Holy crap."

Greg needed to see these and now. Butch might not have been included in the deal, he knew all about it and what Levi's plans had been. I shoved them into my purse and looked out the back office door. I waved Deek toward me.

"Hey, I'm calling it a day. If anyone's looking for me, tell them I had to make a run into Bakerstown. I can be reached on my cell." I glanced around the dining room. Only Darla and Aunt Jackie sat at the committee table. The other table was filled with students from the cosmetology school. "You okay now?"

"If I can't handle six customers by now, you need to fire me." Deek waved me toward the back door. "Fly little bird, the nest will be fine without you

As I headed out to my car, I turned over his words. The kid had sayings as good, or better, than the ancient truth-tellers. I needed to learn from my new part-timer. His mother, Rory, was one of the leading fortune-tellers in the central California area.

I took the small walkway between my building and the one housing Antiques by Thomas. Josh lived in one of the apartments over the building and rented the second one out to his assistant, Kyle. As I came back out onto Main Street, I was almost flattened by a rushing Josh. "Hold your horses, big guy."

He waved me off as he opened the door to Coffee, Books, and More, and disappeared inside. Josh and I had a love-hate relationship. He loved to hate me. I loved making him crazy. He was always coming up with the most stupid ideas to present to the Business-to-Business council. Last year, he'd wanted to cancel our summer festival because it brought in the wrong types. Luckily, everyone else voted him down due to the fact the festival was our biggest money making week of the season. Josh liked his customers rich and old, unlike most of the festival attendees. Mostly because then he already had an in when the estate came up for bid after his customer had gone to the great antique sale in the sky.

I turned right and headed down the street to the police station. I hadn't been lying to Deek when I said I needed to visit Bakerstown. However, I really wanted to check in with Greg and see if we could combine our information and make an investigation plan for the information I'd gathered so far. I felt like, as usual, Greg was out of the process. I knew he was busy, but he'd asked for my help, and I wanted to share this new piece of information.

Esmeralda was knitting when I came into the lobby area. She shook her head. "Sorry, doll. Your man is out on a breaking and entry call down the highway. Do you want to leave him a message?"

I glanced at his open office door and then at my watch. "I guess we can talk at dinner."

"Disappointment doesn't wear well on you. You should be more optimistic. Good things are right around the corner."

I studied her face for any sign of a trance, but Esmeralda appeared to be totally awake and knowledgeable about what she'd just said. Sometimes, the spirits spoke through her and she either pretended not to have heard them, or acted as if her eyes were open but there was no one home.

Today wasn't one of those days.

She sighed. "Seriously, when are you going to start trusting me? You know I have gifts."

"And you know, I don't believe in them." I held up a hand. "Let's agree to disagree on this. I need to head into town. Let Greg know I stopped by, okay?"

"Sure thing." She smiled at me. "You are doing a good thing by the deceased. He's very appreciative of your help in solving his murder."

"Then why doesn't he just tell you what happened and then you can tell Terrance and this will all be over?"

"You know it doesn't work that way. The spirits are all confused when they first travel. They need time to understand what happened. And a lot of the time, they don't want to know what or who did such a horrible thing to them."

It didn't seem as if that was the way communication from the other side should work. If this whole talking to the dead thing was effective, Esmeralda could make her spiritual call, find out who had choked the life out of Levi, and Terrance could go arrest him. But I guess there was that whole thing about looking through a glass darkly. We weren't supposed to be talking to the dead, and they, in turn, weren't supposed to be telling us what they knew.

"You don't have to believe in order for the spirits to communicate, Jill." Esmeralda's comment jarred me out of my circulating thought pattern. "It's enough that they believe in you."

I nodded, not sure how to take that piece of wisdom and promptly changed the subject. "I really have to go. See you later."

Living in South Cove made that statement true, no matter who you were talking to. I probably saw every town resident at least once a month, even the elderly women like Mrs. Davis. She was part of Sadie Michael's woman's group at the church. The group came in to the coffee shop every second Saturday, just for coffee and treats. Most of the women also bought a book after their short meeting. I'd been trying to talk Aunt Jackie into starting a book club at that time that they could join, but our youth book clubs met just after the women came in. We couldn't change the time of that long-running group to add a new one. And the women's group wasn't willing to adjust their coffee meeting to a later time that day. So we were at an impasse.

Not all great ideas worked out. But when they didn't, the failure seemed to be just a matter of certain people being stubborn.

As I drove into Bakerstown, my list of classes and required texts in my purse, I questioned once again why I didn't just order them through my book guy rather than running into the college bookstore on campus. I could say it was because I didn't want to take business away from another store. But to be honest, it was probably more that it gave me an excuse to wander the campus. I loved the way it felt, walking through the courtyard circled by buildings filled with classrooms and offices.

The only thing better than visiting the college bookstore was spending time in the library. Today, I was going to try to find information on The Castle. The Introduction to Business class I'd taken last year had taught us how to look up corporations and nonprofit paperwork in the law library so that was where I was heading first. It was a computer database, so accessing information such as who was on the board and any change in corporation status would show up. The only problem was there was a one- to two-month lag time, so the paperwork would have had to been filed in June or earlier to show up on the search.

If I found what I thought I might, Greg could have a suspect to bring to Terrance's attention by the end of the night.

CHAPTER 11

"There is no way I'm going to a second meeting with that man on the committee." Aunt Jackie's voice trilled over the cell phone. I'd ignored her calls last night when I'd been hoping to see Greg, but the case he was working on was becoming more complex and time-consuming.

And his absence was becoming more frustrating for me. I'd been excited when he asked be to be part of the investigation, sharing the clues and information as it was discovered. Instead, I just kept writing down things in my notebook. I didn't have a clear suspect in Levi's death, but I had some information that I thought pointed a finger at least at someone.

"Look, Aunt Jackie, I don't have anyone else to send. You're going to have to buck up and learn to deal with the guy. It's not that hard. Josh is a good guy." Mostly.

"Send Toby. Or Deek. They could at least knock him out if he talked bad about them. I'm a defenseless woman."

Seriously? No one who'd met Aunt Jackie would ever call her defenseless. "Can we talk about this later? I need to get into the store."

"What, you're not at the shop yet? I thought you were opening at six. What about your commuters?"

"I thought you didn't think we had enough people to make it worth our time." I pulled on a tank over my wet hair. Now, to get on my tennis shoes, let Emma out for a few minutes and then I'll power walk into town. At worse, I'll be five or ten minutes late.

I realized I was talking to a dead phone. I slipped it into my pocket and ran downstairs, my shoes and socks in hand.

Expecting a line starting to form outside when I finally arrived, I was shocked to see no one sitting at the patio tables, ready to give me crap about being late. Instead, the door was open and the smell of brewed coffee wafted out to the sidewalk in front of the store. Julia left the shop just as I was coming up to the door.

"Hey, Jill. Nice morning, isn't it?" With a large CBM travel mug in hand, she got into her BMW and eased out onto Main Street. Hers was the only car on the street I'd seen since I left the house.

I slowly entered the shop but didn't see anyone at the counter. Had Aunt Jackie left the door unlocked last night? But who would have poured Julia's coffee, unless she just went to the back and refilled herself. Julia was determined and tended to take things into her own hands, which made her an excellent executive for her company. But this was odd behavior, even for her.

I glanced at the counter, no money left for the coffee. Then I noticed the cash register ajar. I opened the drawer and there was my typical start-the-day money drawer.

"What the heck is going on?" I asked the empty shop.

A bang from behind me caused me to jump and my hand curled around the pepper spray we kept under the counter, just in case. Toby's idea, but I think he was thinking about Aunt Jackie and me working shifts alone more than just added protection.

My heart slowed as I saw Aunt Jackie staring at me over three boxes of cheesecake she'd brought out to stock the dessert case. She began setting the pre-sliced pieces of heaven onto plates. "Are you okay?"

"You scared me to death. Why didn't you say you were opening the shop when I talked to you?"

She didn't look up from her work. "I thought that it might be apparent, since you weren't here for your customers, I needed to be."

"I was only," I looked at the clock, "five minutes late." Okay so it was closer to ten, but I had been on my way and if she hadn't called whining about the committee, I would have been early. OK, to be fair, I would have been just on time. Honestly, I owed Aunt Jackie a favor and I needed to be nicer. "Thank you for opening. I know it wasn't your responsibility and I do appreciate it."

"I also wanted to finish our conversation. I don't care who you send to next week's meeting, but I will not be attending." Aunt Jackie surveyed the now full display case, threw away the empty boxes and slapped her hands together. I knew that motion. She was washing her hands of the committee and wouldn't change her mind. I guess I was back on the holiday planning committee. The thought made me crave a slice of Sadie's pumpkin cheesecake. And there was one at the back of the display case.

"If you're sure, I guess I'll replace you." I took the plate out, grabbed a fork and took a big bite of pumpkin heaven. With a mouthful of cheesecake, I mumbled, "When's the next meeting?"

"If I'm understanding you through the mush of food, the next meeting is on Friday. Eleven to noon. And it will be held at Darla's winery. The committee voted to each host the meeting on a rotating basis. We have a while before we have to host again." She looked around the empty shop. "I guess this is a perfect shift for you to study. When do your classes start?"

"Next week. I went to get my books yesterday." I held up a hand. "Before you lecture me about how much cheaper I could have gotten them, remember, I was supporting another bookstore. We have to stick together in these hard times."

"I was only going to say that we should consider doing a joint event with the college bookstore and bring in a bigger name by sharing the costs. Who is the manager over there?" Aunt Jackie pulled out a slip of paper and wrote down the basic information I had. Why hadn't I thought of pooling our money to bring in one big author? My aunt was a natural at this marketing thing.

A couple of customers walked in and headed toward the bookshelves. Tourists looking for a beach read. Even in September, the days were warm and it was lovely to spend a day sitting on the beach with a good book.

"I better get going," My aunt nodded at my new customers, like I hadn't even seen them walk inside. "Make sure you throw out some suggestions. That's why they're here and not shopping online. They want the personal touch."

Inwardly, I groaned. My aunt was full of all the selling tips. But sometimes, people just wanted to browse. Alone. Without someone hanging on their heels.

Instead of telling Aunt Jackie that, I nodded. "You know best."

"Don't be a smart aleck. If you don't want to follow my lead in learning how to effectively sell product, don't listen to an old woman. You're probably too hip to learn from my advice anyway." She sniffed and put her purse on her shoulder.

"No, you're right. You've opened my eyes to several new marketing opportunities that I didn't even think of before. You're really good at this." I kissed her on a cheek, feeling just a little bit bad for the shock on her face from my compliment. "I should go see if I could suggest anything for them. Thanks again for coming down. I'll handle the committee assignment for you."

"Just don't forget to attend. We have a reputation to uphold." The shock hadn't remained long. Aunt Jackie went on to tell me all the things I should do as a committee member. My tongue was sore from biting it so much by the time she left. I touched it to check for blood.

Toby wandered into the shop and since Aunt Jackie had left, I ignored the customers who were still happily browsing through our fiction selections. Book people want to enjoy the moment. They don't want to be rushed, or lead to a decision. They'd ask if they had questions. Right now, they were discussing a book on magic I'd read a few months ago. It was a great sophomore outing for the author who lived down the coast.

"What are you doing in so early?" I took in his uniform. "I didn't think you worked on Wednesday nights."

"I don't. But Greg and Tim were out on a call and I had to take Tim's patrol shift. He's taking mine tonight so as soon as I get off here, I'm heading to bed." Toby stifled a yawn. "I wanted to pick up next week's schedule so I could get it on the calendar. Tim wants me to trade so he can go out of town with his girlfriend next weekend."

"When did Tim get a girlfriend?" This was new gossip to me.

Toby shrugged and yawned again. He grabbed his copy of the schedule from the clipboard where Aunt Jackie left them every Tuesday. "I don't know and really don't care. I'm heading home for a shower and a short nap. Then I'll be back at noon."

"I could work longer if you needed a real break." I looked at his bloodshot eyes. The boy needed sleep.

"I'll be fine. I need the shifts. Tasha says the interest rates are going up soon and I want to get locked into a mortgage before they do." He waved the paper at me and headed to the door. "Besides, the vet bill for Emma was an unexpected cost. I'll see you soon."

"Wait, does this mean you've found a house?" I called after him, but either he didn't hear me or he was ignoring the question. Toby's brief stay in my shed was going on over a year now. I liked having him around, but it was getting a little cozy in my driveway now that Greg had moved in. I figured the vet bill was the reason he was so bent on taking extra shifts, not a down on a house. California real estate was pricy. And Toby dreamed of a solid three-bedroom, two-bath ranch with a yard for a dog or, someday, a swing set.

"Can you suggest a few local authors? My wife enjoys romance of all kinds, but I'm more of a history buff. We'd like to support the local community if possible." The man who had been over at the bookshelves, now stood next to me. "You do work here, right?"

I guess the fact I was wearing a Wired Up apron had disguised my bookseller role. "I'm sure I can make you both happy. Let's step over to the shelves and see what we can find."

By the time Toby arrived back to start his shift, I was done. I'd talked to so many people this shift, I just wanted to put my earphones on and run along the beach, ignoring everyone. You didn't know I was an introvert?

I dialed the station as I walked toward the house. When Greg picked up, I started in. "You said you wanted me to looking into who killed Levi, but every time I turn around, you're off chasing down some other bad guy."

"Jill, you have to understand, it's been crazy here." He sighed. "I'm not ignoring you. What, you think I could just forget that one of my friends was murdered?"

"I didn't say that." Man, he was good at deflecting. "I wanted some time to talk out what I'd found. I need someone to bounce ideas off. You said you'd be part of the investigation."

"You're right. I haven't been very available." I heard a door open on his end of the conversation. "Look, can we talk about this tonight? I've got a meeting."

"Fine." I hung up. As I walked down the street, I reconsidered my last words. So I called right back. This time, I got his voicemail. When the beep sounded, I started: "Sorry about before. Do your job. Come home when you can."

This time when I hung up, my heart felt a little lighter. I turned into Diamond Lille's parking lot and beelined it to the door. Time for some potato soup and maybe a small dinner salad to go with it. I was starving and the only thing I'd eaten all day was that slice of cheesecake. I craved real food. And maybe the lack of anything but sugar was why I was grumpy.

Lois sat alone at a booth looking at a menu. I paused by the table. "Are you with someone, or do you want company?"

She looked up startled. The she smiled. "I'd love to have some company. Butch stayed back at The Castle. He's been such a grump ever since Levi was…"

"I'm sorry. Greg told me how close they were." I slipped into the opposite bench and took a menu from Carrie who had followed me to the booth. "It must be hard to deal with the fact Levi is gone."

"I know it is. And I should be more charitable. But that Levi Wallace wasn't the best friend Butch could have. That boy could get my husband into a pack of trouble without Butch even realizing he'd gone off the straight path." Lois sighed and closed the menu. "I shouldn't speak ill of the dead."

"What did you really know about the deal he missed out on because of Levi?"

Lois's eyes widened, but then Carrie came by for our order. After that was done, Lois leaned closer. "How did you know I knew anything?"

"The way you reacted. And honestly? I don't think your husband keeps anything from you. He just doesn't seem the type." I thought about how concerned he was about Lois when she'd faked a migraine to get him upstairs that night. The man wasn't deceitful, but Lois was.

She leaned back into the booth. "You're right. He told me about what Levi had in mind, and I freaked. You have to understand, it would have been our life savings, just to be a small part of the conglomerate. A lot of risk and not very much assurance."

"But Butch still wanted to do it." I guessed aloud. "Because Levi wouldn't let anything go wrong."

"Exactly. You wouldn't believe all the fights we had about this. Finally, he said he was done talking about it and if I didn't want to follow his direction as the head of the house, he guessed we weren't compatible anymore." Lois stopped talking as Carrie delivered our salads. When she left the table, Lois looked at me. "He was willing to divorce me over some stupid deal that was going to ruin us."

"In the end, Levi didn't include Butch." I knew this much was true since I'd seen the argument between the two. "Do you know why?"

"I made Levi a deal. I wouldn't fight him on anything ever again if he left our finances alone. We worked hard to build that nest egg. I didn't want anything to happen to it. Butch may not be able to work this hard for too many more years."

I took a bite of my salad, but Lois didn't continue. I looked up, surprised to see tears in her eyes. "What's wrong?"

She wiped her eyes with a napkin. "I guess Levi got the wrong end of that deal. I didn't have to agree with anything unpleasant, and I would have thought Levi would have made it hard for me right up front. That way he could prove who was really the boss of my husband."

"Did you know what the deal was?" Now I was curious.

She didn't meet my eyes, but what came out sounded like the truth. "I assumed it was a land development deal. But I didn't get the details. Not from Butch or Levi. He kept telling me I was making a mistake. That our investment would double in less than a year. That's when I knew he was feeding Butch a line of crap. No investment doubles in twelve months." She stabbed a piece of tomato and the seed flew out to the table. "Not anything legal that is."

We ate our salads in silence. Then she looked up at me. "I sound like a total witch, don't I."

She made it a statement, not a question, but I answered anyway. "No. You sound like someone who wanted to protect your lives, not just follow along with whatever Levi wanted. I know I'm new to the group, but it seems like Levi was a bit of a bully."

Lois barked out a laugh. "I'm going to like having you around. If we still keep getting together after this total disaster of a reunion. You're a pistol."

As I walked home after we finished lunch, I thought about Lois and Butch and the pitfalls of being married. Especially around the financial decisions made every day. My first husband and I had never comingled funds. He paid his half of the bills, I paid mine, and we both had separate bank accounts. The only thing we did together was file taxes. It was at one of the meetings with our accountant where I'd found out he'd made partner and had never even mentioned it.

When I'd asked him about it on the way home, he confessed that he had been seeing someone else on the side when it happened and had thought telling me about the promotion would give me a bargaining chip in our divorce proceedings. Assuring me the affair was over, he'd assumed we'd go on like before. Instead, I packed a bag and filed for divorce the next week.

Greg and I talked about everything. Since I owned my house free and clear, he insisted on paying for the utilities and a part of the taxes and insurance. With that money and Toby's rent, I was able to save most of the money I got in profits from the business. I wasn't quite sure what I was saving for, except the rainy day my aunt had always warned me about.

Greg seemed to still be paying for debt that he'd accrued during his first marriage. But we did share a travel account and we each slipped money into that account from every paycheck. I would have been as upset as Lois had been in not having a say in the way the money was spent.

I just didn't think it was a good enough reason to kill someone. But as I'd learned over the last few years, logic didn't really come into play when you were talking about murder.

Emotions built a stronger motive. And Lois had been angry at Levi. Even though it seemed as if they'd worked out a compromise, she could have been mad at him for making the deal.

I had a vision of Lois spearing the tomato on her plate as she talked about Levi during our lunch. What was the saying: Hell hath no fury like a woman scorned.

CHAPTER 12

Aunt Jackie's car was in my driveway when I arrived home. She must have used the extra key I'd given her when I'd moved into the house as she wasn't in the car or on the step, waiting.

I heard them in the kitchen as I walked through. Aunt Jackie was talking to Emma like she was a friend, not just my dog. My aunt was feeding Emma pieces of chicken she'd found in the fridge. My lips curved into a smile as I walked in to find her petting Emma's golden fur.

"I didn't expect you. Have you been waiting long?" I put my tote on the table and went to the fridge to pour a glass of iced tea. I returned to the table and sat next to an almost mute Jackie.

She wiped her fingers on a paper towel and took the chicken back to the fridge. "I wanted to run a bridemaid's dress by you."

"You're not getting married until March. Don't you think it's too early to be picking out dresses?" I took a sip of tea. It cooled my throat and kept me from talking for at least a few minutes.

She paused as she was flipping through her planner, looking, I suppose for the dresses she'd clipped out of magazines. I didn't know why she didn't do this all online. She could have the web sites linked. "You act like you don't want me to get married. Is there something you need to tell me about Harrold? Don't you like him?"

"This has nothing to do with Harrold. He's a great guy." I paused, trying to form my next sentence carefully.

"I don't understand. You don't want to be in my wedding? Is that what you're telling me?" Now her voice was tightening and her face was turning pink.

"That's not what I'm saying." I shook my head. "Forget it. I'm not sure why all this over planning is bothering me so much. I guess I think you should just get married. I'll pay for the trip to Vegas. I love both you and Harrold and I'm sure you'll be very happy together." When she didn't respond, I caved. "Okay, show me the dresses."

She pressed her lips together, but flipped through some pages. When she reached the page, she paused and stared at me. "This is about you and Greg, isn't it? You're upset that your relationship isn't moving along. Do you want me to have Harrold talk to him?"

"No!" The word came out stronger than I'd expected. I took a deep breath. "This is not about Greg and me. I'm perfectly happy with where we are right now."

"Are you sure?" My aunt peered at me over the notebook like she was seeing if I was running a fever or showing signs of illness. "I'm sure Harrold would be discreet about his conversation."

"Just show me the dresses." Now I wished I'd just kept drinking my tea and kept my thoughts to myself. Aunt Jackie was a fixer. And apparently in her eyes, I needed to be fixed. I pointed to the least offensive dress. "That one is perfect."

She looked at my one hope and tore the picture out of the book. "I thought I'd gotten rid of that ugly thing."

Moving closer, I tried to imagine myself in any of the other bedazzled and ruffled dresses. Either I'd look like a Vegas showgirl or a Southern belle. I kept the sigh I wanted to let out inside and smiled at my aunt. I asked the only question that mattered: "Which one do you like best?"

By the time she got up to leave, we'd settled on a pink Scarlett O'Hara costume complete with parasol and white gloves. "The umbrella may come in handy. You know how sunny June can be."

I nodded and followed her to the door. "Looking forward to it."

She turned back sharply and peered at me. "Are you sure about me not asking Harrold to talk to Greg?"

"Leave it alone, Aunt Jackie. Greg and I are fine." As if I conjured him with my comment, he came through the front door, almost running into my aunt.

He held his hand out to stop his forward advancement and pulled her into a hug. "My two favorite ladies. What are you doing here? I thought you were closing."

"I'm on my way. Toby said he'd wait until I got back. Although he looks like someone hit him with a tired stick. Good thing he's not driving here." My aunt kissed Greg on the cheek, then wiped away her lipstick. "You two have fun tonight."

He helped her out to her car, then met me in the kitchen. "Why does it always sound dirty when your aunt tells us to have fun?"

"Because you have a dirty mind?" I opened the fridge. "What are you thinking about for dinner?"

"Anything we can grill. I'm so tired of takeout I could scream." He picked up the picture of the dress Aunt Jackie had ripped out of the book. "Is this what you're wearing to the wedding? It's nice."

"I couldn't be that lucky." I told him about the hideous outfit I would be wearing, and to avoid any chats with Harrold for the next little bit. "My aunt thinks we should be moving faster."

"Again, sounds dirty." He took a beer out of the fridge. "I'm heading upstairs for a quick shower and change. If you make a salad, I'll grill those tuna steaks you took out when I get back."

"Perfect." I watched him walk toward the stairs. "And as we're doing that, we need to talk about the case."

"Sounds great." He called back, his tone muffled by the wall between the staircase and the kitchen.

I wasn't sure I believed him.

We didn't actually talk about the case until after dinner was done, the table cleared and dishes in the dishwasher. I had made coffee and served up two slices of the pumpkin cheesecake I'd had for breakfast. Great way to start, and end, a day.

I opened my notebook and started telling him about what I'd learned. When I told him about having lunch with Lois, he put his fork down on the plate. "I can't believe she told you all of that. I don't think she said two words to Sherry in all of the years we went to the annual get-togethers."

"I'm easier to like than Sherry." I stated the obvious. "So what do you think about Butch and Lois? Could either of them have killed Levi?"

He shook his head. "No way. And I'm just not saying that because they are my friends. Maybe Lois had motive, but it sounds like she and Levi came to an agreement and Butch has already admitted he was left out of the deal. If he was angry about that, I'd think Lois would be the one who was in the morgue, not Levi."

"Yeah, I kind of thought the same thing. But from what I could find out from the paperwork Butch threw away, the deal was definitely a takeover of The Castle. I don't think they actually got the sale completed. I checked with the records and the deed hasn't changed hands. It's still in The Preservation Society's name." I sipped my coffee.

"But those electronic records take some time to process. Have you talked to Brenda?" He took my notebook and scanned my notes.

"I guess I can go over tomorrow after work and see what she will tell me. I thought it was odd that she let Levi buy out The Castle for a complete weekend for his private party. I didn't think they did that anymore."

"Find out what made her change her rules, and we might have a lead." Greg pointed to a note about Vladimir and Alana. "Why is this here? He's the owner of the Russian Collectibles, right?"

"Yeah, he lied to Bill yesterday and I don't know why." I took a small bite of the cheesecake and let the gooey yumminess fill my mouth. "I want to remember to stop by City Hall and see if Amy found his business license application yet. Maybe that will tell me what's going on."

"Or maybe he just doesn't want to go to your meetings. Some people aren't naturally social. You of all people should know that." Greg finished off his cheesecake and took his plate to the sink to rinse it before sticking it into the dishwasher. "I've got some reports to finish. Mind if I use your office?"

"Go ahead." Lately it was more Greg's office than mine, mostly because I didn't ever use it. Not for studying and not for business stuff. But it looked amazing. I'd totally repurposed the room when I'd moved in, with a great desk, small love seat, and tons of bookshelves. I just liked doing my homework on the couch in front of the television instead.

Somehow the whole working together on this investigation thing felt less like Nancy Drew and Ted and more like just work. Go do this, go talk to Brenda. And all I got when I reported back was more assignments. I closed my clues book and grabbed the novel I'd been reading earlier. Maybe I was just tired and grumpy. No matter what, I was putting the problem aside and taking advantage of my last free moments to actually read fiction before classes started up again and I was knee-deep in text books.

* * *

Greg was already gone when I woke up the next morning. For someone who wasn't working a murder case, he sure was busy at the station. I'd forgotten to ask him about the break in. I made a mental note to ask him this evening. Toby's apartment was dark, too. Before Greg had moved in, Toby had started having breakfast with me. Mostly because he'd been lonely after Sasha left town and, unknown to me, because Greg had asked him to keep an eye on my investigating. Now, I rarely saw the guy unless he was taking over for me at the shop.

Emma nudged her leash but I knelt and gave her a hug. "The vet said no running for a week. You have to build up your strength."

She licked my face which to me meant, I'm fine, don't worry. I want to run. But I loved my girl and if her vet said a week, we were waiting a week.

"Maybe I'll take you into town later this afternoon for a walk." I patted her side and stood.

A wag of the tail told me she thought that was an excellent idea. And so I said good-bye, locked up the house, and headed into town for my shift. I'd thought about bringing her into the shop with me, but sometimes she'd bark at a random customer. Mostly I thought she might be right on their general character flaws (she hated Josh) but I guess it didn't seem very welcoming to have a dog try to warn you out of the building when you were just trying to buy a coffee.

After I got this college thing done, I'd start bringing her in once a week and see if I could get her settled. As long as the health inspector didn't have concerns. Brad could be a little touchy on department rules. Even if they weren't really rules.

With the commuters all taken care of, I pulled out my laptop and decided to do a little research on our former host, Levi. When I keyed in his name, Google gave me pages of hits and quite a few pictures. Some of him in a tuxedo, some with Jessica, and one that appeared to be his high school yearbook snapshot. I clicked on that one and was taken to a scanned newspaper from Greg's home town.

"Honor student cleared of murder charges. Not enough evidence says DA." I went to the article and whistled. "Football star is laid to rest without an answer on questions surrounding the death of Mike Lord."

Greg hadn't mentioned this. And you would think if one of your friends had been accused of killing another kid—that kind of news would fly through a high school. When I'd tried to follow up on the news article, I'd realized it wasn't a vehicle accident. Maybe that was part of why Butch felt such a loyalty to Levi. I scanned the article for more information, but it was pretty vague about what had happened due to something the reporter called juvenile privilege. Basically, he was complaining that the courtroom and the file had been sealed, limiting his access to the actual facts and, seemingly, giving the paper carte blanche to just plain make stuff up.

I sent the article to my wireless printer in the back office, then looked up Mike Lord's name. If it wasn't about football or his untimely death, there was nothing. At least not online. I wondered if Greg would let me fly back and talk to the people in town. Then it hit me. Most of the group

still quarantined to South Cove and The Castle had gone to school with
Levi. Even if Greg wouldn't talk about the incident, they might. Or at
least their wives might know something. I didn't have anything on my
plate, so it was time to go visit The Castle this afternoon as soon as Deek
arrived for his shift.

Besides, Greg had told me to go talk to Brenda. This was just a few
more people and on a topic he hadn't opened up for me.

The way I looked at it, I was completely in the right here. "Besides,
Greg should have told me."

"Told you what?" Greg stood across the counter, watching me.
"What did you find?"

I closed the laptop. "What are you doing here?"

"Came in for coffee. We're having a meeting and our mayor wants
your coffee, not the stuff we serve at the station." He nodded to the dessert
case. "And I'll take one of those éclairs for the walk back."

"I'm putting this on the city's charge, are you sure you don't want to
take some back for the meeting?" I opened the travel box we provided for
coffee and filled it while Greg waited.

"Make it two then. One for Esmeralda." He leaned on the counter.
"You're really not going to tell me what you were mumbling about?"

I studied him for a second. Why wouldn't I just ask Greg? "Okay, I'll
tell you. I found some articles about Levi being linked to a kid's death
during high school. What happened?"

Greg froze and the pen he'd been playing with dropped from his hand.
"This is why I don't like you involved in investigations. That thing in
high school had nothing to do with Levi. It was a tragic accident. So stop
digging into something that should be kept in the past."

"That's not the way life works you know. Bad things keep coming
back to affect the present." I turned away from him, not liking the pain I
saw reflected in his face. "What happened back then?"

"Nothing good." Greg stood and straightened. "I really need to get
back to my meeting. But Jill, don't go poking bears. If I thought it had
anything to do with Levi's death, I would have told Terrance straight out."

I knew I was fighting a losing battle here. Whatever had happened,
Greg had decided to keep it hidden. I put two éclairs in a to-go box. I
wasn't going to let it go, but I didn't have to make it a federal case, not
without knowing more. "What about the mayor, should I add one more?"

"Heck no, he's big enough as it is." Greg smiled, but his eyes still
watched me warily. I guess he knew I wouldn't give up. He held out a

hand for the bag. "Besides, I kind of like the idea of him not getting a treat. The man wants to cut my budget again."

"You know the council won't let him do that." I handed him the coffee. "Bill's got your back."

"I don't know. Have you talked to him lately? The man acts like he got up on the wrong side of the bed. He came in for our monthly meeting and about bit my head off for missing some report. That's one of the reasons I've been working so many hours. Bill wanted more reports." He glanced at the clock and leaned over to give me a quick kiss. "I've got to go. See you at home."

As he was walking out of the shop, I almost felt bad about not telling him what I planned on doing. On the other hand, he couldn't tell me no if he didn't know. Better to ask forgiveness than permission would be carved on my tombstone.

Two more hours and Deek would be here to take over. I pulled out my clues notebook and started making a list of questions I wanted to ask the gang. Maybe this old incident had nothing to do with why Levi was killed. But I didn't like the fact that Greg refused to talk about it. Didn't he always say that knowing the victim was the best way to figure out why they were killed?

I'd made my notes, cleaned the front of the shop, and completed next week's book order and still had an hour on my shift. For a Friday, this was turning out to be a slow day. I took a book off the Advance Reader Copy pile and curled up on the couch. By the time Deek showed up, I was lost in the world of fantasy built by the author. I half expected my barista to show his elfin ears and talk to me in the ancient language, rather than his surfing lingo.

"Dude, it's totally dead out there. I hear a bus crashed down the road on Highway 1. I don't think we'll see any traffic for at least three hours." Deek pulled his bike bag off his shoulder and deposited it behind the counter. He plopped down next to me on the couch. "I read that book earlier this week. The critics are saying he's the new Tolkien, but I wouldn't go that far."

"I'm enjoying it." I slipped a bookmark to mark my place and then I put the book into my tote. I should have time tonight to finish reading, especially if, as I suspected, Greg would be late. "So how did you get here if the highway is closed?"

"I'm coming from the north. My mom has a house in Bakerstown. The wreck was south of here." Deek sat upright. "Hey, I just wanted to tell you that I'm really digging the job. The kids are great and it's like you're paying me to play and talk about my favorite books."

"You're doing a good job." I looked around the empty shop. "Make sure you have your plans set up for the next book club. And write up a proposal for a young adult author visit when you have time. We haven't done one for a few months."

"Who do you want me to propose?"

I stood and stretched. "Not my job. I want you to figure out who to invite."

"Cool, I can do that." The grin on his face told me that he thought it was more than just cool.

My cell rang. The caller ID showed it was Amy. "Hey, what's up?"

"I found the file you were looking for." Amy paused. "I think you need to see this."

I stepped toward the door. "See what?"

"Just come by." Amy disconnected at her end.

CHAPTER 13

It took me just a few minutes to run over to City Hall. I was out of breath when I pushed through the front doors and saw Amy talking on the phone. She waved me over to her desk. I took a bottle of water out of the cooler that Mayor Baylor kept in the lobby with a big sign: WELCOME TO SOUTH COVE, PLEASE HELP YOURSELF. The free water really was for official visitors only, but what he didn't know got me a bottle every visit. I sank into her visitor chair and cracked open the bottle and waited for Amy to get off the phone.

"Mrs. Davis, I'm sorry, but no one in the police station or the mayor is available right now. Kids like to splash and play in backyard pools. I'm sure no one's being killed." Amy rolled her eyes as she listened to another barrage of complaints from the speaker on the other end of the phone.

I set the bottle down and Amy pushed a file toward me. I opened it and started reading. The application was pretty standard: name, address, what kind of shop they were opening, financials, and then near the bottom, I saw it. Vladimir Petrov had an immigration sponsor listed as part of his record.

"Levi Wallace?" I looked at Amy who nodded and my gaze dropped back to the file. I couldn't believe what I was reading.

She covered the mouthpiece of the phone and whispered. "The phone number isn't Levi's." She waited for me to look back up at her. "The outgoing message was in a woman's voice, although she didn't give her name."

I sank back into the chair and re-read the business application. Had Jessica lied when she'd said she didn't know Vladimir, or his daughter? My thoughts circled around the reason why Levi would be Vlad's sponsor. Could the little girl have been right? Could Jessica be the sister Vladimir claimed was still in Russia? I wondered who I needed to talk to, Jessica or our newest business owner. Or could this just be one of the rare instances where Levi had done something nice without any other reason? Maybe I should just tell Greg or Terrance?

Amy finished her phone call, promising to send a car out to Mrs. Davis' house as soon as there was someone available. I was pretty sure the chore would fall on Tim since Toby was off for a couple of days. "So where was the file?"

Amy smiled and glanced back at the mayor's office. "See, that's another weird thing. The Mayor had it in his locked middle drawer. Lucky for us, I have a key just in case he needs something out of the desk while he's gone."

"So why would Marvin have the file hidden in his desk? Isn't it policy to file it in the file room?"

Amy took the file and pointed to a spot on the top. "The other weird thing is the mayor and Bill have both signed off on the business, but there is no date stamp. Every application that comes into the office is date stamped by me before it goes to anyone else for approval. I never saw the application."

I thought about what this might mean. To Levi's death? Probably nothing. To the mystery of where Jessica came from? Maybe it explained a lot. I didn't know why they would try to keep their familial relationship a secret.

She handed me a new file and I opened it, confused. "It's a copy of the other one. I'm putting the original back into Marvin's desk. If you have to tell people you have it, I understand, but it might cost me my job."

"Greg's supposed to be getting the file too, so maybe he could force Marvin into giving it up without you getting involved. I'll ask him." I stuffed the file into my tote. "I'm not sure it's anything but I do think it's weird."

"Where are you off to now?" Amy looked at an incoming e-mail and shook her head. "Tina has a list of promotions she wants done for the campaign. It's a year away but Tina wants to be prepared, just in case someone dares to run against Marvin in the election."

"Who does she think wants the job?" Greg had told me he was so not interested in politics. And no one on the council had expressed wanting to give up their real life to become mayor. Mayor Baylor may have been a pain, but at least we knew what we got with him.

Amy shrugged. "Actually, I think she has a few other people on her watch list, including Bill. I think he's tired of keeping the mayor in check."

"I'm heading to The Castle to talk to Brenda." And a few others, I silently added. "Greg's been asking me to help with the investigation, but he doesn't seem too interested in the information I'm finding. I think he's jealous that he can't be working the case."

As I thought about his actions, I wondered if I'd nailed the problem. I'd never known Greg to be jealous over anything. Especially not something as stupid as an investigation where neither one of us had the legal ability to do anything.

I walked home to get my car. It was too far to hoof it to The Castle. Besides, I wanted to let Emma outside, so she didn't have to hold it in. My phone message machine had a flashing light. Yes, I still had a real message machine with a tape. My aunt didn't even use one. My message machine had come from the prior owner of the house, Miss Emily. I had added my own outgoing message, but the machine had let me store the earlier one. It was silly, but knowing I could at least listen to her voice, comforted me.

I pushed the button and for a few seconds, all I heard was silence. Then I heard the hesitant voice. "Miss Gardner, this is Josh Thomas. Your next door neighbor in town?" He paused and then kept talking. Like I'd really could have forgotten Josh in the last two days. "I'd like to talk to you about some weird things I'm seeing around town. I don't want to involve the police unless it's absolutely necessary. Maybe it's just cultural differences I'm observing."

The phone went dead. Great, I had another place to stop. I bet Josh just wanted to talk about the wind machines that would keep the ocean smell out of town. Or more likely, he didn't like the kids who were hanging around the bookstore in the afternoons reading and mostly drinking water. I'd let that go, but Josh could be persistent and I didn't want Deek to have to deal with our frantic neighbor.

I got Emma back into the house and took off toward the highway. Heading north, I could reach The Castle just a couple of roads after turning onto the road, but I got to see the ocean for a bit before I had to turn off and head inland.

The sea gulls were playing in the wind and I thought about Emma and our usual runs on the beach. Next week, I promised to myself and my dog. I was at the front gate in less than ten minutes. The ticket booth was shuttered with a big closed sign in the window. I guessed Terrance had sealed up the place after Levi's death or at least didn't want a ton of tourists walking through potential crime scenes. I was sure that Brenda was going to start squawking about the length of time they'd been unable to have tours. It had to affect her bottom line which as a non-profit was hard enough to meet.

I stepped over the chain blocking admittance and headed to Brenda's office. I'd start here and maybe I wouldn't need to talk to the family about Levi's past discretions. I liked wishful thinking—it kept me upbeat and positive, even when I knew my conclusion was totally off.

Fifi, her oversized standard poodle, met me at the door and leaned into me to say hello. Brenda sat at her desk. "You know she's not going to let you go until you pet her. You're one of her favorite people from town."

"I've missed seeing her." I rubbed the dog's tight curls, scratching her behind her ears. "How's the circus? Do you expect to be released from the whole investigation scene anytime soon? I saw you had to close for tours. That stinks."

"You're telling me. And not only am I not getting the tours, now the accountant over at Levi's office is making noises about maybe not covering these expenses. He charged the bachelor party on his personal card and luckily, I'd already billed that out before all this happened. I've been on the phone with his company all morning trying to make sure they will be paying for the food and lodging costs. These people are costing me a fortune." She patted the desk in front of her. "Come sit and talk. I didn't get to see much of you last weekend. What's been going on?"

I wanted to ask *besides the dead bridegroom?* but thought it might be considered rude. I postponed talking about the elephant in the room or the dead guy in the pool and focused on something I knew she'd expect. "I missed you at the Business-to-Business meeting."

"I know but I actually have a good excuse. Terrance came by and wanted me to walk him through the weekend events one more time." She held her right hand up in a salute. "Scouts honor."

When I didn't respond, she dropped her hand and shrugged. "Okay, so I suggested Tuesday morning might be a good time for him to stop by."

"I knew it." I shrugged. "Really you didn't miss much. Bill was in a bad mood. Josh had a list of complaints about the city departments and our new business owner, Vladimir of Russian Collectibles didn't show up."

"So basically, business as usual, except for Bill. He's usually Mr. Sunshine. Mary's been out of town a lot visiting the grandbaby, maybe that's got him twisted."

That idea hadn't occurred to me. I'd have to ask Aunt Jackie if she knew if Mary was in town this week. The two of them were BFFs and before my aunt started planning this wedding twenty-four seven, the women acted more like Thelma and Louise, without the car chase. "Maybe. So how are things here? I bet the gang is itching to go home."

"The former bride-to-be stays in her room. The only time I've seen her leave is for walks around the grounds with the older woman, Lois? And of course, she met with that nice man. The guy who missed your meeting. What did you say his name was? Vladimir?"

"Wait, Vladimir came to The Castle to meet with Jessica?"

"He brought her a small bouquet of flowers to express his sympathy. It was really sweet. She walked right up to him and laid her head on his shoulders and cried. I haven't seen her be that connected with anyone since she arrived last week with Levi." She tapped her pen on the desk. "I guess he found out through the town gossip mill?"

I thought it was more than that, but I didn't want to spread my own gossip without knowing the truth. I just went with the basics. "That was nice of him."

A chime announced an e-mail coming into her computer. She glanced at the heading and sighed. "I don't know what the board wants from me. They know I can't open the museum part until the police say I can and yet, I get daily e-mails asking for an update."

"The board sounds concerned. Wasn't the place doing well?" I tried to make my questions sound conversational.

"You know nonprofits. We're always living on a tight budget. I admit, the strings got a little tighter this year, but nothing we wouldn't have bounced back from." She stopped tapping her pen and pointed it at me. "You've heard the rumors about the society selling The Castle, haven't you?"

"Guilty as charged. Are they just rumors?" I decided to put my cards on the table.

"Mostly. I mean, the board did entertain a few ideas about switching this up to a full-time hotel rather than just renting out a few rooms here and there." That's why they allowed me to accept the bachelor party. It was supposed to be a trial run of what a full-service hotel might entail." The phone rang and she picked up the receiver rubbing her neck as she answered. "The Castle, Brenda Morgan here."

I heard part of the conversation, then she put the call on hold. She turned toward me. "Sorry, I've got to take this. I'll come into town soon and we can do lunch. My treat."

I stood, knowing I'd been dismissed. I wondered if it was another board member on the phone. Did Levi's death change the fact he'd bought the place? Or did it disband the whole deal? These are the things I wanted to know but didn't have time to ask. "Sure, I'll see you soon."

As I walked out of the cottage holding Brenda's office, I ran straight into Lois and MaryAnne.

"What are you doing here?" Lois gave me a quick hug and nodded to the patio around the pool. "We're going out to meet Allison and the rest for a few drinks before dinner. Want to join us?"

"I've got my car so I can't drink, but I can hang out for a while." I fell into step with the women. "So what have you been up to?"

"A big fat nothing." MaryAnne took a drag off her cigarette and blew out the smoke. "I've gone through more cartons here in a week than I typically do at home in a month."

"I hear quitting is hard."

She barked out a laugh. "Dear, I don't want to quit. I just don't want to be smoking nonstop because there isn't anything else to do."

We were getting close to the pool. I put my hand on Lois's arm. "Hey, can I ask you a question?"

We stopped in the middle of the courtyard where the fountain sat. The path went off in four directions around the fountain. She pointed to the brick ledge around the bubbling water. "Sit down, we don't have to rush."

MaryAnne narrowed her eyes, but kept walking. "I'll see you out by the pool."

When she was out of ear shot, Lois leaned closer. "I'm glad she left. She never could hold a secret. So did you find out more about the deal?"

"I'm still working on that. But my question goes back farther. Back to high school actually." I didn't want to show all my cards right now, especially since I could see by the look on her face that I'd hit a nerve. "Did you go to the same high school as Levi and Greg?"

"Of course I did. Everyone here did. Well, except Allison. She was home schooled, but even if she had gone to Foster High, she would have gone years after we did. The girl's a lot younger than Mikey, but I guess you knew that." Her gaze darted back and forth, showing me her nerves.

"So, tell me about what happened to Levi?"

Now, she just stared at the ground. "It wasn't his fault. He didn't do anything to that kid."

"You know that for a fact?" If I acted like I knew what she was talking about, I might get more information than if I kept asking general questions.

"Of course. Look, the guy kept picking on Levi. Everyone picked on him. So one day, Levi played a trick on him. Some sort of chemistry prank that caused the guy's face to turn blue." Lois's lips curved at the memory. "Then the guy sucker punched Levi in a parking lot after a chess tournament. Levi went to the hospital and the guy disappeared. I guess he was worried that Levi would turn him into the cops."

"Wait, I thought he was found dead." I thought about the article. It had said that Levi was cleared of any wrongdoing in the death.

"The guy was stupid. He went out to his father's hunting cabin and accidentally shot himself. Even the coroner said that it was an accident. His dad was part of the city council though and was convinced that his little boy couldn't have died that way. It was sad, really."

"Hey you two, the drinks are flowing. What are you doing out here?" Butch stood at the edge of the path leading to the pool. "Is Greg coming out too?"

"Actually, Greg's working and I need to get back. I've got to take over for my aunt's shift, she's not feeling well this evening." I waved off the margarita he tried to hand me. "Thanks for the talk, Lois. I needed some advice."

She nodded, accepting my lie smoothly. "Of course, any time. We're here until they release us from this prison."

"A prison with drinks, amazing food, and the woman he loves." Butch winked at me. "A man could do worse."

I said my good-byes and then made my way back out to my car. I decided to stop at the shop and pick up some pumpkin cheesecake for after dinner.

I parked the Jeep in front of the shop and was all the way inside before I saw him. Josh Thomas was sitting at a table, watching me enter. I stumbled over my feet a bit. When I got my feet back under me, I turned toward him. "Hey Josh, what's going on?"

"I take it you don't listen to your phone messages?" His voice was low, like he thought someone was listening.

"I heard it, but I've been busy. I was planning on going over to see you right after I picked up dessert for tonight's dinner." I slunk into a chair opposite him. This wasn't going to be a quick conversation. "What did you need to talk about?"

He leaned closer, glanced left and right, then whispered, "I believe our new business owner is a KGB spy."

CHAPTER 14

Greg almost choked on his pasta. "He really thinks that Vladimir is a Russian spy?"

He'd been home when I'd arrived and was already making spaghetti sauce. He'd given me a look when I'd asked him about his day, so I'd changed the subject. Now, we were talking about my conversation with Josh. "He has a pretty good argument."

"What, that he's foreign? Man, I can't believe how bigoted some people are around here. Mrs. Davis has been lighting up my dispatch line for the last month, now Josh is seeing Cold War–spies infiltrating our town under the guise of stacking dolls." He took a piece of garlic bread from the plate in the middle of the table.

I heard Emma's tail start thumping the floor as she watched him tear off a piece, hoping it was for her. I had to agree with my dog. Greg made a mean spaghetti dinner, complete with a first course salad and red wine. Memories of the alley scene from *Lady and the Tramp* filled my mind.

"Actually, he's been seeing a woman show up at the back door early in the morning. She wears a cloak with a hoodie and arrives most mornings at six and leaves no later than seven. And she carries a large tote." I gave Emma a small bite of my bread, hoping to keep her loyalty. If I knew my dog, she could be won over by food, no problem. Of course, she was *my* dog.

"I hate to burst Josh's bubble, but did he ever think that Vladimir has a lady friend? Maybe one he didn't want his daughter to know about? There is still the matter of a wife in Russia." Greg cleaned the rest of his spaghetti sauce off his plate with the bread and pushed his plate away. "That hit the spot. And another thing, how does Josh know this?"

"His apartment windows look over the building Vladimir owns. I guess he can see a lot from that vantage point." I thought about Greg's explanation for Vladimir's mystery visitor, which made much more sense than Josh's conspiracy theory. And it seemed like Vladimir was a bit of a ladies' man since he'd gone to pay his respects to the almost widow with flowers. "Are there even Russian spies anymore?"

"Honey, as long as there are people in power who want to make sure they know what their neighbors are doing, there will always be spies. Now we just have a new bunch of people trying to figure us out and report back to their superiors." He grinned at me. "I cooked, does that mean you'll do dishes?"

"Big game on tonight?" I still wanted to talk to him about the whole high school thing with Levi and the other boy, but for some reason, I held back. Even when I had been talking to Lois, it felt like she was telling me a secret. A secret that even now, years later they didn't feel comfortable discussing. I wanted to be sure that this sore spot had anything to do with Levi's death before confronting Greg with the fact that I knew.

"Preseason game, but it looks like they'll have the new rookie quarterback they got in the draft play for at least a few quarters. I'd like to see how he does in his first national televised game. That alone can mess with a kid's head, especially early on." He kissed me on the head and then grabbed a beer from the fridge. "You can come join me on the couch if you want."

"After I get a few things taken care of first." I fanned the back of my hand over my forehead. "A woman's work is never done."

"Hey, I cooked." He sounded hurt.

"I was kidding." I stood and stacked the plates. "But I do have a few things I want to do before I settle down with a book."

"You mean watch the game with me." He lightly tapped me on the butt. "Let me know if you need help with anything. I don't want to be slacking on my shared chores promise."

Greg was a good guy. A great guy. I shouldn't feel uncomfortable telling him anything. And yet, I held back.

Still.

* * *

Friday morning arrived and instead of the sunny day I'd expected, fog hung on the streets. And dampened my mood. Emma whined when I put on my running shoes, so I relented and clipped on her leash. "We're not running though, just a walk to get you back in the swing of things."

She'd seemed fine since Toby had brought her back from the vet. Probably his quick reaction and frantic drive to the clinic had made this incident a blip on Emma's radar rather than the life-threatening event it could have been. Besides, I loved the way the shoreline looked while the fog was in. The place looked otherworldly.

We wandered up the coastline, no particular hurry. I had to open in just over an hour, Greg was already at the station, so no one waited for us at home. Besides, the walk gave me time to focus on the one question in my life right now. Who killed Levi and why? From what Greg had found out from Terrance, they weren't any closer to finding Levi's killer than I was. Maybe not as close. I just needed to find out what if any of the information I'd found was important

As we made our way back toward the South Cove beach parking lot, I noticed two figures on the observation deck, looking out to the ocean. The man was tall and dark, but I couldn't see his face from where I stood. The woman—and it was definitely a woman, as her loose brown hair billowed out into the wind—stood next to him, staring at the waves. I did that a lot. Just sat and watched the waves. It calmed me.

Emma barked at a seagull and the woman turned to look our way. She said something to the guy and then they turned and left. I guess they didn't realize anyone else was out here. Disappearing form my view, the only thought I couldn't shake was the woman looked like Jessica. A lot like Jessica.

When we got home, Greg's truck was back in the driveway. Had I been wrong? Had he not left? Or had he just not been in bed and I assumed he was gone? No, the house wasn't that large that I could avoid running into him. He must have forgotten something and come back for it.

He was sitting at the kitchen table when I came in. "Hey, I've got to run upstairs and shower before I go to work. Want to join me?"

He didn't answer, so I slipped into the chair next to him. "Whose laptop?"

"What?" He stared at me as if he didn't even know who I was. He slammed the lid of the laptop. "Oh, it's one from work."

Greg stood and jetted out the back door. No good-bye, no see you tonight. And worst of all, no answer to whose Mac he held in his hand. I knew the city didn't pay for laptops, except for ones for the mayor, Greg, and Bill Sullivan. All the other employees had desktop personal computers. And the patrol cars had laptops, but they were attached to the cars. And *no one* had an Apple product. Especially one that was that expensive.

I watched out the kitchen window as he pulled his truck out of the driveway. Had he thought I'd already left for work, that's why he brought the laptop here to check out? I looked at the clock. If I was going to get a shower and still be on time to open, I had to go.

No one waited for me at the door. But within ten minutes the shop was filled with Friday commuter regulars. I loved talking to these customers about their big city jobs. I'd been one of them for years before I'd moved and opened Coffee, Books, and More. I knew how hard it was to get through the day in the grey cubicle jungle.

One of the last customers I served that morning was a real estate agent. "Rumors are flying about the new owner of The Castle. Have you meet them?"

"Where did you hear about the sale?" I'd just searched all the new filings and there was nothing.

"Someone from the records department is leaking information to my boss over at the real estate agency." The woman flipped her too perfect hair. "Of course, it could just be gossip. Last year, the story was that Sandra Bullock was moving to town and buying up property. You see how that turned out."

Well, there was no movie star living in our little tourist town. I didn't think anyone famous would like living here, mostly because of all the visitors we get. I suspected they liked gated communities and ten acres plus of land. I had to agree with my customer, rumors did seem to appear with no real reason—except this wasn't the first time I'd heard that The Castle had been sold.

I called Brenda to chat but I got her voice recording saying she was unavailable for the weekend. She must be taking some time after the bachelor party that wouldn't die. She listed John, the guy we'd met last Friday as the contact person. I hadn't realized he was her assistant. As I was pondering this new information, the phone rang, startling me.

"Coffee, Books, and More, this is Jill." I looked at the clock. Nine, not a good sign. Typically, a call this early this would mean someone couldn't do their shift. I grabbed the schedule. Toby was off until Monday due to his job making South Cove safe from drunk drivers so it had to be Deek calling.

"Hi, Doll. Just calling to remind Jackie about the meeting today. I hope she's feeling all right. She seemed a little out of sorts at the last meeting." Darla came just a few words from actually asking what was going on with my aunt. I thought it must be an interviewing technique. Asking without asking.

"She's fine. Distracted with this wedding planning. You know she and Harrold are getting married next June, right?" I went with the obvious. There wasn't anyone in the world my aunt hadn't told about the upcoming wedding. Or probably invited. I checked my watch. I could attend the meeting, then head over to Diamond Lille's for Friday clam chowder. It would be my reward for attending. If I kept rewarding myself with food for attending the meetings, by the time the festival was over, I'd gain five to ten pounds.

"Of course, I should have thought about that. Well, tell her to bring a calendar. We're going to start planning dates this meeting."

"Actually, I don't think she's going to be able to continue." I left it at that, hoping Darla would say they didn't need anyone to replace her, but I got a little gasp.

When she gathered her breath, she sputtered. "I need her. You don't understand what goes into planning one of these festivals. I can't do it without her."

I sighed. Time to fall on the sword. "Don't worry. I'll replace her."

"Oh, Jill, that would be lovely. We need all of the members to make a successful festival." Darla droned on and on about the community spirit and teamwork needed to pull off one of these events.

Finally, when she took a breath, I lied to get her off the phone. "Sorry, someone just came in. Excellent customer service is essential, you know."

I took a book to the couch, but instead of reading and losing myself in the story, I brooded over the new responsibility I'd just accepted. It wasn't like I didn't want to help, but my fall schedule was overloaded as it was, especially with the math class the college was making me take for the degree. I don't know why they felt I needed something like Algebra to run my coffee shop, but my advisor hadn't seemed willing to give me a pass on the class. My mind was wired for words, not numbers.

I was still grumbling when Deek showed up for his shift.

"Hey boss man. What's the story today?" He grabbed a cup of coffee and plopped down on the couch next to me. "Why are you in the doldrums?"

"The what?" I didn't move. I didn't have the energy.

Deek laughed. "The doldrums. Haven't you ever read *The Phantom Tollbooth*? You look like you're wiped out and not wanting to do anything."

"I'm kicking myself for saying yes to another project when I'm pretty sure I can't get the ones I have done." I took a sip of my now cold coffee. "I'm an over committer. Isn't there a self-help group out there for people like me?"

"Probably, but the down side is you have to go to more meetings and their coffee isn't primo like ours." He leaned back into the couch. "Tell Uncle Deek what's going on. Maybe I can help you adjust. I'm excellent at this time management thing. One year I took nineteen credits and ran the fantasy book club over at the college. Man, those guys could come to blows over what series ruled. No one ever beat out Tolkien for our top spot though. I guess we were traditionalists."

"I said I'd take Jackie's spot on the festival planning committee. With classes and my shifts, I'll hardly have time to see Greg, much less meet at least weekly on this festival."

"You need to delegate."

My laugh came out a little too bitter. I started holding up fingers. "So I have Aunt Jackie, who already bolted from the job. Toby who needs at least a few hours of sleep a day. Nick, who is actually back in school, so the drive would be killer, even if he had time. And you."

He nodded. "Exactly. You have me. I'm down to my last year so I'm only taking four classes this semester and next. I have time and brain cells to spare."

"You'd want to represent us at the winter festival planning committee?" I rolled my shoulders. This could work. Hope seeped into my body, making me come out of the doldrums as Deek had called my mood. "It's a lot of coordination and a huge time commitment."

"You'll be paying me right?" Deek sipped his coffee. "I could use some real-world experience in this team building project management thing. I'm kind of tired of reading case studies."

"I'm paying you for your time. And today, I'll even cover your shift while you're gone. If you can get them to schedule these meetings just before your shift, that would be awesome."

"Then I'm your guy. Who knew this coffee shop job would be so fun? I get to work with the kids on weekends, and now, I get to plan a winter wonderland." Deek rested his arms on the back of the couch, apparently enjoying the new responsibilities.

"Well, at least as wonderland as we can get down here in the land of sun and sand." I glanced at my watch. "Your first meeting starts in fifteen minutes at the winery. You better get going."

He finished his coffee and saluted when he stood. "Your wish, my command. Or something like that. See you around noon. You sure you can handle the volume?" He looked around the empty shop.

"Fridays don't get going until after school lets out. You'll be busy around three with the cool kids." I picked up my book. "If I'm lucky, I'll get to read a few chapters before you get back."

I was lucky and by the time Deek returned all excited and filled with news from the committee, I'd finished half the book. I tucked it into my tote for later, and headed out of the shop, leaving Deek in charge.

I stopped by City Hall to see if Amy wanted to join me, but she was already eating at her desk. "Sorry, I had Lille's deliver. I'm on phone duty since Esmeralda is out today. Some sort of convention."

"For fortune-tellers?" My stomach rumbled. I hadn't remembered breakfast either at home or when I got to the shop. Which was so not like me. Between Greg's unusual behavior and the Darla call, I'd been too upset to eat. That never happened. "I'd like to see that schedule."

"Exactly. What are their sessions titled? I don't see dead people: What happens when your connection goes off?"

"Or Gypsy costumes: Do we have a responsibility to dress the part?" I loved talking with Amy. She had the same warped sense of humor as I did.

"What about, Eating for your muse: What foods keep the dead away and what foods bring them closer?"

At that my stomach growled again. And Amy's phone rang. "I've got to get back to work. I'll see you at Sunday brunch?"

"Eleven, at Lille's." I turned toward the door and heard Amy's routine script as she answered the phone.

"South Cove Police department, how may I help you?"

Diamond Lille's was packed so I had to settle for a small table in the corner. After giving Carrie my order, I sipped on my iced tea and opened the book I'd been reading earlier.

I was halfway done with my soup and all the way lost in the book when loud voices drew me out of the story and back to reality. The diner had cleared a bit while I was reading, but the booths were still all filled. And the angry voices came out of the one around the corner where I couldn't see the occupants.

"I suppose your boyfriend would have paid more attention to you during a meal." The man's voice was too tight, too loud. I felt bad for the woman on the other end of the discussion. He wasn't listening, just reacting from pain. I'd watched this conversation before with when I was a family law attorney. Typically, when a spouse had evidence of infidelity, by the time they got to me, they were calm.

Tiny, the chef, walked by me on his way out to the far booth. I could imagine the arguing couple would be hustled out of the diner quickly.

Lille didn't appreciate anyone messing with her customers. I returned to my book, trying to zone out the voices when I recognized the woman who flew past me toward the restroom door.

It was Allison, her face swollen with tears.

CHAPTER 15

Toby was sitting out in a lawn chair in front of the apartment shed when I arrived back home. Emma lay at his feet. I'd given him a key for the back door when he'd moved in. He used it sparingly, mostly to let Emma out during the day when I was working. Toby loved my dog almost as much as I did.

"Hey, what are you doing awake? Don't you work tonight?" I opened a second chair that had been leaned on the side of the shed and sat. Emma came up to give me kisses and then sat on my foot, claiming me as her own.

"Couldn't sleep so I thought I'd keep Emma company while you were gone. I expected that you'd be home earlier. Did Deek come in late?"

Leave it to Toby to notice my extended hours.

"Actually, he took over our assignment on the festival committee so I watched the store until he got back. Then I went to Diamond Lille's for lunch." I closed my eyes and let the sun warm my face. Maybe I'd take a nap this afternoon. Allison and Mikey's fight at the diner had left my nerves on edge. I hated listening to people fight. Probably a holdover from when I was a kid listening to first my parents, then my mom and step dad. No matter where it came from, loud, angry voices made me crazy.

"Anything exciting happen?" Toby reached out and scratched Emma on the chin. "Especially at Lille's?"

"How did you find out so fast?" I knew Toby was hooked into the gossip mill, but this was ridiculous.

"I got a text from Tim. I guess Lille called the station after she sent Tiny out to break things up." Toby yawned. "He said he saw you walking out of the diner when he pulled the cruiser into the parking lot. He wanted to make sure you were okay."

"I was fine. I didn't fight with my husband in a public place." I closed my eyes, remembering how hurt Allison had looked when she ran to the restroom. "What did Tim do? Did he have to arrest Mikey?"

Toby barked out a laugh. "No way, he didn't want to explain to Greg that he arrested one of his best friends."

"Greg's buddies sure have made things interesting around here." I shook my head. "It was just supposed to be a fun weekend. Now, one person's dead, and people are fighting. It's like those chickens that fight each other when the heat gets turned up high."

"Terrance needs to figure out who killed Levi and fast. I don't think legally he can ask those people to stay around much longer." He stood and stretched. "And I don't think we'd like it if we had to see much more of them. Sometimes old friends are best left in the past. That's why high school reunions are only a weekend. Any longer and you realized which ones are really bat-crap crazy."

He folded his chair. "I'm heading to bed. Glad to see you're home safe. I thought maybe you'd get involved and tick the guy off. You tend to go all Wonder Woman and try to save the day when people are being hurt."

"That's not true." Well, I guess it was true a little. "Besides, Allison wasn't hurt. Mikey yelled at her but he didn't hit her, at least what I heard. Did he really hit her?"

"No, but I bet they'll either be seeing a marriage counselor or a divorce lawyer as soon as they get released from The Castle." He rubbed Emma's head. "I'll see you tomorrow."

"Sleep well." I folded my own chair and walked with Emma to my back door. Glancing at my watch, I had a few hours before Greg would come home. And it was Friday, so we might go out for dinner rather than cook. I pulled my book out of my bag. Time to finish the story.

* * *

"Where are you?" Greg called out from the living room. I hadn't heard him drive up as I'd fallen asleep on the swing. I had almost finished the book before my eyelids were drooping and soon, I was in dreamland.

"Out here," I said as I struggled to sit up. The book fell and hit Emma who had been sleeping under the swing. She jumped up like someone had attacked her, turning to bark at the book now on the porch floor.

Greg came outside, the screen door banging behind him. The sound made Emma give up her hunt for the vicious book and she ran to greet him. My dog was picky with who she loved, but she loved some people with all her heart. Greg knelt and gave her hugs. "Before you ask, I've already heard about Allison and Mikey. That's why I'm a little late. I went up to The Castle and talked to them both."

"Is she okay?"

"Mad as hell, but okay." He stood and gave me a quick kiss. "Mikey's going to have to work hard to get himself out of the dog house for this."

"Who did he think she had an affair with?" I thought I already knew the answer, but it wouldn't hurt to get independent confirmation.

"Levi. I guess he had a habit of seducing Mikey's wives. Which explains why he kept coming up with a new one every few years. Too bad about Allison. I kind of liked her." Greg sank into the swing next to me, picking up my book and handing it to me.

"So could he have been so mad he killed Levi?"

Greg looked at me, fatigue filling his eyes. I could see the idea had been considered and already discarded. "I really don't think Mikey could do something like that. I know, I know, people deal with jealousy in different ways, but Mikey?"

"Love makes people do strange things." I pointed out the obvious. "But you don't think that's what happened."

"I'm sure Terrance is investigating all angles." He turned away and put his forearms on his knees. I couldn't be sure, but it seemed as if he was avoiding looking directly at me. Body language experts would surmise that Greg was either lying or holding back something. Right now, I'd have to agree.

"Greg?" I put my hand on his arm to get him to look at me.

He stood up like he'd been shot with a cattle prod. "Let's forget all of this and go out to dinner. I'm calling a date night truce. No talking about Levi or the gang, or anything else that could be considered as a negative conversation. We're just a couple in love tonight."

I still wanted to know about the laptop and what had really happened during high school, but I knew he'd been working hard and trying to keep the gang from going off the deep end after Levi's death. The group had seen Levi as some sort of pack leader. And now, there was a gap in leadership. Either the group would disband and go their separate ways, or someone new would step in and take over. I realized Greg was waiting for a response. "Date night sounds great. Where do you want to eat?"

After changing into our more formal duds—black jeans and a blue dress shirt for him, a sundress and crocheted sweater for me—we left the house. I beelined to Greg's truck and the passenger side, but it was locked.

I looked inside. The laptop sat on the passenger seat.

I heard the click of car locks behind me. As I turned around, Greg was holding my Jeep's door open for me.

"I thought we'd take your car. I need a little break from old blue."

I moved over to the other side of the driveway and settled into the seat, moving my dress out of the way so he could shut the door. The guy was sneaky. He knew I was curious, but right now, he wasn't talking. I gave up. Tonight, was going to be just about us. Come hell or high water, as my grandpa used to say.

The high water mark arrived with dessert. Greg got a text on his phone. He picked it up, read the message, then typed a quick response. I held my fork over the chocolate lava cake that had just arrived with a cup of really good coffee. Greg had his own apple and pear tart. "Do we have to go?"

"Actually, no. That was Butch. He wanted to apologize for Lois telling you the story about Levi and the football player." He took a bite of his dessert. "Why didn't you say something?"

I set my own spoon down. "It's not like we have talked a lot about Levi's death since you sent me on an investigation that you don't seem to want to know anything about."

"That's not true. We've talked every night about this." Greg didn't look at me.

"So tell me the rest of the story. Was Levi involved in this kid's death?" I twirled my spoon in the cake, wanting to take a bite, but holding back for his answer.

"No. Not in the way you think." Greg sipped his coffee and leaned back in his chair. "I'll tell you, but it has to end here. This is the past and has nothing to do with his death."

"You're totally convinced of that fact?" Now I decided to focus on my dessert and let Greg tell the story at his own pace. "If you are, I'll leave it alone."

"I know you. If you don't have all the answers, you can't leave something alone." Greg motioned the waiter for more coffee and we waited in silence while he refilled our cups.

I finished off my dessert during the wait. Hey, a girl's gotta eat, right?

"So this guy was bullying Levi. Bad stuff. Taking his clothes out of his locker, beating him up after class. Any time he found him alone, Levi would suffer some new kind of humiliation. We tried to keep him in sight. Butch became his body guard and the rest of us filled in when Butch couldn't be there. Finally, Levi got fed up. He hacked into the kid's computer and found something." He sipped his coffee.

"What did he find?"

"Copies of every test for every class the kid was taking that year. Rumor after the suicide was his father bought the kid's access to higher grades in exchange for supporting the boosters. Our football star who was all but moved into his dorm at Stanford was hiding a secret." Greg shrugged.

"So Levi threatened to expose him?" Now I got it. The kid killed himself rather than be outed as a cheater by the runt he'd been bullying. "And the kid couldn't take the chance of losing his scholarship, no longer being the golden boy. So he killed himself."

"Honestly, I'm surprised he didn't kill Levi instead." Greg played with his spoon in the tart. "The kid's dad was all up in Levi's face that he had killed his son. And honestly, maybe he had. But not by his own hand. The police investigated, ruled it a suicide, and left the parents to grieve. Levi told the guys what he'd found, mostly because he was scared that Mike Lord's dad was going to kill him."

"That is so sad." I placed a finger on my lips. "What about the father, could he have killed Levi?"

"He moved away years ago. I heard he was killed in an auto accident in Boston. Before you ask, there was no other family." Greg waved the waiter down for the check. When it came, he held out a hand. "Can we go home now?"

I could see that telling the tale had drained him. What was it about old friendships that kept us tied to the past and the secrets so tightly?

The ride home was quiet and when we reached the house, he paused in the living room. I stopped at the bottom of the stairs, watching him. "Do you want something to drink?"

"I think I'll stay up for a while and listen to music. Do you mind?" He met me at the stairs.

"Do you want company?" I had to work in the morning, but I could power through with a few hours of sleep. I pushed his hair out of his eyes. He needed to get it trimmed. Of course, I liked his hair a little longer but he said it made him look like Dustin Austin, our resident lost in the sixties hippie.

"Actually, I'll just put on headphones and chill." He reached up to kiss me. "All this stuff with Levi has me feeling melancholy."

"Reliving the glory days?" I tried to make my tone teasing. I didn't want to leave him alone, but I knew he didn't want me there. Not tonight. Tonight he was going to grieve his friend and the life Levi would never live. He'd held himself out as the strong one for too long. It was time for him to release his friend to the fates.

His lips curved into a small smile. "Honey, as far as I'm concerned, the years since I met you are the glory days."

Emma paused at the bottom of the steps and finally chose to join Greg. I didn't blame her. I wanted to be in what had been my office, sitting on the loveseat next to him. Instead I climbed the stairs, drew a hot bath, and then poured myself into bed after the water cooled.

* * *

Saturday morning, the alarm woke me. I reached over to turn it off and noticed Greg's side of the bed empty. Either he'd never come to bed, or he was already up and busy with weekend tasks.

I showered, got dressed, and then wandered downstairs to find him. A note sat on the kitchen table. I poured myself a cup of coffee, then picked it up, reading it aloud: "I'm going out with Jim and the guys on the boat. We're doing our own kind of wake for Levi. I forgot to tell you last night. Love Greg."

For a second, I was angry. I didn't mind that he was going out with the guys, but something about the whole thing bugged me. It had been the same feeling I'd had during the weekend. Girls against the guys. The other women seemed resigned to not being part of the conversation. I wasn't. And Greg had never treated me that way. Until now.

"Get a grip, Jill." I chided myself. "He just lost a good friend."

The stern talking-to didn't make me less mad, but it did make me realize I was going to be late for opening if I didn't get moving. My phone rang as I power walked to the shop. It was Amy.

"Hey girl, do you have plans today?" Amy was chipper even at ten to six in the morning.

I waved to Harrold who was setting up a new train in his display window. I loved The Train Station, even if I didn't want a model train. It was fun just watching the kids hang around the window, especially during the holidays when Santa rode the rails. "Besides working until ten when Deek takes over, no. Why?"

"I'm taking you to the city for shopping. I've heard there's a new designer opening up shop and I want to see what they have."

"You're not much of a designer girl, are you?" Amy lived in either swimsuits or for work, long shorts and light flowy tops. If you opened a dictionary to California girl, her picture appeared.

"Justin is taking me to a faculty dinner next month and I need something formal. I'm going crazy. Just say you'll come with me. You have excellent taste. And you know formal. You used to do that, right?"

I smiled. As an attorney, I knew formal attire in and out. "My firm used to make us attend charity events. If you don't find anything you could just look in my closet. You might have to have them taken in, but I've got a ton of gowns and cocktail dresses just gathering dust in the third bedroom."

"You really should take those to Vintage Duds and consign them," Amy told me, and not for the first time. "Just because Sherry runs the place, doesn't mean it's the devil."

I wasn't going to argue the fact, but I wasn't sure Amy was right. In my mind, Sherry and her store were the enemy. We made plans for Amy to pick me up at the shop exactly at ten. As I walked past the consignment clothing store, I knew one thing: I wasn't going to take my lovely dresses into Vintage Duds and have Sherry bad-mouth me. We might not be mortal enemies, but I wasn't her favorite person—even if I hadn't been Greg's new relationship.

CHAPTER 16

We had not one but three dresses in the back of Amy's VW Bug when we left the city. One was the typical little black dress. One, a shift silk number in an aqua green made her look like a tall glass of water. And my favorite, a bubbly blue cocktail dress that I thought made her look like a princess. She couldn't choose one over the other so she bought all three, presumably with the idea she'd make a decision later and take two back. I had a feeling all three would stay in her closet long after the date to return for a refund passed. As we drove through Bakerstown, I remembered the conversation about the sale of The Castle. I hadn't been back to look up new filings since early in the week.

"Hey, if I buy us an early dinner, will you stop at the college for a few minutes? I need to research something." I pulled out my notebook and checked my to-do list. The fact that rumors were beginning to surface made me wonder if my computer search had just been too early. Without turning my head, I threw the winning punch. "We could go to that seafood place you love."

"Sure. And I could go check out Justin's office and see if he's around." Amy turned the car onto the road that led to the college. "I'm going to give him a fashion show with the new dresses tonight. I hope he likes at least one of them."

"I'm sure he'll love all of them." Justin adored Amy so whatever she loved, he did too. She parked in the administration parking lot and we walked into the quad. The library was on the right and the history department, where Justin taught, on the left. Amy flipped back her blond hair, smoothing it as if there might be some strand out of place. There wasn't. "Meet back here in twenty minutes, then it's off to dinner."

"Sounds like a plan." I headed toward the library. Not only did I want to check the real estate title filings, but I also wanted to research Levi's company. I didn't know a lot about prenups that I hadn't learned through celebrity rag gossip, but I suspected the prenup could hold a clue to the reason he was killed. Or maybe my curiosity about Jessica's new wealth was clouding my judgment. Were those kind of documents public domain since Levi was answerable to the board of directors? I made a note to go visit Jimmy Marcum on Monday. He'd kind of slipped my mind and as I landed at an empty research table, I made a note in my book for Monday's to-do list.

Greg always joked that if it wasn't on my list, it wasn't going to happen. Especially after he saw my planned 'impromptu' date nights on my calendar. So sue me, I like to know what's happening in my life.

I keyed in my student password and accessed the county real estate filings. It didn't take me long before I'd found it. The Castle had been purchased two weeks ago and now instead of being owned by the nonprofit board, it was owned by one person. Jessica Lorraine Cole. So Levi hadn't bought the property, Jessica had. As I waited for the deed filing to print, I thought about Jessica and her background. Where had she gotten the money to purchase something that expensive? The original board had brought in several different investors to purchase it from the estate. But Jessica bought it all by herself? Something didn't add up.

Tucking the printouts into my notebook, I did a search for Wallace Software, Inc. Several different websites were listed, but when I narrowed the search for ones in North Carolina. I found Levi's company. Opening the website, I saw a large plot of land with a modern building including solar panels and some sort of rain water collector and filter system. I went to the About Us page, and Levi's picture and bio was front and center. He'd been the heart behind the company. The website hadn't been updated since the death and his email address still was listed at the bottom of the page under a banner that read: QUESTIONS? ASK OUR CEO.

I scrolled through the other names, not knowing what I was looking for and then I found it: A brand-new addition to the board. Lois beamed happiness in her picture. Apparently, Levi had given her more than just his promise to keep Butch out of the big deal. What was going on with these people?

"Are you ready?" Amy spoke behind me.

Closing the browser, I logged out and stood. "Starving."

As we walked toward the car, Amy chatted about how crazy crowded Justin's office was. "He has books stacked up against the walls. I think

I'm going to buy him a bookcase for his birthday. What do you think? Too impersonal?"

I'd been lost in thinking about the circular relationships between Levi, Lois, Butch, and the rest of the gang. And more importantly, how did Greg fit into all of this? The group seemed to feed off of Levi and his activities. Now that he was gone, what would happen? And was it a good or bad thing? I turned to Amy and grabbed on the last thing I heard her say. "Bookcases are nice."

"You aren't listening. I could have told you that Justin was kissing some co-ed in his office and you would have responded with the same line." Amy paused as she stood by the driver's side door, looking over the car toward me. "What's got you thinking?"

"Nothing, everything. I'm just going in circles with this thing." I opened my door. "Let's go eat and talk about anything but Levi's death and who killed him. I need some downtime."

As we drove to the restaurant, I got a text from Greg: Will be late.

I texted back: No worries. I'm having dinner with Amy.

It took a few minutes before I got another text. This one read: Have fun. I love you.

How many times have we had this same text conversation? The difference was before it was on nights where he had to work late. Now he was out with the guys. Why did it feel so much different? I said a silent prayer for his safety, then texted back: See you at home.

* * *

When I got home, Greg was still out with the boys. I assumed if he was back at The Castle, drinking with the guys, he would sleep there. He took his driving seriously, even if it was only a few miles to the house. He'd told me several times that he'd only have to get pulled over once for drunk driving and he'd lose his job. And he liked his job. Even if he wasn't head of the South Cove Police Department, I didn't think he'd do anything dangerous, like driving impaired.

* * *

I opened a soda and sat at the table, going over my Who-killed-Levi notes. Greg had told me that the high school thing was a dead end, but I googled the names I found in the article anyway. When I found Mike

Lord's father's obituary, I crossed the thread off my lists. No one, except the five friends and Lois, knew or even cared about the long ago suicide.

I looked at the other suspects on my original list. Butch and/or Lois— the only wonky thing I couldn't explain was her new position on the board. It didn't mean Lois had killed Levi, and in fact, I didn't think she was strong enough to strangle him. Maybe Brenda, she had motive, especially now that I knew The Castle had been sold. Brenda didn't seem like a killer though. And she wouldn't put her dog in jeopardy of needing to find a new home but maybe knowing the place had been sold and she'd be out on the streets made protecting Fifi a stronger motive? Besides, The Castle wasn't in Levi's name. If that the sale was the trigger, Jessica would be on Doc Ames' autopsy table.

"Stop checking people off the list because you like them. Think with your head, not your heart," I chided myself. Jessica. Maybe she'd killed her soon to be husband because he found out, what? That she'd bought The Castle out from under him? And then why was she so distraught over his death. If she was acting this grieving widow role, the woman was putting on an Oscar worthy performance. Besides, I didn't know what the prenup said. And like Lois, would Jessica be strong enough to choke Levi? Doubtful.

Allison, on the other hand, had strong arms due to her obsessive swimming. Mikey apparently already knew about the attention Levi had given her. I didn't think it had crossed the affair line, but I was sure since Allison was wife number five, Mikey might be a little quick to judge. I drew a box around the couple. I didn't understand why they had been fighting in the diner. They both were definitely staying on the naughty list.

By the time I'd finished adding in my notes from today and closed the notebook, it was nine. I grabbed the book that I was only pages from finishing and took a fresh soda into the living room. Sinking into the couch, I opened the book and proceeded to fall back into the story.

Five minutes later, my cell rang. I'd set up Greg his own ring tone, so I knew who was calling. "Hey, lover. Are you drunk dialing me?"

A female voice chuckled in my ear. "No, but if you want me to talk dirty to you, I could entertain you for a few minutes."

The voice sounded familiar. "Brenda?"

"Yep. Your boy here is almost passed out, sitting out by the pool. I'd leave him here to sleep it off, but with the track record these fools have had this week, let's just say I don't want to find another dead body." I heard Greg in the background asking for his phone back. "Hold on, I think he wants to talk to you."

I heard a few bangs and swear words telling me that Greg had dropped the phone at least once, but soon, he came on the line. "Hey baby. Brenda says she doesn't care where I go, but I can't stay here. Can you come get me?"

This was a first. I'd never had to go pick up my drunk boyfriend before. Even in the bad relationships I'd had prior to moving to South Cove and meeting Greg. I looked longingly at the book. Then I tucked the bookmark back into the same spot I'd just removed it from. I would get this book finished. It just might be tomorrow. "I'll be there in five minutes."

I hung up the phone and grabbed my tote and keys. Emma looked at me, her tail wagging slowly. "If you promise to stay in the car, you can go."

A bark from her sealed my decision and I grabbed her leash, just in case, from the front table. "Let's go."

She ran outside and sat at the gate, waiting for me to open it. Then she ran to the car. The dog knew things. I would swear she could understand what I was saying, as long as it was basic words and commands. I let her into the back, threw my tote on the passenger seat, and took off to rescue Greg, or really Brenda from Greg.

The parking lot had one extra vehicle in the visitor spaces in front of the ticket booth. The Closed for Business sign still sat in the booths window. I checked the door on Greg's truck. It was locked. I peered in and saw the laptop on the front seat. That laptop was bothering me.

I walked into the compound and headed toward the pool area. A man stepped out of the shadows from behind the ticket booth.

"What are you doing here?" He grabbed my arm, swinging me back to face him. A whiff of whiskey filled the space between us. Fear filled my body as I tried to see who it was. But the courtyard was too dark.

I shook off his grip. I wasn't going to let some drunk tell me where I could or couldn't be. I took a deep breath, then squaring my shoulders, I asked, "What's it to you?"

"This is private property. You can't just come in here and wander around. I should call the police." Now the man shook a dirty finger in my face.

"Go ahead. I know the deputy who's on tonight. I'm pretty sure I won't be the one going to jail for trespassing." I knew now I was just pushing my luck, but the guy had scared me.

"John, what are you doing?" Brenda rushed to my side. "Are you okay, Jill?"

"I'm fine, but your guard dog needs to step back." I glared at the older man who, now, after he stepped into a light, I recognized as one of Brenda's employees. "Geez, do you welcome all your guests like this?"

"I didn't know you were expecting anyone. She just came in from the front like she lived here or something." John glared at me. "There are too many people here now. The antiques are going to be hurt or worse."

"I think worse already happened, John. You can go home now. I've got this." Brenda put her arm around me. "Sorry about that. He's very dedicated to The Castle."

"I'm not sure dedicated is the word I'd use. Obsessed maybe?" I realized I was shaking now that we'd stepped away from the man. "Anyway, I'm here to pick up my guy. Is he still awake?"

"Barely. I'm guessing he can walk. I think what kept him afloat was he was sober when they got here. I guess he was the designated driver. His friends on the other hand—I think their wives are going to have to use a bell cart to get them to their rooms." Brenda shook her head. "As annoying as it is, I love the income that they're bringing in, especially since Terrance still hasn't given me the go ahead to reopen for tours. The board is going to crap when they see the take for the month."

I turned my head, watching her as she talked about The Castle's finances. She didn't know it had been sold. That was obvious. Well, I wouldn't be the one to tell her. Especially since she'd just rescued me from the angry John.

"Jill!" Greg stood knocking the chair he'd been sitting in over. "You came to rescue me."

"I always will." I responded with the scripted response from a television show I loved. I hadn't thought he'd been paying attention, but I guess he had. "Are you ready to go home? I'm sure Brenda wants to call it a night."

"Brenda's a sweetheart." He grinned at her. Man, I hadn't seen him this in-the-wind ever.

I took his hand and led him to the Jeep where Emma greeted him with a high-pitched whine. She'd stuck her head and half of her body out of the window, trying to get closer to him. I opened the passenger door while he greeted the dog.

"Hey sweetheart. Did you miss me?" He gave Emma a hug and almost fell over. Apparently everyone was a sweetheart tonight.

"Get in the car and we'll go home. Then you and Emma can have your love fest." I gently moved him toward the open door.

"I love you too." He patted my face and then fell into the seat. "You are the cornerstone of my life. I don't know what I'd do without you."

"Let's hope you don't have to figure that out." I moved the one remaining leg still out of the Jeep onto the floorboard and slowly closed the door, hoping he wouldn't move.

I walked around to the other side of the car and got in. Starting the engine, I backed out of the space and then left the parking lot. A Journey song came on the radio and Greg turned up the volume to almost ear splitting level. As he sang along, I turned down the volume just a tad so my speakers wouldn't blow. When the song ended, Greg leaned back into the seat.

By the time I pulled into the driveway, Greg's singing had been replaced with Greg's snoring. I shook his shoulder. "Wake up. We're home."

His head lolled to one side and the snoring got louder.

I got out and opened the door for Emma who jumped down and followed me to the gate. "I guess Greg's sleeping out here tonight."

Emma turned and looked back at the car and barked.

Then we both went inside and went to bed.

When I awoke the next morning, I smelled bacon and coffee. Greg must be awake. Emma wasn't in the bedroom anymore, abandoning me for the chance at human food. I slipped on capris and a clean tank and headed downstairs.

When he saw me come in, he went to the coffeepot and poured me a cup. He sat it on the table and pulled me into his arms.

"I'm sorry." He held me tight.

When he let me go, I sat at the table. "I assume you're apologizing for me having to go get you last night?"

"I shouldn't have gotten that wasted. I could blame it on the heat from being on the boat, then we drank too much when we hit The Castle, and of course there was Levi, but they're all excuses. I should have been more careful." He nodded to the stove. "You want me to make you an omelet? Or are you seeing Amy for breakfast?"

"Actually, since we spent yesterday together, brunch was canceled, so I'd love one." I started to stand. "What can I do to help?"

"Just sit there and drink coffee."

Emma came to me and nuzzled my leg. Then she made a circle and plopped down onto her bed. Sunday morning at home. When did we become a Rockwell painting?

"So how was the fishing trip?" I didn't want it to sound like I was checking up on him, but I wanted to know if he'd found out anything that might shed some light on Levi's death.

"Unproductive. Mostly we just sat around and told Levi stories. The guy will be missed." Greg chopped an onion while he talked. "I didn't realize how much he'd helped the rest of the group. He got Butch his job on the oil rigs in Louisiana, his company hired David as the real estate agent in most of their land deals, and Mikey, well, he actually works for the company in marketing."

"And Lois is on the board for the company." The words were out of my mouth before I thought about if I'd planned to tell Greg this or not.

He stopped chopping, turned and looked at me. "Seriously? How did you find that out?"

"She's on the company website as a new board member. Didn't Butch tell you?" I sipped my coffee, watching him.

"No. In fact, he said she just signed up to do some volunteer work because she was bored all the time. I wonder if he knows about this." Greg dumped the onion into a bowl and started chopping green peppers. "We were teasing him that Lois runs the household. The guy just has his debit card and a credit card in his wallet. He has no knowledge about their financial status at all. He said Lois handles everything. At least she does since Butch lost their savings in one of Levi's schemes a few years ago."

"Don't expect me to be your accountant when we get married." I teased. "I have enough trouble keeping the books for the shop. I'd hate to have to juggle everything."

The toast popped up and Greg spread butter on the bread. Then he brought me a plate with a jar of strawberry jam. "I like that."

"What? Toast?"

He kissed me on the top of my head. "No. You said 'when we get married.'"

Crap, I had. "I didn't mean…"

"Don't go all backpedaling on me. I just thought it was sweet." He tapped a finger on my investigation notebook. "What else do you have in here that I don't know about?"

I walked him through the suspects as I saw them, adding the part about Lois and Butch at the end. "Honestly, I don't feel right about any of them. Last night, Brenda acted like it was business as usual for The Castle. I don't think she has a clue it's been sold or that Jessica is the new owner."

"I talked to Jessica last night. She's considering leaving North Carolina. She says it has too many bad memories for her to go back there. She's meeting with the attorney next week to see what her options are before the estate is probated." He went back to the stove and started sautéing the vegetables. Greg did omelets right. It wasn't fast, but the results were yummy. "I didn't get the feeling she was measuring The Castle for drapes or that she even knew about owning it. Are you sure it's her?"

"I looked at the legal filings. There were too many rumors floating around about the sale for something not to be happening. I can't believe

Brenda hasn't heard something yet." I tore off a scrap of crust and gave it to Emma.

"After we eat, I need you to drive me to The Castle."

"I doubt if anyone is up at this time. Your friends looked pretty trashed when I saw them on the patio." I licked a bit of jam off my finger. I loved warm toast with butter and jam. It hit my happy spot.

"I want to get my truck. Then I need to show you something." He set a plate with a huge three-egg omelet in front of me. "I found Levi's laptop in the truck. I guess he left it there after our last fishing trip and didn't have the chance to go back for it. Jessica told me the password last night."

"Don't you think you should give it to Terrance?" I focused on my plate, not looking at Greg's back, now cooking his own breakfast. This subterfuge didn't feel like him. If anyone was straight up and by the book, it was Greg.

"I will. I just want to see what he was thinking. It's the last contact I'll ever have with my friend. I'd like to do it alone." Greg grabbed a plate and slid his omelet on it. Then he turned to me. "If you'll help me get through it. I need you."

"I can do that. But if I go to jail for police obstruction, you're going to have to get me out." I started eating. I needed to have one good meal before we started skirting the law. It was part of the investigators handbook. Or at least the one I was going to write someday after I made all the mistakes first.

"Honey, if you get arrested, I'll be sitting in the cell next to you." He turned my face toward him, wiped a bit of jam off the corner of my mouth with his finger, and then kissed me. "We can be the couple who bonds together in our cells."

"With our schedules, it might be the only way we actually have time to talk." I went back to eating. "This is really good. I'm glad you're around to cook on weekend mornings. I may have to change up my brunches with Amy."

He squeezed my shoulder, then went back to eating. When his head was turned away, he said, "I'm good at other lazy Sunday morning activities, too."

CHAPTER 17

The drive to The Castle was quiet. There was no one on the road at seven on a Sunday. Well, except for the old pickups filled with weekend anglers heading to the marina to take out their boats. It was lovely. Except for one thing. We were going to get a dead man's laptop to see what mess he'd gotten himself into.

Happy lazy Sunday to me.

Was it bad that I was excited about the investigation again? I loved working with Greg on putting together the puzzle. I was back to feeling like one of those television investigating couples, like Bones, but unlike the characters in those stories, I didn't have any real skill I brought to the investigation except for my curiosity. And my mad love for reading mysteries. That had to count for something, right?

Greg dug his keys out of his pocket and leaned inside the passenger door. "I'll see you at home."

He didn't even wait for a reply. I wondered what he thought might be on that laptop. Whatever it was, the anticipation of finding out had put him in a bad mood for days. I waited for him to start the truck and ease it out of the parking lot. Old blue, as he called the truck, had been having starting issues for a few months. I told him he should get a new vehicle, but he said that was like throwing away a clock that just needed new batteries. Although I noticed he hadn't gotten the truck into the shop yet either.

We didn't talk a lot about finances, but I knew that his last marriage had left him pretty strapped, mostly because he took on the debt that Sherry had charged on various credit cards. I figured he must be getting closer to paying it all off, but who knew? I guess one day we were going to have to have that discussion. I was debt free, including my newish Jeep. I'd wrote a check for the transaction a few years ago out of what I called the Miss Emily Fund. The money had been left to me by a friend who had been murdered. Although the woman had been old, her death still carved a hole in my chest and I'd missed her every day. The good news is she also left me her house and I'd hung her paintings all through the place as I redecorated to make it mine.

Well, mine and Greg's now. I hoped he considered the place home. He used the word often enough and he'd always called the dump he'd lived in before, the apartment. Not I'm going home, just I'm going to the apartment to sleep.

I was still pondering these unanswerable questions about our relationship and what it all meant when we arrived back home. Emma barked through the glass when she saw Greg's truck pull in next to us. And just a few seconds after Greg parked, Toby pulled his truck in next to Greg's.

I waited for all the engines to shut off, then let Emma out. She ran to the front of the vehicles where Greg and Toby were leaning on the truck hoods and talking.

"Hey, how was your shift?" I took in his rumpled uniform and bloodshot eyes. He was tired to the bone.

"Busy. Three guys are cooling their jets in the drunk tank this a.m.. I suspect one of them at least has a high-price lawyer that will be calling in Judge Harrison from the golf course about midday. I finished up all the reports so if you do get the call, you're ready." He nodded to Greg. "Sorry to ruin your weekend."

"You didn't drive drunk, they did. And if they do call me in, I might just take some time getting there. Being locked in a jail cell has a way of making people think about their actions and consequences, even if they have good attorneys." He slapped Toby on the back. "You just keep doing your job."

"I'm hoping that tonight will be a little calmer. Last night, I'd just get back on patrol and another idiot would take off from the winery. I wish Darla had an attached motel where her inebriated guests could go sleep it off." He pulled at his rumpled shirt. "Any chance I could use your washer and dryer this afternoon, once I get some sleep? This is my last clean uniform. I guess I didn't plan well this week."

"Just drop your laundry off before you go to sleep. I'm doing ours today, I can get yours done too." I thought about my taxi service to pick up Greg last night. So many people started drinking without thinking about the exit strategy. I bet if I hadn't been here, Brenda would have bundled Greg into one of the guest rooms at The Castle. We were family in South Cove.

He shook his head. "Not part of the deal. I can do my own laundry."

"I know. Let's just say I'm feeling generous today. Bring it over and I'll get it done." I folded my arms. "Discussion over."

"You better listen to her, dude." Greg chuckled. "I've seen that look before. Besides, you don't want her to grumble all day about this and make me miserable, do you? Give a guy a break, will you?"

I playfully slapped him on the arm. "Just for that, you're helping with the laundry. Or better yet, you're on bathroom duty today."

"Evil. She's just evil." Greg put his arm around me as we left the driveway. Toby went to his apartment to grab his laundry and drop it off on the back porch. Greg and I went to the kitchen to open the laptop and see what was really going on in a dead man's world.

We putted around the laptop-shaped elephant in the room until after we'd started laundry, cleaned the kitchen and made out a list of chores for the day. One of which would be to run to Bakerstown for groceries. If Toby was right, and Greg was going to be called into the station, that task would fall to me. But I wanted to make sure I got his thoughts on what we needed before I left. Shopping in another town made the list more important. We couldn't just stop in the local grocery for an item or two we forgot from the last shopping event.

Finally, everything was planned and we sat at the table, staring at the laptop.

"So what is the password?" I asked as he lifted the lid.

He smiled and cut his eyes toward me. "Little star. That was his nickname for Jessica. And apparently, he used it on all his passwords since they'd met." He typed out the word little, the star symbol and the numbers in the year. The screen bloomed to life with a picture of Jessica and Levi at some charity event. They looked happy. "She's broken."

I felt the tears well behind my eyes. "I would be too."

We sat for a moment, lost in our own thoughts about what was and what could have been and for me, how happy I wasn't in Jessica's spot right now. With Greg being in law enforcement, the idea that something tragic could happen was always in the back of my head. Police officers were shot all the time. Sometimes for stupid reasons. I hoped I'd never have to deal with the situation.

"She really loved him. I wish you could have known the Levi before he became the jerk you met. He would give someone the shirt off his back. But ever since he passed the seven figure mark in annual salary, he started to change. I guess money does that to people." Greg cleared his throat and clicked open the flashing email icon. Email hadn't stopped coming in since Levi's death. Either these people didn't know about the murder, or they thought the account was being monitored. So many were condolence letters. Today's equivalent of a sympathy card, I guessed.

Greg scanned through a few and then went into sent mail. He scrolled until he found one addressed to Allison. He looked at me and asked, "Mikey's Allison?"

I shrugged. "Only one way to find out."

"Honestly, I didn't want to know." He held his finger over the mouse. "Pandora's box is now opening. Regrets need to be boxed up and taken out later."

"Are you sure?" I knew he was joking around, trying to make light of how he was feeling. There was a reason the investigation had been taken out of his jurisdiction. Sometimes during an investigation, you found out things that friends and family didn't want or need to know. "You can just turn this over to Terrance."

"I'd rather know what I'm turning over." He rolled his shoulders. "Levi was my responsibility. Even though he was my friend, he died in my town. On my watch."

He opened the email. All of my hopes that it was just friendly chatter about the upcoming bachelor party ended with the greeting Levi had used, My Lovely. The email just went downhill from there.

"Listen to this," Greg pointed to the screen, then read the section aloud: "*Don't worry about Jessica and Mikey. I'm sure we can find a place in that huge castle to be alone for at least a few minutes. No one will ever find out. One time, and I'll leave you alone, if that's what you want. But baby, I want you so bad my teeth hurt.*"

I didn't say anything. Obviously, Levi had been seducing Allison, whether or not she'd taken him up on his offer. Mikey must have found out based on his outburst at the diner.

"What a jerk." Greg shook his head. "He always wanted what someone else had. Sherry told me he'd tried to woo her at one of these reunions. It was one of the reasons we didn't attend more than one as a couple."

"Sorry, Greg. I know you liked the guy."

He shook his head. "I loved my friend. I didn't know this guy. Maybe it was partially our fault. Once the guys at school started picking on Levi, we were always excusing him for everything. He didn't know better. He was socially awkward. He grabbed my prom date's butt during dinner when I was in the restroom. I told him to knock it off, but I could see he was proud of getting away with it. I guess with more money and power, he kept getting away with it."

I didn't know what to say. So I focused Greg away from his trip down memory lane to the present. "You don't think Mikey killed him, do you?"

"No. I mean, I don't think so. I talked to Mikey yesterday about the fight at the diner. He's convinced Allison is seeing someone now. Apparently, Levi put it in Mikey's head that since she wouldn't sleep with him, she must be sleeping with someone else. Nice guy, right?" He thrummed his fingers on the table. "Maybe we should go talk to both of them. I don't see how it will kill their relationship any more than this already has. And we can get Mikey and Allison off your suspect list."

"I'll talk to Allison and you talk to Mikey?" I liked the divide and conquer technique.

"Sounds like a plan." Greg went to close the laptop but I put my hand out to stop him. "What?"

"Is there anything directed to Lois? About the board appointment?" I scanned the email addresses, trying to find one that looked like hers.

Greg scanned the list too. "Looks like it goes back two weeks, then it's automatically dumped. I suspect if she's on the website already, the deal was done way before two weeks. They still haven't taken Levi off and he's been dead a week now."

The words echoed in the kitchen.

He shook his head. "I don't think I'll ever get used to saying that word. Where are you in the laundry? Do you have time to take a quick run over to The Castle?"

I glanced at the clock. It was nine. "Do you think anyone's awake?"

He shrugged. "If they're not, they will be."

I changed over Toby's first load of laundry to the dryer and put his whites into wash. I'd have his basket ready and sitting on his porch way before he even woke up. I liked doing laundry. It calmed me in some weird way. Take something dirty and stained and make that all go away. Too bad life wasn't like that.

We took my car back to The Castle. This was my the third visit to the place in less than twenty-four hours. It was a personal record. And of course, there was the one visit where I'd accused Craig of trying to block the council's blessing on the Mission Wall project. If I'd known how long it was going to take to get the decision through the California Historical Society, I might have let that one alone.

I'd brought my notebook and as Greg drove, I made a few new notes on the Mikey-Allison suspect page. Greg glanced down. "Does that really help you when you're thinking about the investigation?"

"Sure. You have case files and the murder board to play with. I write everything down, including things that are totally outlandish and then I prove them wrong. As I whittle out all the things that couldn't be true, the one thing that could be true starts to stand out. And, it makes me focus on what hasn't been eliminated." I thought about my first investigation. Miss Emily's death had been devastating to me and when I thought Greg and the police department were going to rule it a natural death, I'd been incensed. My notebook from that was more of a journal of all the things I thought were strange and that the police, well, Greg, were ignoring. The more I looked into Miss Emily's life, the more suspects I had in her death. And more motives.

"It looks messy." Greg turned the car into The Castle parking lot. "I don't know how you keep track of everything."

"You should have seen my first notebook for Miss Emily. Now that was confusing." I closed the spiral notebook and shoved it into my tote. I knew exactly what I wanted to ask Allison. And if I could get some time with Lois, it would be a twofer trip. "Let's go investigate."

"Honey?" Greg put his hand on my arm. "You realize that we have no authority to even be looking into Levi's death. So you need to go slow with any accusations."

I turned and gave him my million-watt smile. "Honey? I never have any authority. You're the one who has to get used to my world."

Mikey and Allison were having breakfast, alone, out on the patio. When they invited us to join them, I pulled up a chair and Greg frowned as I sat down.

"We've already eaten but I'd love some coffee." I glanced around at the empty pool area. "Greg, why don't you and Mikey go find us a waiter?"

"I need to talk to you anyway." Greg nodded at Mikey. "Do you mind?"

We watched the men walk away and then Allison handed over her cup and the full carafe of coffee on the table. "You can have mine. I don't drink coffee." Her lips curved into a smile. "At least not anymore. I hear it's bad for the baby."

My eyes widened. "You're pregnant?" Now that just made the whole thing touchier. Before I thought about it, I blurted, "Who's the father?"

Allison frowned and sat down the coffee after filling my cup. She blew out a sigh. "I thought that was you in the diner. You must have heard our fight. I didn't tell Mikey I was going to the doctor and he thought I was sneaking around."

"Which you were." I sipped my coffee. "But for a different reason."

Allison shrugged. "I didn't want to tell him until I was sure."

I decided to put my cards on the table. "You said Levi had wandering hands recently."

"He did." She focused on the fruit on her plate, not looking at me. "You can ask any of the women."

"We found his emails to you. Were you having an affair?" I watched her face.

"No! He wanted to. After Mikey and I got married and he introduced us to the group, I started getting emails from Levi. At first, they were just friendly. Then he asked if I wanted to have coffee with him." She leaned back in her chair, remembering. "Mikey was out of town and I told him that."

"But he still wanted to have coffee," I guessed.

She laughed, a short sound that didn't have any humor. "He said he knew. And he wanted more than coffee. I've been avoiding him ever since."

"Did you tell Mikey?" I knew the answer but I needed her to confirm.

"What, that his oldest friend was trying to bed me?" She shook her head. "Levi threatened to tell him, and I said to go ahead. My hands were clean in this. The worst thing I did was respond to his friendly emails. Before he started hitting on me. I told Mikey everything after Levi died. After the fight. I told him I didn't do anything."

I believed her. As dedicated as she had been to swimming, she seemed just as committed to making her marriage work. Even if it had problems like a friend trying to break them up. But Levi hadn't really wanted Allison, not for long term. He had Jessica. No, he just didn't want Mikey to have something he hadn't.

I decided to change the subject. I'd compare notes with Greg later. "So when's the baby due?"

"April. If it's a girl, I want to name her after Mikey's mother. We haven't decided on a boy's name yet."

From the look on her face, it was clear that Mikey had suggested the one name Allison would never call her child. Levi. Oh, the fun of being a couple. She finished her fruit, then put her napkin on her plate. "Sorry, I need to go lay down. This being knocked up has made me crave naps."

"Congratulations and I'll be rooting for you."

She looked at me sadly and I realized she thought I was talking about the marriage, not the pregnancy but it was too late to explain as she scurried away. I poured myself more coffee and waited for Greg to return.

"Hey, what are you doing out here all alone?" Lois plopped down in the chair that Allison had just vacated. She waved down the waiter who had finally arrived and handed him the dirty plate. "Bring us more coffee and mimosas."

I held up a hand. "Just coffee for me."

"You really need to lighten up." Lois waited for the man to leave. "So what's up? Why are you here today? Upset that your boy went out drinking with the rest of the guys last night? They needed the break."

"Actually, I wanted to talk to you."

The mimosa and coffee had arrived and the guy handed us a small menu. Lois waved it away. "Bring me the biscuits and gravy plate."

The guy looked at me. "Really, coffee's fine."

She laughed as he left. "You eat like Allison. I swear that girl only eats fruits and seeds."

I wondered if that was all she could keep down, but Allison's condition wasn't my story to tell. "Greg made omelets this morning."

"Being the good boyfriend to make up? That sounds like our Greg." She sat the drink glass down, already half gone. "So what did you want to talk about?"

I set my coffee cup down and decided to be direct. "Why did Levi put you on the board for his company?"

CHAPTER 18

Lois finished off the rest of the mimosa and waved the waiter down for another one before she answered. "How did you find out?"

"The website. You're listed as one of the board members." I sipped my coffee and watched her. "The picture is great by the way."

"It's not what you think." She grabbed the glass from the waiter and chugged it. Then she handed it back. "Another one. Please."

I focused on the coffee, letting her settle and decide what she wanted to tell me.

"Look, Levi owed us. He owed Butch. That whole thing during high school. He had Butch go tell the kid what he'd found. And threaten him. Butch said he was scared, but I think even then, Levi liked having people do things for him. Everyone thought he was so sensitive, but he played the victim role with grace."

"Butch didn't…" I paused, wondering if she'd tell me if he had.

Lois's eyes widened. "Butch didn't kill the kid, if that's what you're asking. He just cornered him after football practice and told him to leave Levi alone. Or his secret was going to be all over the high school by the next day."

"So he shot himself."

"That same weekend. The team played Friday night, he told his dad he was going up to the cabin afterward. When he didn't come home Sunday, the old man drove up to see what was wrong." Lois filled her cup with coffee. "Butch felt responsible. He came to me after school when we found out and just cried. Levi needed to pay for that."

"So you told him to put you on the board."

Lois nodded. "Not my best moment, I'll agree. I didn't want to blackmail him but we were struggling and the board money is easy. Four meetings a year and I make over six figures. No wonder the rich keep getting richer. Even if it's just for a couple of years, that would build up our retirement account."

"What happens now that Levi's gone?"

Lois tapped one finger on the table. "I have a contract. A valid one. They don't need to know why Levi picked me to fill the opening. And yeah, the chance I'll get a second term is unlikely, but I'll give them everything I can for the next four years. Then, we'll see."

I finished off my coffee, thinking about Lois's words. She had a reason for Levi to stay alive since his support kept her on the board. Nothing I'd learned this morning pointed toward a possible murder suspect. In fact, it eliminated several. I wondered how Greg was faring with Mikey.

"Hey big guy. How are you feeling this morning?" Lois's gaze went over my head and I realized the boys were back from their chat.

"I haven't drunk that much since the last reunion I attended." Greg pulled up a chair and sat next to me. "I'm beginning to think that you're the problem, missy."

"You've always been in love with me, admit it." She smiled and I could see the mimosas were making her eyes a bit glassy. "Only Butch won my heart first and I could never be unfaithful."

"You broke my heart. Almost ruined me for other girls." He put his arm around my shoulder. "At least until I met Jill here. She's the real deal."

Lois's lips were tight and I could barely see the red lipstick that she kept leaving on her mimosa glasses. "I'm happy for you. It's time you found someone who really cares for you."

Mikey didn't say anything, but he pushed away his almost full plate. He looked at me. "Where'd Allison go?"

"Upstairs to lay down." I said.

Greg looked at me as if questioning what I did to make her leave, but then Lois spoke up. "What is wrong with that wife of yours? She's either obsessively swimming in the pool or she's crashed out way too early."

"Allison's fine." He ran a hand over his face. "She's going to have a baby."

Greg slapped him on the back. "Hey, man, you didn't tell me that. Mikey, a father. What's the world coming to?"

As they exchanged congratulations and good wishes, I snuck a peek at Lois's face. Under the bright smile lay a sadness she couldn't hide.

When we got home, I rotated laundry and brought out a basket of clothes to fold in the kitchen. Greg was looking at my notebook.

"So, what did Mikey say?" We'd talked about the baby on the way home, but not about the affair.

"He told me he was concerned that Levi was going after Allison. Apparently, the rest of his marriages had failed because of interference from Levi. He'd promise these women the moon, then once he got them in his bed, he dumped them." Greg unloaded the dishwasher as he talked.

"And yet, Mikey stayed friends with him?"

Greg shrugged, obviously uncomfortable with the subject. "He blew it off. Thought it was his own fault or the woman's fault, whatever. But deep down he knew. And I don't think he was really in love until Allison. Then the thought of losing her made him crazy."

"She told me she didn't do anything with Levi. But he was always pushing her. Trying to get her to meet him, sending little gifts to the house. No wonder Mikey thought she was having an affair. Levi made it look that way." I folded clothes as I talked. "But she wasn't falling for it. I think she's pretty strong."

"She'd have to be to put up with that." Greg closed the dishwasher and grabbed a pair of pants out of the basket. He folded quickly. "What's next on the agenda once we get these folded?"

"Do you want to take a chance at running to Bakerstown for groceries?" I looked at the clock. It was one. I'd at least finished washing Toby's uniforms and by the time we got back, the other load would be dry too.

"Sure. Even if they get the judge off the golf course, they can cool their heels a few hours while I handle some of our household chores. You're going too, right?" Greg paused, looking panicked at the idea of grocery shopping by himself.

"You know you are perfectly able to do it by yourself." I smoothed the last set of pants and hung the three dress shirts from the chair. "But yeah, I was planning on riding along, if you buy us lunch at the drive-in."

"Sounds like a plan." He set the laundry basket on the floor.

I glanced around the kitchen. We'd almost knocked out all the cleaning in just a few hours. This couple thing had its advantages. "Your friends seemed to be very stuck in gender roles. Lois is the fifties housewife. Butch the bread winner. Even Mikey wants Allison to stay home and raise his offspring."

"We grew up in Iowa, what can I say?" Greg sank into a chair and opened a soda. "Women took care of the home, the men put food on the table. It was how we were raised."

"But you're not that way?" I spread my hands, indicating the clean house.

"My mother worked full time. I had chores from the time I was in school. And when I was married to Sherry, if I didn't do it, it didn't get done. So I guess I'm the exception to the rule." He pushed an unopened can toward me. "Sit, drink. We're almost done, we can take a break."

I joined him at the table. "I really like this. I'm glad I asked you to move in."

"Is that how you remember it?" he said with a laugh. "Whatever you need to tell yourself. Hey, let's take a walk down at the beach after we get back. I think Emma's getting a little stir-crazy being locked in the house."

"Maybe she'll learn not to eat everything she comes in contact with then." I reached down and scratched behind her ears. "But yeah, it sounds lovely, if you don't get called out."

"I'm thinking positive. Besides, once I get to the station, it will be a quick in and out. Those big shot lawyers like to make these kind of appearances quick. Otherwise, rumors start flying about who exactly they were bailing out." He grabbed the keys to the Jeep from the wall hanger. "Do you have a list?"

"I have one on my phone, unless you need something too." I still wasn't used to buying his toiletries, but I figured it would become second nature, sooner or later. "Who exactly did Toby lock up?"

"Why do you think I know?" Greg put on his Cheshire-cat grin and sunglasses. "Let's go woman."

"Can we stop by the police station and take a peek?" I followed him out the back door, making sure Emma stayed inside. We kept the front door locked, even when we were home now. Especially since I was nearly robbed this summer.

"I'm not running a zoo." He opened the car door for me. "Besides, you'll see it in Monday morning's news. If Darla follows up on the lead I'm going to leak to her."

"You're a tease, Greg King." I slipped into the car and buckled my seatbelt.

The next few hours were just domestic bliss. We didn't talk about the case, his group of friends staying at The Castle, his ex-wife, or anything that could derail the conversation. It was fun. Like a date should be. Even if that date was stocking up on groceries and other supplies.

Greg did get called out later that evening. I guess the judge didn't answer his phone on the course. We'd had dinner and were sitting out on the back porch sipping iced tea when his phone rang. Toby had stopped by around four and picked up his laundry. He didn't look like the living dead anymore.

I went inside and turned on the television, mostly for background noise. Then I opened the book I'd been trying to finish for a few days. Tomorrow I didn't have to work, but I had my first class of the semester so I knew recreational reading time would be limited for a few months.

I brewed a cup of tea and curled up on the couch. Lights flashed in the window and I considered hiding in the bathroom until whoever it was that had just pulled into the driveway went away. Instead I went to the front door and stood at the screen door, watching my aunt carry her wedding planner up my steps.

"Jill, how did you know I was here?"

"Wild guess." She was a little out of breath so I took the book from her. In the few days since I'd seen her, it must have gained five pounds. "What have you added to this? All the wedding songs from 1960 to today?"

"No. But that's a good idea. I hadn't thought about the music yet." She sat her purse on the table, then strolled to the kitchen. "Do you have coffee going?"

I followed her, grabbing my teacup as I passed the coffee table. Someday she wouldn't ask me that question all the time. Or, then again, maybe not. My aunt was an acquired taste, but her tenacity made me smile. I pointed out the obvious. "No. It's seven o'clock in the evening. No coffee. But the water should still be hot for tea."

She sniffed but grabbed a cup and fingered through my tea selection. "Did you get these from Kathi?"

"Most of them. She's trying to get me educated on the joys of tea. I hate to tell her the truth. I like the fruit ones the best." I sat at the table, moving my murder notebook under a pile of bills I'd taken out to give to Greg. We were sharing costs, but he tried to pay all of the utilities since the house was free and clear. I thought it was over kill, but he was stubborn. "So what brings you out on a Sunday night?"

"I wanted to talk to you about the engagement party. I talked to Amy today and she and Justin are having one. Do you think it's too late for Harrold and me?"

I groaned on the inside. I had hoped that the conversation wouldn't be about the wedding, but I should have known. "If you want an engagement party, we'll have a party."

"Well, you don't have to sound so excited about the idea." Aunt Jackie sat down next to the book. "I was just thinking since this will be the last time either Harrold or I get married, we might want to throw out all the stops."

Now I felt like a heel. "You're right. I'm sorry, it's been a long day. A party sounds fun. Where do you want to hold it?"

She opened her book. "I need your help. Of course the easy answer would be The Castle. Or even South Cove Winery. But we'd have to call in favors for both of these since they don't typically sponsor these types of events."

Of course, according to the event planner, this was exactly the type of event the new owner of The Castle planned on having. "Oh, I don't know, The Castle might just be perfect. Go talk to Brenda tomorrow and if she gives you any trouble, I'll call her. I'm sure she owes me a favor or two."

Okay, so Brenda owed me a lot. Mostly for keeping her out of jail when her ex-husband was murdered. It's surprising the number of times that when a person is killed, it's a loved one or former loved one who did it. Which brought me back to Jessica or honestly, anyone in Greg's group of friends. What were the stats that the victim knew the killer intimately? Fifty percent? Seventy-five? Ninety? I wanted to Google it, but my aunt would consider that rude, especially since she was still talking about the engagement party.

"And I want those tea lights spread all through the pergola that's around the pool. That's what they're called right? The mini lights." My aunt glanced up from her scribbling and stared at me. "Jill?"

She'd caught me daydreaming. "Fairy lights. I think they're called fairy lights now. Tea lights are the candles that Esmeralda uses during her voodoo sessions."

"Now, dear, Esmeralda doesn't do voodoo, she is a fortune-teller. It's quite different. I would have thought you knew that as close of friends as you two are." My aunt wrote down fairy lights, then made a quick drawing of their required placement.

"We aren't close friends." I argued. "She's a neighbor and sometimes we talk, but it's not like me or Amy or even Sadie."

Although as I thought about it, I hadn't seen Sadie lately either. I was bad at this friendship thing. Brenda had said as much when she told me she never saw me anymore. I wasn't one of those girls who got a boyfriend and dumped all her women friends, was I?

I made a mental note to stop by Sadie's bakery tomorrow. I'd have to be early since the woman got up at four to make the desserts she then delivered late morning. I don't know how she did it all. And she was continuing to volunteer at the church. Although I secretly thought that was more to impress the single Pastor Bill than a true calling from God. I looked around for the lightning bolt to strike me down for being human. Nothing. Just my aunt watching me.

"Are you tired, dear?" She reached out a hand to feel my forehead. "You don't feel warm. Maybe you're getting sick."

"Sorry, I'm fine. I was just thinking about," I paused, not wanting to say exactly, then I just grabbed the first thought. "Sadie. I haven't seen her since Nick's going back to school party."

Nick was my part-time summer and school holiday help, and Sadie's pride and joy. He was killing it at college

Nick must have been on Aunt Jackie's mind, too. "That boy is going to go far in this world. No small-town life for him. I just hope he keeps his feet solidly under him."

That was my hope for him as well, but so far, Sadie had raised a really good kid

"So I think we have a good plan for this. Shall we set a tentative date for late October? Will that work with your school schedule?" My aunt checked the paper calendar she kept in her purse.

Paper. Everyone else I knew kept their calendar on their phones, but I don't think my aunt even realized her smartphone had the app. Or email. She was just starting to text. She loved sending me reminders of chores to do in the store when she was upstairs watching her shows. I think it made her feel like she was managing from afar.

"As long as it's not a Monday or a Wednesday, I'm good." I was only taking two classes a semester. It would take me a bit longer to finish up the MBA, but I liked the mix of working and school. Each had its joys and drawbacks and I never got bored which made me happy.

"Let's go for the weekend before Halloween. I don't really want to feel obligated to do some sort of costume theme." She wrote the dates in her notebook. "I'll run by The Castle tomorrow and let you know how it goes Tuesday morning."

I watched as she started putting away her glasses. Our planning session was over, apparently. "This was fun," I lied.

"You don't have to patronize me. I know event planning isn't your strong suit, but I got used to bouncing ideas off Sasha and with her off to the city, I need a new partner in crime." She kissed me on the cheek. "Oh, I meant to ask, how was the festival planning meeting? I hope you didn't over extend yourself with tasks."

"Actually, I didn't take on any." I could see my aunt's response in her eyes, so I held up a hand, stopping her. "Deek is our representative on the festival committee and he's loving it."

"Deek?" My aunt wasn't quite sure what to think of our new employee, except that he needed to put on some weight. The guy was skinny. "Are you sure he's qualified?"

"The guy has two degrees, one in marketing and is a semester away from getting his MBA. If he didn't love school so much, he'd be running his own Fortune 500 company by now." Well, that and if he would wear something besides the jeans and T-shirts I'd always seen him in. "The fact he almost had a minor in English literature makes him a perfect employee. Although I doubt we'll keep him long."

Aunt Jackie put her bag over her shoulder and went to lift the book. I waved her away. "I'll carry it to your car. It's going to be enough for you to haul it up all those stairs to the apartment. Maybe you should think about dividing it into volumes."

"If I do that, the volume I want will always be upstairs and I'll be running more than I am now." She let her lips curve into a smile. "Besides, they say weight lifting is good for us older folks."

I went with her out to the car and watched her go. As I walked back to the house, I notice the extra cars and light on at Esmeralda's. She was doing a reading. I kind of expected there to be brightly colored auras floating around the house when she did one of these, but as usual, all I saw was the starry California sky. I hoped the spirits were treating her well this evening.

Then I went inside and read. I was going to finish this book if I had to stay up all night. Book hangover was a real thing. They needed a support group for people like us.

CHAPTER 19

I was finishing the last page when I saw the lights in the driveway again. This time I didn't get up. I figured it was Greg, coming home from the station. The key turned in the lock just as I was closing the book with that satisfied sigh I got when I loved the ending. I would definitely put this book on our Staff Picks shelf. Deek had suggested the feature as part of the newsletter he developed for us. Now, we had a monthly column of Staff Picks as well as a cute shelf near the coffee counter of the books. I had to admit, sales were rising.

"Hey, I thought you'd be asleep." Greg dropped his keys into the basket on the table near the door, then went into my, his, office, to put his gun in the safe. That was another thing he'd brought from the apartment. A gun safe and several actual guns. It wasn't like I was afraid of them, I'd just never had them in my house before.

He stopped at the couch and kissed me, then picked up the book I'd laid on the table. "I should have known what you'd spend your free evening doing. This any good?"

"Excellent." It was a thriller and I knew Greg had liked the author's last book. "You should read it."

"Maybe I will. I've had some free time lately, especially with you going back to school. I get a little lonely here with Emma by myself." He sat next to me.

"Yeah, especially on nights you don't have some sort of game to watch." I pointed at the television. "I didn't think that television even knew such games of skill existed. We were more of a romantic comedy house before you moved in."

"Totally, not true. I watched games over here a lot before I moved in. The television loves it when I'm in control of the remote." He bent his head back over the couch and sighed. "I'm beat. I hate it when the lawyer thinks he has to put on a show for his client. I wanted to tell the guy that it wasn't up to me when he got released, it was the judge who had left him stewing all day while he did eighteen holes. But that would have gotten me into hot water with the DA."

"Sounds like hell." I didn't envy Greg's job. A lot of it was being political. "So who was the big shot, you going to tell me?"

"I am." When he saw the shock I felt register on my face, he laughed. "Don't get your hopes up, it wasn't someone famous."

"I'm just surprised you're going to tell me."

He ran his hand through his hair. "It might have something to do with Levi's death. Well, not really, but it was a fallout from the death."

Now he had me totally confused. "What?"

"The guy is some big shot nightclub developer. I guess Levi had set up a meeting with him for this weekend and when he heard Levi was gone, well, he started drinking." Greg brushed Emma hair off my yoga pants. "I heard he's an angry drunk, especially when a multi-million-dollar deal goes south."

"So Levi *was* planning on turning The Castle into some exclusive club. I don't understand why are the papers in Jessica's name?"

"Taxes maybe? A shelter against his company's stock holders? He thought he was being clever?" Greg yawned. "Who knows what went on in Levi's head."

"You ready for bed?" I brushed the lock of hair that kept falling into his eyes back away from his face.

"Definitely." He started to sit up and then sank back down into the couch. "What are you doing tomorrow?"

"I have class in the evening." I didn't know what he was looking for. "The shop's closed on Mondays."

"I mean about the investigation. You're not planning on doing any snooping around tomorrow, are you?"

I shrugged. "I'm not sure what I'd do. We kind of eliminated all of our suspects except Jessica and I can't see me going up to a grieving woman and accuse her of killing Levi."

"Yeah, that's where I am too. After finding the laptop, I thought we'd have a good lead there, but it was only Levi's warped mind going after something he couldn't have."

"You know the group is going to change now that Allison is expecting a baby. You may stay friends, but I can't see a weekend like this with a toddler running around." I unfolded my legs from under me and stretched.

"Honey, when Levi died, that changed the group forever. I doubt there will be any more of these annual get-togethers. We'll do phone calls and Christmas cards, but the gang won't be the same. One weekend a year wasn't enough to keep us close, like we once were. And Levi was the driving force that kept those going. Now, we'll be sucked into our own separate lives."

I didn't know if that was a bad thing or not, but I kept my opinion to myself and went to let Emma out one more time. Greg set up the coffee for the next morning and then it was time for bed.

As I drifted off to sleep, Greg curled around me, his arms pulling me into a hug. "If you're wondering, I'm happy with the life we have. This is where I should be."

I felt my lips curve into a smile, then I went to sleep.

* * *

Greg was gone by the time I woke on Monday. Emma nudged me awake, and then whined while I got dressed in my running clothes. It was like she knew I'd planned on taking her down to the beach today. She had a sixth sense about some things. Like runs and when Greg brought home pizza from Bakerstown's Godfathers.

Maybe she did understand what we said more than I realized. Anyway, she knew we were running this morning. The morning was gorgeous and as we ran, I felt my head clear for the first time in months. We were down the coast and turning around before I knew what was going on. Emma was running in the surf, playing with the birds that liked to hunt for bits and pieces of food with each wave. One would fly up, land a few feet away from Emma, wait for her to get close, then fly up again. As we neared the parking lot, I called her from playing with her friend and clicked on her leash. A man and a woman sat on the steps to the deck that led to the parking area. This time, I recognized them.

Jessica and Vladimir looked up when I approached. He started to stand, but then Jessica put a hand on his arm. "It's too late to hide, father. Good morning, Jill. Who's this?" She reached a hand down to Emma who gave her kisses. I'd never seen her warm to a person she'd just met that quickly.

"Emma, meet Jessica and Vladimir." I smiled. "Emma's my running partner."

"I would have thought that police man of yours would run with you." Vladimir petted Emma's head. "He should keep you close. It's not safe for young attractive women to be alone."

"Papa, don't scare Jill. She's being cautious, she has Emma."

"And pepper spray, just in case." Jessica's words filtered through my head. "Wait, he's your father?"

Vladimir nodded. "Guilty as charged. My Jessica is my first born. She looks just like her mama did at her age."

"Why are you keeping your relationship a secret?"

Jessica moved over on the stair. "Come sit. We need to talk."

She told me about how she had saved money and used a 'service' to come to the United States when she turned eighteen. But as things go, finding a job here in America was harder than she'd imagined. So she got hired on at a strip club in Texas. "Not the best decision, but I was a kid in a strange country."

I had never met a former stripper before, but I admit, I was a little naïve. "So what happened?"

Jessica smiled, but her eyes shimmered with tears. "Levi found me. He kept coming into the strip club, talking to me, paying for my time and all of a sudden, the manager came to me and told me I was fired. Go, he said. A car is waiting for you in back."

I listened, Emma laying at my feet watching us.

"The only person in the car was the driver. He took me to a condo on the better side of Houston. Levi was there, cooking breakfast. He turned to me and said, 'Welcome home.'"

Now the tears were falling. I put my hand on her shoulder. "He bought you?"

"He saved me. We started dating, he told me I was free to do whatever I wanted, but I enjoyed spending time with him. Eventually we fell in love." She patted her father's knee. "I asked Levi to bring over Papa and Alana last year when Mama died. It took a while, but now we are all here. Legally." She added as an afterthought.

"Wow." That was some story. An immigration story gone good. And Levi had been the hero in the whole thing. I'd heard so many bad things about the guy, I had doubted his ability to be thoughtful or selfless. This was the guy Greg remembered and why they stayed friends. "So what are you going to do now?"

She leaned against her father. "I'm moving here to South Cove. I can work in Papa's shop. According to my attorney, the prenup Levi signed will keep me from needing money, and maybe I'll start some sort of charity to help girls who want to come over to the US, without going through the coyotes I used."

"I think that would be a lovely use of Levi's legacy." I guess Greg was right, we were all out of suspects for Levi's murder. The wife to be didn't kill him. I didn't think the father-in-law had anything to do with it, especially since he had more to gain if Levi stayed alive. I decided to head to town and talk with Greg about this new twist. I stood and brushed sand off my running pants. "You do need to tell Terrance about your father though. It might make you look guilty if he finds out on his own."

"There are no more secrets." Vladimir said, making a gesture like an umpire did when he called someone out. Apparently, no matter where men came from, they were still all about the game. "We will go into town today and tell them everything."

Another reason I needed Greg to know—so if anything went wrong, he could help clear up any misunderstandings.

"I'll see you around then." I smiled at Jessica. It was nice that she was staying in South Cove. I hoped she and I might become friends. I looked at my watch. If I stopped by the station to see Greg, I'd miss Sadie. I made a mental note to call her and invite her to the Sunday Brunch group. We'd have to move it a little later or earlier, since she wouldn't miss church, but it would be fun to have another regular.

My heart was light as I showered and got ready for my day. I packed my school bag, left it by the door, then grabbed my tote and walked into town.

I stopped by the shop and took out a box of cookies to ease Greg's Monday. While I was there, I grabbed another book off the Advance Reading Copy pile that seemed to grow overnight. I might have a few minutes here and there to start reading. When I arrived at the station, Esmeralda was at the front desk. She peered at the box. "Cookies?"

"Yep. Is he available?"

She glanced at the door and then at the box again. "Depends."

"On what?" I knew what she wanted, but we could play this game.

"On if one of those cookies has my name on it." She waved me closer. "Show me what you have girl. I didn't have breakfast and I'm starving."

I opened the box and she picked out two of the large chocolate chip walnut cookies that Sadie had baked on Saturday. We'd get all fresh desserts tomorrow morning, so I needed to get rid of the leftovers anyway.

She glanced at the phone display. "He just finished his call. Go on in."

"Thanks." I knew Esmeralda liked me. Her cat loved me. But first and foremost, she was Greg's employee-slash-guard dog. If he'd told her he didn't want to see me, no amount of cookie bribes would get me through that door.

Greg looked up when I entered and his gaze dropped from my face to the box. Seriously, I could get a complex here if I didn't know firsthand how amazing Sadie's desserts were. "You didn't have to stop by. I did scramble some eggs this morning before I left the house."

"I need to update you." I closed the door behind me. No use everyone overhearing our conversation.

He waved me over to the couch. "You know they think we make out when you close the door."

"You're just dreaming." I opened the box and took out a cookie. I still had some coffee left in my travel mug. Greg grabbed his cup and sat next to me.

"So what's up? You told me you weren't investigating today." He took a cookie out of the box and bit into it. His face lit up like a little boy with a train under the Christmas tree. "Sadie is a baking genius."

"Yes, she is." I told him about the meeting I'd interrupted between Jessica and Vladimir. When I'd finished, he'd eaten two cookies, but hadn't said a word. I narrowed my eyes at him. "You don't seem surprised."

"I just found out myself, I promise. The mayor had some questions on Vladimir's business license application so he asked me to dig into his background. I got the report from the private investigator this morning."

I sank back into the chair and sighed. Even when I thought I was two steps ahead of Greg, really, I was behind or just even. And that was running flat out.

"I still have one question though," he mused, considering his third cookie. He grabbed it, then looked at me. "What is she doing with The Castle?"

My eyes widened. I hadn't even asked. "I don't know. She didn't say."

"Which means you forgot to ask." He ate the cookie.

"I was a little taken back about the whole story. How crazy would it be to make your living at a dance club?"

"Gentleman's club is the PC name. Or not PC name. Besides, there's a lot of bad in the world that we don't typically see here in South Cove. That's one reason I like working here." He sipped on his coffee. "Face it Jill, we're pretty sheltered."

"I like being sheltered." I thought about Levi again. "So this basically wipes out all our suspects in his killing, right?"

"I believe so. Maybe it was a random, impulse event. Strong emotion can lead people to do strange things." He glanced at his watch. "Sorry, but I've got a meeting with the mayor to tell him what I just told you about Vladimir."

"You told me first?" For some reason, knowing this made me smile.

He went back to his desk to grab a file. "Of course I did. You're my partner in crime."

"I'm heading into town early tonight and grabbing dinner before class. You going to be okay?" I put my tote on my shoulder and stood.

"For dinner? Honey, I didn't starve before we moved in together. I think I can handle one meal on my own." He kissed me as he ushered me out of his office, then shut the door. "Besides, there's a game on tonight. I'll pick up takeout from Diamond Lille's and Emma and I will eat in front of the television."

"You're teaching my dog bad habits." I waved at Esmeralda as I headed to the door.

"I know you're not talking about eating in the living room, you do it all the time." He paused at the reception desk and watched me.

"Of course not. I'm just hoping she doesn't get hooked on watching college basketball. I'll have to send her to rehab if we ever break up."

He shook his head. "Who said you're ever getting rid of me?"

As I walked back to the house, thoughts about Levi and his entourage circled through my mind. The one thing I hadn't totally nailed down was the sale of The Castle. Aunt Jackie was stopping by and talking to Brenda today. Maybe she'd pick up some gossip. Jessica had mentioned that Terrance had been making noises about letting them return to their normal lives in a few days. I suppose he was at an impasse with the investigation like we were. I hated to think Levi's killer was going to get away scot-free.

I had a list of housework I needed to get done, including cleaning the bathrooms that had seemed to slip off Greg's list yesterday. I had four hours, give or take, to get as much done at the house before I needed to leave for class. Especially if I was going to make a stop at the library to see if I could find anything else about the sale of The Castle.

My list took me less than three hours and even with a shower, I had time to start the book I'd tucked into my tote. I'd also brought it with me as a dinner companion. Now, I was sitting at the library, with a good hour to spare before class. This time would be eaten up with homework probably as soon as the first class was over. Right now, I was enjoying my quasi-student state and spending time in the library. I booted up the computer, put in my password, and found the legal records for the sale of The Castle.

I re-read the document four times. Nothing new. Nothing showing me that Jessica didn't know she now owned one of the most historical sites on the California coast.

"Have I told you how cool it is that we're closed on Mondays?" Deek plopped into a chair next to me. "I got three classes in today and only have to come back for one on Thursday night. Are you taking Professor Andy's accounting class this semester?"

I turned toward him. "Next semester. Then it's all about numbers for the three months. I told you how much I hate numbers, right?"

"It's all a part of the game. You have to know the numbers to know if you're successful." He pulled out a protein bar and unwrapped it. Holding it toward me, he asked, "You want one?"

"No." I didn't have to tell him that eating or drinking in the library was prohibited. I just hoped he wouldn't get busted while he was sitting with me in the small computer section of the research wing. "I ate earlier."

"Mom's doing some class tonight so I'm supposed to feed myself. I think I'll go to the Burger and Brew and watch the game." He pointed with his half-eaten bar to the screen. "What's that?"

"The legal filing of a property sale. I'm trying to find out who actually bought the property." My head was beginning to throb and I figured a migraine was in my future. I was getting as good of a fortune teller as Esmeralda, at least where these headaches were concerned.

"Did you look at the filing page?" Deek reached over and with a few keystrokes, a new page listing all the details of the transaction appeared. In buyer and filer, Levi Wallace was listed. As new owner, Jessica Cole's name appeared. "The dude bought this and just gave it all to some chick?"

I nodded, scribbling down several bits of information including the name of the attorney who actually filed the paperwork. It looked like I was going to be seeing Jimmy Marcum tomorrow after all. Maybe he could shed some like on Levi's motives.

Or maybe, just maybe, there was a darker reason for the change in ownership. If so, did the fact that Jessica was the sole owner of The Castle put her in danger too?

CHAPTER 20

Greg was asleep when I got home and when I woke up, he had already left for work. He said he got more work done in the first two hours before anyone else showed up than he did all day.

For me, the quiet gave me time to think. And usually, read. After the coffee commuter group had dwindled down to nothing, I opened my laptop to see if Jimmy had a website that listed office hours. Jimmy Marcum was an old-school lawyer, the type you'd see in reruns of Perry Mason or something. I think he still wore a suit to work every day, even if he wasn't appearing in court. The other thing was I totally trusted him to be as honest as he could about a situation.

I updated my investigation book which now only had one open page entitled Jessica and The Castle. It sounded like a Nancy Drew mystery. I listed off the questions I wanted to ask Jimmy and then tucked the notebook back into my tote bag. As soon as Toby arrived to take over the shop, I'd run into town, see Jimmy, and pick up lunch. Then I would head home to work on the five chapters the professor had assigned as reading for next week. This class just might break me.

But I was Wonder Woman. I could run my business, investigate murders, and pass Math for Business Decisions. At least I hoped so.

I opened the book I'd started yesterday and began to read. I was picking out a new book to carry with me when Toby walked into the shop. I'd finished the other one, but it hadn't given me that sigh of happiness when everyone was okay at the end of the book. Instead, it had made me anxious and wondering if the heroine would ever find the right guy or keep a job. I hated books like that. I wanted the happily-ever-after. Which, again, was a testament to my Pollyanna side.

"Thanks for doing my laundry." Toby slipped on an apron and washed his hands in the sink. "You don't know how much I needed that extra couple hours of sleep."

"Don't tell me you're turning into a washer woman for everyone in town." My aunt appeared from the back office, dressed in a cashmere twinset and pleated pants. She set the baby-blue outfit off with a single strand of pearls—which I knew were real—and dark blue flats. One of her more casual outfits. She'd given up on heels years ago, saying her days of waitressing at the coffee shop had ruined her legs forever. "You already have one man to take care of, you don't need two."

"I only did it this one time." Why was I explaining myself to her anyway? It wasn't her business. Then I realized I had it wrong. Everything was Aunt Jackie's business, at least according to her. She had her purse and the wedding planning book. "Why are you so dressed up?"

"I went to talk to Brenda yesterday but no one was there." Aunt Jackie poured herself a travel mug of coffee and took a sip before continuing. "I thought you and I could go over this morning and get this party all nailed down. I have things to do that I can't until I have a confirmed date and place. Like ordering the invitations. I found several possibilities online last night."

I glanced at the clock. Jimmy's office was open until five. And Aunt Jackie had to be back for work around three. I could still do this and get my reading done before class reconvened next week. It changed up my plan for the day, but I knew when my aunt had her mind set on something, it was going to happen.

"Sure, let me grab my purse and keys." I paused in front of Toby. "I'm glad you got some sleep. You've been looking a little like the walking dead lately."

He glanced at Aunt Jackie who was now inventorying the dessert case as she waited.

"You're out of Key lime cheesecake. I'll bring one up for you." My aunt disappeared into the back room.

"This Sasha thing has got me more wound up than I'd expected. Seriously, who gets this worked up over a break up?" He grinned as Aunt Jackie returned with a cheesecake box.

Toby took it from her. "I'll get that set up. You two just go and have fun."

"I'll have her back in plenty of time for her shift. We're just heading up to The Castle."

Toby started plating the cheesecake and I grabbed my tote. Apparently sharing time was over. He had come a long way from the playboy he'd been when Aunt Jackie had first hired him. Who'd knew that the guy actually had deep feelings and a strong yearning for family and connectedness. Once, during his first year with us, he'd been dating two different girls and they'd both shown up at the hospital when he'd been attacked. That had been awkward.

"Don't forget to stock the new books that came in yesterday," my aunt called back as we left the shop. "I can't be carrying those heavy boxes out to the front by myself."

As we went to the back parking lot where she parked, I looked at her. "Doesn't he always stock the new books on Tuesdays?"

"Of course, dear."

Now I was confused. "Then why did you remind him?"

She handed me her keys and then walked over to the passenger side. I guessed I was driving. "Because he needs to know what he does is important and why."

I thought it was more like she wanted to put on the guilt trip just in case he got busy and was unable to complete his to do lists but I didn't say anything. A tune from *Phantom of the Opera* blasted from the speakers as soon as I turned on the car. My aunt liked her show tunes loud. We made our way up to The Castle with little conversation. My aunt looking small as she sat in the passenger side with her wedding planner book on her lap. It was a good thing the wedding was in June since the book was growing so fast, soon she wouldn't be able to carry it without a handcart.

Greg's friends' cars still sat in the parking lot when we arrived so I guessed Jessica's wish that they'd be released hadn't come true. I wondered what Terrance was thinking and if he'd found out about the sale of The Castle. Maybe he'd already worked that line and found it to be a dead end. This is why people needed to talk. I could share my information and he could share his. However, he'd probably arrest me for obstruction of justice or some stupid thing if I told him even half of the stuff I'd found out.

We parked the car and as we walked toward the ticket booth my aunt stopped. "Lock the car."

"What? No one's out here." I looked around at the deserted lot. The closed sign had still been on the welcome sign out by the highway. I bet Brenda was having a cow by now. I hate to be in Terrance's shoes.

She just stood there, her eyebrows lifted, not answering me.

"Fine, I'll lock the car." I double-clicked the remote so she could hear the beep-beep sound from the car, then shoved the keys into my jeans pocket. I unlatched the chain that kept people out and opened the way for my aunt. We headed into Brenda's office in the first building on the right.

It was empty. No receptionist. No Brenda. I walked over to the coffeepot and put my hand on the half-full pot. It was cold. "I don't think she's even been here this morning." I backed up and looked at the door for some kind of sign saying she was ill or where the guests could go if they needed help. Nothing.

It was creepy empty. Like one of those places in Stephen King's *The Stand* after Captain Trips took out most of the world with its genetically modified flu bug. I met my aunt's gaze. "Was this the way it looked yesterday?"

She slowly scanned the room. "I think so. None of the computers were on. The coffee was at that level. I went to check to see if it was still warm so I could fill up my travel mug."

So what ever had happened, it had happened yesterday. Visions of all the zombie movies I'd ever watched came into my head. If this had been a movie, we would have heard the door open behind us and the hive swarm in to eat us.

But this was real life. And like Greg had just said that morning: Nothing bad happened in South Cove. At least, not as bad as the rest of the world. I backed out of the office. "Let's look around and see if we can find anyone."

The pool area was empty. The tables cleared and waiting for their guests to come and eat. I went back to the fountain and turned toward the main house. That's when I heard the scream. I waved at Aunt Jackie to stay where she was and then inched my way up the path. I could see the house and the large windows for the dining room. A woman stood by the window waving her hands and screaming. It was Lois. A man pulled her away from the window, then came back and glanced around. I flattened myself against the wall and hit Aunt Jackie who was standing behind me.

"I told you to wait at the fountain." I whispered through clenched teeth.

She flattened next to me and whispered back. "Who was screaming?"

"Lois. I think someone has the group locked up in the dining room." I thought about what to do next. Quickly, I devised a plan. "Why don't you take my purse, go back to the car, drive down the hill and call Greg?"

She shook her head defiantly. "New plan. You and I go back to the car, drive down the hill, and call Greg. Do you really think I'm going to leave you alone here?"

"Please? Someone has to watch to make sure they don't leave with the hostages. I don't know what they want, but if this has been going on for at least a day, I don't think they are looking for ransom or planning on keeping those people alive." Greg would be devastated if all of his old friends were killed over a period of less than a week. "Use my cell phone. The number listed under Greg goes to his cell. If he doesn't answer, call 911."

"You know I don't know how to use that stupid phone of yours." She paused, I could see she was seeing the value in my plan. "All right, but I'm going to use my own phone and just call 911. I know how to dial that."

"Be careful and go slow. I don't want him seeing movement. I doubt that they can see the parking lot from there, but you never know." I hoped I wasn't sending Aunt Jackie off to be shot. I just felt that she'd be safer, locked in her car than hanging out here with me. I would wait for Greg to show up just watching the windows and making sure they didn't leave.

My legs already ached from crouching and I'd been hiding here for only a few minutes. This staying still and quiet was going to kill me. I started running through the reasons they had been taken hostage. Money. Well, that couldn't be the reason. Jessica was the only one with any chance of having big money and she had to wait for probate on Levi's estate. Maybe they'd tried to kidnap Levi and failed so they thought they could get ransom from his company for his soon to be wife?

Then why hadn't they called someone yesterday? Aunt Jackie had been here yesterday to talk to Brenda and had found the office in the same state as it was today. That thought made my blood chill. What if she'd been here when it happened? My aunt might have been one of the people locked in that dining room.

I glanced back down the path, but no one appeared. Too early for the cavalry. I went back to my mental musing. So not money, or at least it wasn't the obvious reason behind this.

Maybe he was obsessed with someone? Again, I'd have to put Jessica as the target. She did work at a strip club for a while. Which totally explained the attitude when we saw her get off the elevator when this circus of a bachelor party first started. But Allison might be the girl too.

Allison was sweet, kind, and a little obsessed herself, but at least her obsession was swimming. Could she have had a rabid fan that didn't like her retirement plans from the sport?

Now I just felt I was reaching.

I looked down the path another time.

Nothing.

This waiting thing was hard. Maybe I should have snuck out with Aunt Jackie. We could have both been safe, sitting in her car at the bottom of the hill. Something poked me in the leg. I arched my back and pushed my hand into my jeans pocket. I pulled out Aunt Jackie's keys.

Crap. She wasn't safe or out of danger because I had her car keys. I stared down the path, hoping she'd figured out how to use my phone and that Greg really was on his way. If not, I needed to inch my way back to the parking lot without being seen and then tuck her in the car and take off.

The keys jangled in my hand and I realized I was shaking. I took a deep breath and with one last look at the now empty window, I stepped back on the path.

"I'm sorry Jill, but you have to come with me." Brenda stood in front of me blocking my way.

I dropped the keys into the soft dirt behind me, hoping they wouldn't make a noise. Maybe if Aunt Jackie came back, she'd find the keys where I'd been. Maybe.

"Brenda," I put on a smile. "I was just looking for you. My aunt was wondering if you would rent her the pool area for her engagement party."

She looked at me like I was crazy.

Since she didn't say anything, I kept chattering. "She sent me here to beg you for a favor. Of course, she couldn't come herself because she has a shift coming up at the coffee shop."

Brenda's eyes widened and she glanced down the path. "Don't tell me she's here too?" She shook her head. "Just keep your mouth shut about her and maybe he won't notice."

Now I was confused. Brenda seemed concerned about Aunt Jackie. She couldn't be part of the kidnapping if she was helping me. "What's going on, Brenda?"

"I can't tell you. We don't have time. If we don't get back to the house soon, someone is going to die."

CHAPTER 21

Brenda grabbed my arm. Her grip was tight. She hissed into my ear as we walked. "He saw you from the window. I don't know why you keep getting yourself in these kind of situations, but this time, your luck might have just run out."

I stumbled on a cobblestone and she pulled me upright. Fear pulsed through my body and I didn't know what was going on. Only that we were going in the exact wrong direction from safety. "Why are you helping him?"

Brenda pressed her lips together as she pushed me through the oversized door into the marble foyer. "Because I have to." She pointed to the door on the right. "That way."

I felt like a death-row prisoner being taken to the execution chamber. Brenda's fingers were clawing into my arm, and I knew, the time to try to run had long past. I might get to the entry door, but not much farther before she caught up with me. I tried to calm my breathing and without thinking, I whimpered, "I don't understand."

"Just be quiet. Tell him you came to see me about a booking. Then shut up." She hissed into my ear before shoving me in front of her and into the room.

I blinked, trying to adjust my eyes from the dark foyer back into sunshine. The tapestry drapes that hung on the wall of windows that overlooked my hiding place were pulled back, letting sun into this room for the first time, probably since the antiques had been brought in from Europe. Sun and tapestries didn't mix well.

Lois and Butch were sitting at the table across from where I stood, their arms tied behind them with gags in their mouths. Lois pleaded with me with her gaze, but she didn't realize I wasn't there to help, I was just as lost as she was. Looking around the room, I saw that all of Greg's friends were seated similarly around the table, gagged and bound. Jessica sat at the head of the table, no gag, but her arms were tied. She gave me a slight nod and I realized she thought she could still talk her way out of this.

Maybe the years of self-protection as a young woman had given her hope, even in this situation. Or maybe, she knew someone, probably her father, would eventually come looking for her.

I just hoped it wouldn't be too late.

"Sit down." A man standing near Jessica waved a gun at me. "Use those curtain ties to bind her to the chair. But be careful. They are delicate. We don't want to be ruining any of the furniture."

"Blood splatter would really mess up these antiques." I didn't move, waiting for him to actually look at me. I thought I knew who it was, but I wanted to be sure. "Why are you doing this?"

This time, he left off his study of Jessica and turned toward me. John Anderson, the man who'd been so animated about taking care of The Castle each and every time I'd run into him stared at me, but instead of the thoughtful man I'd seen when I first met him last weekend, now a wild animal seemed to be living behind those eyes. I was afraid I had given him a good idea.

"She didn't mean it," Brenda stepped closer to me, holding out the drapery tie back. "She only came by to ask about holding an engagement party out by the pool."

"More people getting drunk and ruining The Castle?" John shook his head. "Would you party at the Louvre? Or in St. Patrick's Cathedral? Why do people think it's perfectly fine to desecrate this historic site?"

I shrugged off Brenda's hands as she tried to guide me into a chair. "The party is for my elderly aunt and her boyfriend. I'm pretty sure it will be as calm and respectful as a tour of any religious chapel in the world. Are you saying my aunt is destructive?"

I didn't know if going on the defensive was really a good strategy, but mostly, I was just waiting for Aunt Jackie to get a hold of Greg. If she couldn't make my phone work, she could call from the office. The office door was still open and she could lock herself inside while she waited. Or maybe she'd come back to the spot where she'd left me and found the keys. Either way, I needed to give Greg time to get up here and save us.

"No one respects the artifacts like they should." He pointed the gun at Brenda. "Her husband was the worst. He stuffed drugs inside priceless vases, just to hide them from customs. He treated The Castle like his own little pharmacy."

"Craig is dead." And his murderer was in jail, or was he? If the drug lord hadn't gotten tired of Craig two timing him, John would have killed him just to save The Castle. "No one here did anything bad to the campus. You need to let us go." He laughed and pointed to Jessica. "She was going to turn this place into a night club. People drinking, throwing up," he choked up a bit before he continued, "smoking in rooms like this? What do you think it would have done to the furniture? The artwork? People like that don't deserve to be alive."

"She didn't plan on turning The Castle. Levi did." At this, Jessica's head turned toward me, her eyes narrow. "Levi was the one to blame, but he's already gone. You dealt with the threat. Now, this is just overkill."

"I can't step back now. What, do you think all these people are just going to forget about being tied up for a day? Are you?" He shook his head. "No. As soon as I let you go, you'll run to your boyfriend crying. And I'll be in jail. Who will watch out for The Castle then?"

"I will. You know I love the place. Even when I was married to Craig, I worked to try to get the place set up as a historical landmark. I'm still working on protecting it." Brenda stepped closer to the man. "Why don't you give me the gun, then you can leave, and I'll take over."

"You won't even have a job in a few days," he poked Jessica with the gun barrel. "Thanks to this she-devil. She will make sure her dead lover's plans go on. Honoring his memory, isn't that what you told that one over there?"

He pointed at Lois, who shook her head, unable to talk.

Jessica tried to turn her head to look at him. "I was talking about the money he left me. I didn't even know that he'd bought The Castle until you told me last night."

"Then why is it in your name?" John growled.

Jessica let a single tear drop from her eye. "Because he loved me, you idiot. He loved me and you killed him." She jerked against the ties that held her. If she'd gotten loose, I thought she would have rushed him and knocked him over. And probably gotten shot for her efforts.

"Likely story." John turned away from her like he was bored with the conversation. He looked at me, and then back to Brenda. "Why isn't she tied up yet?"

Brenda nodded to me. "You need to sit down."

I didn't look at Brenda when I responded. "I'm not going to sit."

John stepped away from Jessica and toward me. "I can't depend on you for such a simple thing like tying this girl up. How can I trust you to take care of The Castle?"

The doors behind him burst open and John jerked and dropped the gun he'd just pulled out. He followed it to the floor. Toby ran over and kicked it away, then put John's hands behind him and cuffed him.

Greg was holding me. I hadn't even seen him walk in, I'd been too busy watching the show as John fell. He held me away from him and scanned my body with his gaze. "Are you all right?"

I nodded, tears filling the back of my throat. But I wouldn't cry. Not here, and not in front of that maniac. "He killed Levi."

Tim and Brenda were walking around the table, untying and ungagging the group. Lois piped up when I said that. "He said it in front of all of us. He killed Levi because he thought he was opening a nightclub here."

"Stupidest thing I've ever heard. It's too far away from anything. Greg's department would be getting rich on the DUI fines alone." Butch grumbled, rubbing his wrists. He pulled Lois into a bear hug. "You okay kiddo?"

"I have to pee." She extricated herself and with Allison, MaryAnne, and Jessica, and disappeared out of the dining room.

"How long have you been in here?" Greg asked Mikey.

Mikey rubbed his wrists. "I think he started bringing us in about four yesterday. I thought everyone had taken a nap or something. I was one of the last ones to be knocked out and then dragged in here."

Greg looked down at John. "I wonder if he was on Terrance's radar. He sure wasn't on mine. I didn't even think about him when I was listing off suspects."

"No one did. He was invisible. A guard for The Castle. But when things started to change, he reacted. I think he went a little mad." I leaned into Greg's side, watching as John slept propped up against the wall where Toby still stood over him. I saw Toby had added ankle shackles to John's binding. I bet it was the first time Toby had gotten to use that particular tool from his police belt.

"Well, I better get Terrance called in on this. I guess if John confessed in front of all these witnesses, he'll probably do the same when he wakes up from the little nap Toby gave him." Greg squeezed me. "Can I say, I'm getting a little worried about how I'm always finding you in these particular situations?"

"Don't blame me. This was all Aunt Jackie. She wanted to talk to Brenda about having her engagement party here." I looked around for my aunt. "Where is she, by the way?"

"Crap, I told her to lock herself into Brenda's office and not leave until

I came back." He looked over at the group. Brenda, who had overheard, stepped closer.

"Let me go get her. I don't want to be here when Jill tells you it was me who brought her into the mix." Brenda gave me a quick hug. "I'm so glad you were one step ahead of us all. I thought we were all going to die."

Greg looked at me. "Do you want to explain?"

I told him about how we'd seen Lois banging on the windows and how I'd sent Aunt Jackie back to drive out of here and call him, but I realized I had her keys. "So, did she call from the office or did she figure out my phone?"

He grinned. "She called 911 from the office. When Esmeralda answered, she said all Jackie did was gripe about how useless your cell phone was. It took her a couple of minutes to calm down enough to tell her what was going on."

"I forgot about the lock. Don't cell phones let you call 911 without keying in the code?"

He shrugged. "If they do, Jackie couldn't figure out how to make it work. I think she threw it across the parking lot. I bet you're going to have to buy a new phone."

"If I do, she's paying me back." I glanced around the room. The friends were all gathered in a huddle, whispering. "I think your friends need some Greg time."

He shook his head. "I need some Jill time."

"I thought you were calling Terrance?" I asked as we walked out of the room and toward the pool area.

"Toby can handle it. I want to take a few deep breaths before we go back to the station to this cluster." He pulled two chairs close and faced them toward the large Grecian designed pools. "So what's your plan for the weekend?"

"Studying. You wouldn't believe how much homework they gave me on Monday. I'm kind of scared to go to my Thursday class." I ran the tip of my finger over the back of his hand that he had on my jean-clad leg. "What did you have in mind?"

"I think we should drive up to Napa, find some little bed-and-breakfast, and walk around the city, drinking wine and buying trinkets until we have to drive back on Sunday." He stared out at the pool. "What do you think?"

I leaned my head on his shoulder and watched the birds flying over the water. "I think I can study later."

CHAPTER 22

The next Monday was our monthly staff meeting. We sat around the table, drinking coffee and eating what was left over of last week's desserts. Deek watched my every move, following me from table to counter and back as I brought over the food. Finally, when I couldn't stand it anymore, I spun around and confronted him. "What do you want?"

"Man, I can't believe you did that. Weren't you scared? From what I heard, you all but wrestled the gun out of that guy's hands." Deek's eyes widened. "Were you shot?"

Toby started laughing, then he was choking, and finally, after my aunt slapped his back a couple of times, he groaned and stared at me, a small smile still on his face.

"Okay, that's just stupid. Do I look like I was shot?" I sat the chocolate cheesecake with mini chocolate chips on top of the table, then pushed Deek into a chair. "Look, can we talk about business, not what happened at The Castle last week?"

"I've got a few items on my list." My aunt took a sip from her coffee. "First, I want to know how the holiday festival committee is going. Deek, do you want to update us?"

"I thought we'd talk about what happened at The Castle." Deek looked at the three of us. Toby, Aunt Jackie, and I had all been in the middle of the take down. John was in the Bakerstown jail after Terrance and Greg talked a while about turf jurisdiction. Honestly, I think Greg was glad to release him since his station only had a small holding area and he would have had to pay the county for John's stay while the court system decided what to do with him.

The man was crazy. There was no doubt. But he did kill Levi. As well as kidnap and hold eight people hostage for more than a day. Well, nine, if you count me, but I was only there for a short time. From what I pieced together from the others, he went around and either drugged or knocked out everyone who was at The Castle on Monday afternoon. He sent all the staff home, saying Brenda was upset about the overtime. And when the hostages woke up, they'd been tied to a chair in the dining room.

He claimed he just wanted to find out who the new owner of The Castle was, since Brenda had been informed that morning that the property had been sold. She'd been in shock and had confided in him. She thought John would be an ally in her grief over losing The Castle since he loved the place as much as she did. But really, he loved it more. More than anyone could have known.

"We caught the bad guy, he's in jail, discussion ended." I smiled at the other two. "I'm paying you to come to this staff meeting so we can talk about the business, not South Cove gossip." I took a bite of the chocolate cheesecake, then waved my fork at him. "So tell us what's going on with the festival."

"Jeez, you guys keep your secrets close." Deek muttered and took a sip of his coffee.

Toby elbowed him. "I'll tell you all about it after the meeting. I'll even show you how I cuffed the guy."

I shook my head. Knowing Toby, he'd leave Deek cuffed out in front of the store while he took care of some made up business. "Don't let him put cuffs on you," I warned. "You might not get them off for a while."

Toby grinned. "You're ruining all my fun."

"The festival?" Aunt Jackie prompted.

Deek swallowed hard, glancing side-eyed at and then actually moved his chair away from Toby an inch. "So, yeah. We're expanding Santa's workshop to include stations up and down Main Street. I said we would talk about opening the food truck in front of the store and only selling hot chocolate and some sort of holiday cookie. We'd need to make it reasonable enough for the kids to buy."

"It's going to mess up traffic on Main Street." My aunt shook her head. "I'm not sure it's safe to have the food truck out front. It's too big."

"Oh, I should have said, we're closing Main Street from Beal to Diamond Lille's. It will be pedestrian only, except for the train." Deek bounced in his chair.

"The train?" Toby looked at him like he was crazy. "We don't have a train."

"Harrold said he knows a guy who runs a trackless train for a traveling circus. I guess the place is shut down for the winter, and the guy will run it on weekends for us for the entire festival."

"You're closing Main Street for six weeks?" I shook my head. "Seriously?"

"Just for the weekends. They already checked with the pigs," he glanced at Toby, "I mean, the cops and they have a second way out of town that won't be blocked. That's why we have to stop at Beal Street. If we closed all of Main, it would block all traffic out of South Cove."

I wondered if Greg had been the one to approve this plan or if it had been our mayor and Greg was going to just have to work around it. But I didn't want to curb Deek's enthusiasm for the process. "So what else should we know?"

"There isn't much left to tell, a lot of the stuff is still in the planning stage." He looked at his notebook, scanning the next couple of pages. "One more thing, we're all dressing like Santa's elves from Thanksgiving until New Year's."

"I'm not." Toby didn't even look up from the book he was scanning. I'd brought out all the Advanced Reader's copies from the back, put them in the middle of the table, and told the group everyone had to take at least three. "I already have to wear a uniform for one job, I'm not dressing up in a costume for the other one."

My aunt sniffed. "Red and green just aren't my colors."

They all turned and looked at me. "There is no way I'm going to be the only one dressing like some stupid elf. Maybe you could suggest we all wear Happy Holiday T-shirts or pins."

"Ha, gotcha." Deek slapped the notebook down on the table. "Darla wanted the elf thing, but everyone voted her down. Including that old dude next door. He didn't find it funny at all."

"If Josh had a different disposition, he could be an excellent Santa." My aunt pulled a book out of the pile Deek had made. "I'll take that one."

"Now, Aunt Jackie, Josh has lost a lot of weight. I don't think you could call him Santa size anymore." I didn't comment on his demeanor. The guy was definitely more of a Grinch type.

Deek pulled a new book out of the pile to replace the one my aunt had stolen from him. "The guy is cool. He knows a lot about old stuff."

"If we're done talking about Josh Thomas, maybe we could get back to the meeting?" Toby picked up a second book and started scanning. He loved reading nonfiction, so having him even pull a few of the novels we'd been overwhelmed with was a surprise. We really missed Sasha, especially in the reading and reviewing part of the job. "I'd like to grab a nap before I have to go in tonight."

We finished up our meeting with the few items I had and the many items my aunt wanted to remind everyone about. Including turning the pots off when they closed. After the guys had left, I confronted her. "What was that? You're the only one who closes. Why did they need to sit through a through explanation on how the close works?"

"Because they may need to do it someday." My aunt filled her travel mug with the last of the coffee. "What if I'm gone?"

"Then I'll close." Sometimes she took this preparation thing way too seriously.

She walked over and checked the lock on the door, again. "And what if you're gone?"

"When are we ever both gone on the same day?" I watched her as she kept her back to me. "They won't remember anything you told them and now they got an hour's overtime so you could explain your job. So what's really going on?"

"It's probably nothing, but my doctor wants me to see a specialist about the arthritis." She stood looking out the window onto Main Street. "I just may need to take some time off, that's all. And besides, there's the wedding to think about. Who's going to close when Harrold and I are in Europe?"

"Do you want me to go to this appointment with you?" She still wasn't looking at me, so I knew she was concerned. Which may have been why she was so crabby lately. I'd put it all on the stress of the wedding. I put a lift into my voice, trying to lighten the mood. "We could make a day of it. Maybe lunch and shopping at the art galleries you love?"

"Don't be silly, Mary's coming with me." I saw move her hand toward her face to wipe at her eyes. Now I was concerned. But when she turned back, a smile curved her lips. I knew it was fake. "Although I do appreciate the offer. You always were such a sweet girl."

"If you're sure. I can adjust my schedule and go with you and Mary. Just let me know." I'd lost this battle even before I knew we were fighting. My aunt prided herself on her independence. For her to be seeing a specialist, well, that would seem like giving up to such a strong-willed woman. I walked to the office and grabbed my tote and a light sweater. "I'm going home. I'm tired, grumpy, and I have a ton of homework to do before tonight's class."

"I'll talk to you tomorrow." Aunt Jackie started up the stairs, then paused. "Thank you. I know you care but I want to do this on my own."

I used the back door to leave, locking up after myself. My mind was on Aunt Jackie and why her primary doctor was sending her to someone else.

I didn't know much about her health issues, just what she'd let me know, but the next time we talked, I was going to sit her down and hear the whole story. She didn't need to be keeping all this to herself. Or maybe she wasn't. Maybe she and Harrold talked about these things. I shook my head, knowing the answer before I even thought of the question. Mary was going with her. If she'd have told Harrold, he would have been the one to go. She was holding back on both of us.

I checked the lock a third time before heading to my car. I didn't need people getting into the shop and either joyriding through my supplies or sleeping in the back room. We didn't have a homeless problem in South Cove, but every once in a while, Greg found someone sleeping on the beach. Then he'd take the guy to the holding cell and let him sleep there. The next day, he'd tell the guy to get out of town, and so far, everyone had. I was hoping our luck would hold.

But as everyone knows, luck only takes someone so far.

The pretty silver and blue doll I'd admired when I brought the women from the bachelor party to town was gone from the window when I approached Russian Collectibles. Someone must have bought it last weekend. Had it only been just over a week since Levi's death? So much had happened.

The small blond girl came out of the store with her jump rope. She took one look at me, dropped the rope, and ran back into the shop. I could hear her yelling for her papa. I picked up the rope and was about to put it on the table that sat on the sidewalk when Alana, Vladimir, and Jessica stepped out into the morning light. Jessica stepped forward and took the rope from my hands. "Jill, so nice to see you. We were going to visit you at the coffee shop."

"The shop is closed on Mondays." I brightened my smile. "But we'll be open at six tomorrow morning and I have a great kid's book collection. I'm sure your sister will love shopping for books with us."

"That's not why we were coming to visit, but yes, we'll bring her there soon. She needs to read more to learn about her new home." Jessica waved the little girl closer. "We have a gift for you for helping me get out of that terrible situation."

Vladimir stepped aside and Alana stepped forward, a large gift bag in her hands. She smiled shyly at me and said, "Thank you for saving my сестра." She glanced at Jessica who shook her head. "My sister," Alana corrected.

I knelt to her level and took the bag. Sitting it on the ground, I pulled out the doll I'd been admiring. Someone, probably Vladimir, must have seen me focus on that particular item when we'd walked through town that day. He'd be a terrific shop owner because he watched and paid attention to details. Like what doll I liked.

"This is lovely, but I didn't…"

Jessica held up her hand. "I know you didn't mean to rescue us from John, but we'd been in that room for over twenty-four hours by the time you arrived. I think much longer and he would have started shooting." She glanced down at her sister and stroked the little girl's hair. "I don't know what I would have done."

"John was a little crazy." I knew he loved The Castle, and it was that love that had eventually sent him over the edge.

"He was a bad man." Vladimir stepped forward and put his arm around his older daughter. "Jessica has had her fill of bad men in her life. Now I hope she finds a good one."

"Papa, we talked about this. Levi was a good man. Besides, I don't need a man to take care of me. I'm going to help you out with Alana and the shop." She smiled at me. "My father is a true romantic. He believes in love."

There were worst things to be called. "Since we're talking about The Castle, have you decided what you're going to do with it?"

Jessica sank into one of the chairs. "Jimmy Marcum had a letter for me with the legal papers. Apparently, Levi saw how much I loved the place, and knowing that my papa was here, he decided to give me my own business to run. It was his wedding gift to me."

"That's some wedding gift." Levi could be a generous man. Or he could be a royal butt. The man had been complicated.

Jessica laughed. "I'd gotten him new shirts. He was always complaining that his buttons fell off after a few washings, so I bought him five tailor-made shirts for his suits. I spent over a grand on the stupid things and I thought I was being extravagant."

"Well, he out did you there." I stood, carefully returning the stacking doll into the bag. "I'm sure he would have loved the gesture."

Jessica wiped tears from her eyes. "Now those shirts along with the rest of his clothes are going to a charity where they help people get jobs. Those guys are going to walk into their interviews dressed to the nines."

I could see the pain in her eyes; she'd loved Levi, no matter what we'd found out about the guy, he'd saved her and she loved him. She shook away the tears forming in her eyes.

"Anyway, you asked about The Castle. Brenda and I had a long talk and she has some great ideas on how to get the place back on its feet financially. I hired her to manage it. The prenup left me enough money to burn, so I guess I'll burn it by taking care of that landmark."

The Castle had always been a big draw for tourists to South Cove. So much that the mayor loved supporting the business in any way he could. Now that Jessica owned the place, I was sure he'd try to become hers and Vladimir's best friend. Politics. It was something I could think about later. Right now, I was just glad the place wasn't being closed or turned into a night club. It had found someone who loved it just the way it was.

As I walked home with the gift bag feeling heavy in my arms, I felt lighter than I had for a while. We had two, no, three new residents of South Cove. And I thought they would fit in just right.

CHAPTER 23

Jackie had been out of sorts all day. She'd spent yesterday in the city with Mary and now, the day of Amy and Justin's engagement party, she didn't seem to be all that interested in the event she'd spent the last two months helping plan. We were at The Castle, doing the final touches to the party that was scheduled to start in ten minutes.

"Aunt Jackie, are you okay with the gift table being over here?" I waved my hand toward the entry area. People could come into the patio area, drop off their coats and gifts, and then head straight for the bar. But before I moved on to talking to the bartender, I wanted her blessing on where everything had been set up.

In a pink lace dress, with white flats, she looked younger than her years. Harrold had arrived a few minutes earlier and sat talking to Greg over near the pool. She looked at me, then at the patio. "It's fine."

I stepped closer, unsure of what I'd just heard. She didn't seem to be in a party mood. "People will be arriving any minute. Do you need something? Are you all right? Is this about your doctor appointment yesterday?"

"You ask too many questions." My aunt put her hand over her mouth, trying to call back the sharp words. She took my arm and pointed me toward the kitchen. "Look, why don't you go check on the caterers. We don't want the guests to be without food."

"Sure, I can do that." I paused before I left her side. "But, are you sure you're all right?"

She put a hand on my shoulder. "I'm as good as I need to be." A smile creased her lips, but I could see she didn't feel it on the inside. Something was bothering her. I knew I should have gone into the city with her and talked to her doctor. But she'd wanted to make the trip with Mary, and had too much homework to press my point. "Go check on the caterers and then find Amy and Justin. They need to be enjoying this."

"We need to do a girls weekend in the city sometime before the holidays." I hugged Aunt Jackie quickly. "Especially since soon you and Harrold will be newlyweds and won't want to leave each other sides."

"I think we're a little old to be clingy, dear." She glanced over at Harrold who seemed to be arguing football with Greg. She glanced at her watch. "Go check on the caterers. I'd hate to disappoint everyone with no food."

I walked away, but something made me turn back to look at her before I disappeared into the main building. She was staring at Harrold, and I swore I saw a tear drop fall from her eyes. Something was definitely wrong and she was going to tell me. I just wouldn't press her tonight.

Brenda met me in the lobby. "We have a problem. The wine delivery hasn't arrived."

"Let me call Darla. I'm sure it's just a hiccup, although they should have been here hours ago."

"We have a case to start the night out, but that's not going to last long. And we don't have any champagne for the toasts." Brenda checked her phone. "I texted your aunt hours ago, but didn't hear back from her. She told me not to bother Amy. And then I kind of forgot. This is all my fault."

"It's not your fault," I consoled Brenda as I stepped toward the counter to use the land line. Why had Aunt Jackie not responded? After planning this event for months, it wasn't like her to not follow up on every last detail.

It took me almost a half hour to find the mix up and get the wine on its way to The Castle. Then, I went into the kitchen and checked on the caterers. The party had started by the time I returned to the patio.

"You look lovely." Greg whispered in my ear as I paused by his side. "Your aunt knows how to throw a party."

"She does." I glanced around but didn't see her nearby. I pointed to the bandstand. "Justin and Amy just arrived."

Greg handed me a glass filled with an amber liquid. "Apparently, they were low on wine when I got our drinks. I see they just brought out a new case. Do you want me to get you some or will the beer work for now?"

"I'm dying of thirst. I'll deal with the beer." I watched as Vladimir and Jessica walked up to us.

"Lovely party. I'm so happy you invited us." Jessica kissed me on both cheeks and her father followed suit. "I love the way the lights make the patio seem so magical."

"You look stunning." Jessica was decked out in a long dark blue gown with silver heels. Around her neck was a single diamond, large enough to sparkle in the dim light.

"The one thing I do have is party clothes. Levi liked me to look the part of the rich guy's arm candy." She smiled, a little sadly. "It's been hard being just a normal girl for a while."

Toby stepped into the circle and slapped Greg on the back. "You clean up good, boss."

"I could say the same about you." Toby had on a black suit, with a light blue dress shirt, open at the neck.

"Jackie would kill me if I showed up in jeans and a T-shirt. Where is she, anyway?" Toby looked over at Amy and Justin, then quickly looked away. I could see the pain of his own recent breakup still affected him.

I glanced around, but still didn't see my aunt. "She didn't seem to be feeling well. Maybe Harrold took her out for a little air." I turned back into the circle to see Toby staring at Jessica. He saw me and blushed, then stepped out of the circle.

"I'm on the way to the bar. Does anyone want something?" He paused.

"I'll come with you. I haven't had a shot of vodka for years. Maybe Jessica will have to drive her papa home tonight." Vladimir looked at Greg. "What about you, police man? Do you want to drink with the Russian spy?"

Greg laughed. "I take it you've heard the rumors."

"If I was a spy, I would have more money in my bank account." Vladimir held out his hands. "Unfortunately, you only have a poor Russian shopkeeper in your little village."

"We love having you here." I wanted to kill Josh who still hadn't given up the idea that Vladimir was KGB.

"And you aren't as poor as you play." Jessica put her hand on her father's arm. "Go drink with your new friends. Just make sure you don't take off without me. I'll play designated driver tonight."

"We have drivers available to take people home." Toby said. "We hired college kids from Bakerstown. They'll drive you home, leave the car and the keys with you, and then someone picks them up to return to The Castle."

"See, you can drink a bit too." He pulled Toby into a hug. "Come my friend. Let's talk."

Jessica and I stood and watched as the men made their way to the bar. "I'm afraid my father is feeling at home. You may not like him as much once you get to know the real man."

"Don't be silly. Everyone has their own odd habits. Around here, especially." I watched the mix of people drinking, eating, and talking. Everyone from town was here. Well, everyone except my aunt and her soon to be husband. If they had snuck off to have a little alone time in one of the guest rooms, I was going to kill her.

"Toby, he seems like a nice guy." Jessica was still watching the bar area. She turned to me. "Is he seeing someone?"

"No, he and his last girlfriend broke up late summer. Sasha was an amazing girl. He was lucky to have her, but she went off to build a career." I stopped talking and looked at her. "Wait, are you saying you're interested in Toby?"

"I didn't say any such thing. It's way too soon for me to even be thinking about a future." Jessica blushed. "But he is a nice guy, right?"

I watched as Toby and Greg stood talking to Vladimir. "Toby's the best." Jessica wandered off to greet someone else and to get away from me asking any more questions. I liked the possibility of Toby and Jessica. I just didn't know if either of them were ready to move on from their last relationships.

Brenda stepped toward me and took my arm. "You have a phone call."

"From who? Everyone I know is here at the party." I glanced at her face and stopped short. "Is Aunt Jackie okay?"

"How did you know…" Brenda shook her head. "Never mind, I don't want to know. Just follow me. She says she needs to talk to you."

I hurried after Brenda, winding through the maze of paths and around the fountain that was alight with the little tea lights and appeared to be pulsing blue and silver water through the stone angel statue. I took a deep breath, hoping that my aunt hadn't needed to be taken to the hospital. She'd been acting off and snarky all day, but I thought it was the upcoming party. My aunt liked things to be perfect. And when they weren't, she got annoyed. Aunt Jackie lived that mantra: If Mama ain't happy, no one's happy.

Brenda waved me into her office, then picked up the phone on her secretary's desk. "I just happened to be in the office putting away the receipt from the winery delivery, and the phone rang. If the wine hadn't been late, I wouldn't have been here."

I took the handset she held out for me and took a deep breath to settle me after nearly running into the office. "Hello?"

"I need you to handle the party." My aunt was direct and sounded fine. "There's an envelope with Brenda that has everything you need to do listed out. Amy's your friend, you should be handling this anyway."

I closed my eyes, pushing away all of the possibilities that had run through my mind. "Are you all right? Where are you? The hospital?"

"Why would I be at the hospital?" My aunt asked, a level of frustration in her voice. "I'm fine. I just need you to do a favor for me. Is that too much to ask?"

"Where are you? Why aren't you and Harrold at the party?" I leaned on the desk, and noticed Brenda standing a few feet away, trying not to eavesdrop but looking as concerned as I felt.

"Just deal with things, please. Harrold dropped me off at the apartment and he's gone home to his house."

I blew out a breath. "Seriously Jackie, you are driving me crazy. You worked for months with Amy on this party. She's going to want to thank you. You can't just walk out because you decide you don't want to stay. Come back and at least say how happy you are for Amy and Justin. She's going to think something is wrong."

I didn't hear anything on the other end of the line after my tirade. Well, good, maybe I'd woke her up. I couldn't believe she was doing this. There was a time to be a diva but this wasn't it. I softened my voice, "Aunt Jackie? Do you need Greg to come and get you and Harrold?"

She blew out a breath. "That's just it dear, there is no more me and Harrold. We just broke up."

"*What are you talking about*?" I envisioned Harrold's face every time he looked at my aunt. The man was in love. And I'd never seen Aunt Jackie happier. "It's just pre-wedding jitters. Amy's engagement is making you nervous. By the time June comes along, you'll be excited to start your new life."

This time, the silence went on longer. "I don't think you're hearing me, dear. I broke off the engagement this evening." I heard the crack in her voice. "Harrold and I are not getting married in June."

The line went dead and I was left holding the handset, my mind unable to wrap around what my aunt had just announced. This was crazy. My gaze met Brenda's. "This isn't good."

"Is she okay?" Brenda liked my aunt. Everyone liked my aunt. She took the handset out of my hand and listened for the dial tone before setting it back on the phone. "Are you okay? You look a little sick."

"She went to the doctor yesterday and, today, well, let's just say she's not herself." I shook my head. "I don't know what's going on, but I'm supposed to handle the rest of the party. What do you need me to do?"

The music slowed and as the band leader stepped toward the microphone, my heart was beating fast. I didn't like being in front of so many people. This is why Sasha or Aunt Jackie handled the author events. I was better behind the scenes. Greg stood next to me. "Are you okay?"

I looked up into his eyes and smiled. "As much as I can be. Seriously, Aunt Jackie knows how I feel about these things."

The music died and the band leader waved me toward the microphone. My dress shimmered in the lights from the stage and for a second, I felt like a princess. I glanced at Greg who nodded, giving me the strength to make the announcement.

"So, we're so glad you all came out to celebrate with us." I wetted my lips. I'd put on lipstick earlier, but I was sure, I'd bit it all off now. My teeth were probably glossy red. I ran my tongue over the top row and hoped it didn't show. The crowd stepped closer to the stage, and for a second, the murmuring stopped, waiting for me to continue.

I took a deep breath and jumped in. "We're here to celebrate the upcoming marriage of Amy and Justin." I continued my impromptu speech about Amy, our friendship, and how much I liked her with Justin. The words took over and my nervousness fell away. I finished up and called the couple forward.

The crowd was silent for a minute then, as Amy and Justin made their way up to the stage, they started clapping. Amy hugged me and whispered in my ear. "Thank you."

"I love you." I stepped away from the microphone and let Justin talk with Amy staring adoringly at her soon to be husband. Greg met me at the edge of the stage.

"You did great." He squeezed me. "Do you want to go talk to your aunt now?"

I shook my head and angled him to the bar. "Nope. I want a glass of wine, and maybe another, and then we're going to dance and help Amy and Justin celebrate their upcoming nuptials. I'll talk to my aunt tomorrow."

That was an understatement. I knew something had happened to cause this change of heart for my aunt. And I knew it wasn't Harrold's decision. I wasn't ready to find out why she'd made this decision, but it would be tomorrow.

Tonight I was taking the Scarlett O'Hara way out and I'd dance while Tara burned.

Tomorrow would be soon enough to dig through the damage.

Don't miss the rest of
The fabulous Tourist Trap Mysteries
Available now
From
Lyrical Underground!

And be sure to check out Lynn Cahoon's
CAT LATIMER MYSTERIES
A Story to Kill
And
Fatality by Firelight
Available from
Kensington Books
Wherever books are sold

Photo Credit: Angela Brewer Armstrong at Todd Studios

ABOUT THE AUTHOR

New York Times and *USA Today* best-selling author Lynn Cahoon is an Idaho expat. She grew up living the small town life she now loves to write about. Currently, she's living with her husband and two fur babies in a small historic town on the banks of the Mississippi river where her imagination tends to wander. *Guidebook to Murder*, Book 1 of the Tourist Trap series, won the 2015 Reader's Crown award for Mystery Fiction.

In the gentle coastal town of South Cove, California, all Jill Gardner wants is to keep her store—Coffee, Books, and More—open and running. So why is she caught up in the business of murder?

When Jill's elderly friend, Miss Emily, calls in a fit of pique, she already knows the city council is trying to force Emily to sell her dilapidated old house. But Emily's gumption goes for naught when she dies unexpectedly and leaves the house to Jill—along with all of her problems...*and* her enemies. Convinced her friend was murdered, Jill is finding the list of suspects longer than the list of repairs needed on the house. But Jill is determined to uncover the culprit—especially if it gets her closer to South Cove's finest, Detective Greg King. Problem is, the killer knows she's on the case—and is determined to close the book on Jill *permanently* . . .

**In the California coastal town of South Cove, history is one of
its many tourist attractions—until it becomes deadly . . .**

Jill Gardner, proprietor of Coffee, Books, and More, has discovered
that the old stone wall on her property might be a centuries-old mission
worthy of being declared a landmark. But Craig Morgan, the obnoxious
owner of South Cove's most popular tourist spot, The Castle, makes it
his business to contest her claim. When Morgan is found murdered at
The Castle shortly after a heated argument with Jill, even her detective
boyfriend has to ask her for an alibi. Jill decides she must find the real
murderer to clear her name. But when the killer comes for her, she'll
need to jump from historic preservation to self-preservation . . .

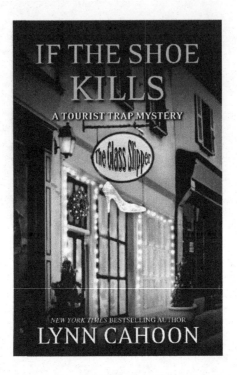

IF THE SHOE
KILLS

A TOURIST TRAP MYSTERY

The Glass Slipper

NEW YORK TIMES BESTSELLING AUTHOR
LYNN CAHOON

The tourist town of South Cove, California, is a lovely place
to spend the holidays. But this year, shop owner Jill Gardner
discovers there's no place like home for homicide . . .

As owner of Coffee, Books, and More, Jill Gardner looks forward to
the hustle and bustle of holiday shoppers. But when the mayor ropes
her into being liaison for a new work program, 'tis the season to be
wary. Local businesses are afraid the interns will be delinquents,
punks, or worse. For Jill, nothing's worse than Ted Hendricks—the
jerk who runs the program. After a few run-ins, Jill's ready to kill the
guy. That, however, turns out to be unnecessary when she finds Ted
in his car—dead as a doornail. Detective Greg King assumes it's a
suicide; Jill thinks it's murder. And if the holidays weren't stressful
enough, a spoiled blonde wants to sue the city for breaking her heel.
Jill has to act fast to solve this mess—before the other shoe drops . . .

Jill Gardner is not particularly thrilled to be portraying a twenties flapper for the dinner theater murder mystery. Though it *is* for charity . . .

Of course everyone is expecting a "dead" body at the dress rehearsal . . . but this one isn't acting! It turns out the main suspect is the late actor's conniving girlfriend Sherry . . . who also happens to be the ex-wife of Jill's main squeeze. Sherry is definitely a master manipulator . . . but is she a killer? Jill may discover the truth only when the curtain comes up on the final act . . . and by then, it may be far too late.

KILLER RUN

A TOURIST TRAP MYSTERY

She's running on empty...

THE MISSION WALK

NEW YORK TIMES BESTSELLING AUTHOR

LYNN CAHOON

Jill has somehow been talked into sponsoring a 5k race along the beautiful California coast. The race is a fundraiser for the local preservation society—but not everyone is feeling so charitable . . .

The day of the race, everyone hits the ground running...until a local business owner stumbles over a very stationary body. The deceased is the vicious wife of the husband-and-wife team hired to promote the event—and the husband turns to Jill for help in clearing his name. But did he do it? Jill will have to be *very* careful, because this killer is ready to put her out of the running...forever!

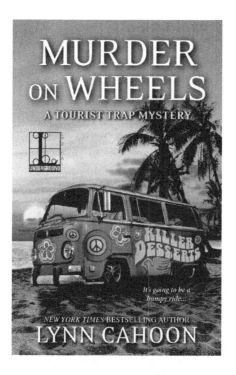

**The food truck craze has reached the charming coastal town of
South Cove, California, but before Jill Gardner can sample the
eats, she has to shift gears and put the brakes on a killer . . .**

Now that Kacey Austin has got her new gluten-free dessert truck up and
running, there's no curbing her enthusiasm—not even when someone
vandalizes the vehicle and steals her recipes. But when Kacey turns
up dead on the beach and Jill's best friend Sadie becomes the prime
suspect, Jill needs to step on it to serve the real killer some just desserts.

TEA CUPS
AND
CARNAGE

A TOURIST TRAP MYSTERY

Tea Hee

OPEN

The kettle's about
to boil over...

NEW YORK TIMES BESTSELLING AUTHOR

LYNN CAHOON

**The quaint coastal town of South Cove, California, is all
abuzz about the opening of a new specialty shop, Tea Hee.
But as Coffee, Books, and More owner Jill Gardner is about
to find out, there's nothing cozy about murder . . .**

Shop owner Kathi Corbin says she came to South Cove to get
away from her estranged family. But is she telling the truth? And
did a sinister someone from her past follow her to South Cove?
When a woman claiming to be Kathi's sister starts making waves
and a dead body is found in a local motel, Jill must step in to
clear Kathi's name—without getting herself in hot water.

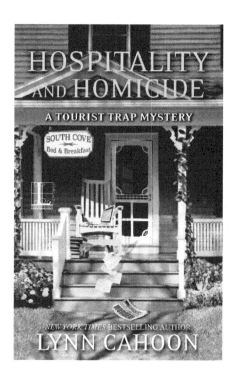

A visit to the serene coastal town of South Cove, California, could make anybody feel refreshed and inspired. But as Jill Gardner—owner of Coffee, Books, and More—discovers, some folks won't live to tell about it . . .

Mystery author Nathan Pike checked into South Cove Bed & Breakfast to compose a compelling novel, not commit murder. But things get real when a rival B&B owner ends up exactly like the victim in his draft—undeniably dead. As Nathan prepares to complete his magnum opus behind bars, Jill's the only one who can prove his innocence and deconstruct the plot of a twisted killer!

Printed in the United States
by Baker & Taylor Publisher Services